A CASE OF CLOSURE

A Bertrand McAbee Mystery

Joseph A. McCaffrey

authorHOUSE®

AuthorHouse™
1663 Liberty Drive
Bloomington, IN 47403
www.authorhouse.com
Phone: 833-262-8899

Published by AuthorHouse 12/22/2022

ISBN: 978-1-6655-7871-4 (sc)
ISBN: 978-1-6655-7872-1 (e)

Library of Congress Control Number: 2022923540

Print information available on the last page.

LIST OF BOOKS BY AUTHOR

OTHER McABEE MYSTERIES

Cassies Ruler
Confessional Matters
The Pony Circus Wagon
Scholarly Executions
Phantom Express
The Troubler
The Marksman's Case
A Byzantine Case
A Case of Silver
A Went Over Case
The Demosthenes Club
The Case of the Bear

All of the above titles are also available in audiobooks; *The Case of the Bear* is pending. Please refer to Audible.com.

REVIEWS OF EARLIER MCABEE MYSTERIES

Cassies Ruler

If you love mysteries, you have plenty here to keep you glued to your book until it unravels at the end. While a violent account, it reflects the subject at hand and makes for a good read.

- Illinois Standardbred

Confessional Matters

The good guys and bad guys in the religious hierarchy and other disciplines are wonderfully characterized, and the action seems very much like what you read in the newspapers nowadays.

- The Leader

The Pony Circus Wagon

The pre-WWI historical background and international intrigue distinguish this gripping and at times addictive mystery from the standard whodunits.

- Kirkus Reviews

Scholarly Executions

The author hits the ground running with a resolute mystery. An intelligent, intuitive detective who steers clear of guns in favor of a team of talented cohorts.

- Kirkus Reviews

The Marksman's Case

Classy ex-classics professor Bertrand McAbee and his multicultural mystery-solving posse go the distance with a former military sniper turned vigilante. An entertaining mystery, although not for the gun-shy.

- Kirkus Reviews

A Byzantine Case

McCaffrey's mystery thrills with well-drawn characters, solid procedural details and strong storytelling. Historical intrigue and well-narrated suspense make this adventure an absorbing mystery.

- Kirkus Reviews

A Went Over Case

In this thriller, a dying man hires private investigator Bertrand McAbee to find the whereabouts of his brother, missing for nearly 30 years. In his 10th outing, a steadfast gumshoe proves he can handle anything...

- Kirkus Reviews

DEDICATION

For Rosemary Ocar the Mayor of Brookwood

CHAPTER 1

"Dr. Richard Pruitt?" The female police officer from Davenport asked, a little too gently for his tastes. He noticed that her partner, not much older than the students he taught at St. Anselm, stayed quiet and behind her.

Pruitt responded, "Yes. Something wrong officer?"

"I'm a patrol officer with the Davenport P.D. My name is Linda Carney, and this is Walt Protsky my partner." Protsky tipped his hat. "Is there somewhere we can talk?"

"Sure. Come to my office." He led the pair up to the third floor where his office was located. They weaved around four corridors of the building named Anselm Hall. Pruitt was unnerved but he tried to conceal it. He figured the pair had some bad news. Linda Carney had a tougher look about her, short hair with a ribbon of white over her right ear, enlarged brown eyes, and lips that when shut were zippered shut. Late 20s maybe. Both of them paced side by side with him. Along the way he saw two colleagues from the Education Department. They looked askew at the three of them, as though he was being arrested. They then averted their eyes, offended by the sight. He imagined the faculty rumor mill would be set afire shortly.

Anselm Hall was a long red building of four floors. It was the foundation structure of the college. The original part was built sometime in the 1880s, from then it underwent several additions. From the outside the red-bricked structure looked straight. However, walking inside of it one found that there was a small unevenness from one to another of the additions. Pruitt's office was on the far west side. He frequently felt that he was descending as he approached his office on the third floor.

He pointed to two seats to the side of his desk. He imagined that the disarray of the office probably offended the two cops. What did you expect from him after 43 years in the same office? Neatness? "So. I am Dr. Pruitt. How can I help you?"

Linda Carney, clearly in charge, said, "We have come with some questions and some news. Please bear with me." He nodded. "Do you have a sister?"

"Two. One is in Denver in a convalescent home. The other lives in Rock Island. Agatha. Why do you ask?"

"Can you give me Agatha's address?"

"2615 12th Street," he said, now with fear and alarm in his voice.

"Your sister's body was found in the house today by the Rock Island Police Department. We are here on their behalf. I'm very sorry. Her identity was confirmed by a neighbor.'"

Richard Pruitt looked at the pair of them in disbelief. He said, "She had just moved there a few months ago. She wanted to be in that neighborhood in case she needed assisted care. There is a huge convalescent center a few blocks away. I can't believe this. How? She was in fair health," his voice somber and wandering, trance-like.

Linda Carney said, "The house is unfortunately a crime scene I can't say anything more. The Rock Island P.D. wishes you to come over there directly. If you are unable to drive, we would be more than pleased to drive you over there. But there is an urgency for your presence."

"I'll go right now unescorted. A crime scene? What does that mean exactly?"

"Sir. We were not given any particulars, just the barest of information. That Department has become overwhelmed by Covid. We are doing this as a professional courtesy. I'm very sorry about this." With that said they left.

Richard Pruitt, 72 years old, got up from his chair. Feeling faint he sat down again. There was no sense calling his sister in Denver. She was in full-blown dementia. There was no other immediate family. He felt terribly alone. Finally, he arose and headed to the faculty parking lot.

Linda Carney got into her squad car and dialed Hugh Concannon the lead detective in Rock Island. She had been warned by the Davenport Desk Sergeant to be careful when dealing with Concannon. The word on him was that he was a mean-spirited son of a bitch. "Don't chat with him. When you've told Pruitt and you're sure he'll get over there tell him that and just hang up." Accordingly, she did just that and when about to disconnect he yelled "Well where the fuck is the bastard? That all you can tell me?"

"Yes sir. He'll be there directly." She disconnected. "Enough of that crap," she said to her silent neophyte partner.

Concannon looked out through the kitchen window. He saw the white Prius pull up along side of the curb. Besides his unmarked Ford there were two black and white squad cars in the driveway leading up to the unattached single car garage. He observed a white haired man, aged looking. He was too heavy for his own good. His shoulders were slouched, he had thick glasses and appeared to be in some sort of fog. A dumb, absent-minded professor geek of some sort. In Concannon's mind there were slots that held different kinds of people. It was important to drop everyone into one of them. Pruitt was an easy match. He went to the front door and opened it. Pruitt entered hurriedly. "Detective Concannon, Rock Island P.D. This is your sister's residence?" Pruitt thought that Concannon was trying to yell at someone in Chicago, 170 miles to the east. "Come in and sit down here in the living room. Your sister's body, murder victim, is in her bedroom. I'll want you to I.D. it in a few minutes. Where were you last night? About midnight to 3:00 a.m.?"

"What?" Pruitt asked in confusion as he saw the mayhem in his sister's house, she was so fastidious. 'Everything in its proper place' she'd say. All he saw was disarray. It seemed a tornado had struck, resembling an experience of the type he had while at Southern Illinois University, years back as an undergraduate.

"Home. Sleeping where…"

"Anyone with you?" Concannon interrupted him.

"No. I live alone."

"That's convenient," he said with a snarl.

"I want to see my sister. What happened here?"

"You will. Don't you worry. The medical examiner is in there. Just hold your horses until he's done. Tell me about your sister," he demanded.

"My sister is dead and you're treating me like a suspect, really?"

"Damn right. As far as I can tell you're nearest of kin. Of course you're a suspect. Don't you watch TV?"

"No. I don't watch TV. I'm here to attend to my sister for God's sake," Pruitt said angrily.

"There's no urgency there. She's dead. Murdered. Last night. Until I think otherwise you're a prime suspect. Now back to my question – tell me about her. Details."

"She's a former librarian. University of Iowa. She lived in Iowa City most of her adult life. Moved back here, we are a Rock Island family, about three months ago. Now it ..."

"No." Concannon put up a restraining arm. "You have to wait until the medical examiner clears the scene."

Concannon had a long square face. His eyes were a light gray, suspicious, and given to a perpetual squint. His mouth, twisted a bit, created a snarl of sorts, his voice matching up to it. He appeared to be in good shape, about 6'2", probably in his late 50s. An unpleasant man all around, thought Pruitt who imagined that Concannon held every resident of the 40,000 or so citizens of Rock Island, Illinois, to be prime suspects. He wondered how on earth that a man of this ilk was given this job. How many people did he cause pain to, his callousness a quality that he nurtured.

"That's it? You think that'll pass. Condensing your sister's life into a few evasive sentences. Why in hell would she move from Iowa City to here? What was behind that? Your pleasing company?" He said with dismissive sarcasm.

Pruitt was a gentle man, retiring in manner. Concannon was pushing every button he could in an effort to evoke a reaction from him, but to what end? Pushed enough, he looked Concannon square up, "That's it detective. I've had enough of your manner. From now on you can question me with my lawyer present."

Concannon, taken off guard that the wimp pushed back shook his head in exaggerated disbelief. He said, "Have it you way mister, you'll talk plenty by the time I'm finished with you."

Seconds later a small, balding, bespectacled man, came out from his sister's bedroom. He went to Concannon and said in a low voice, "Okay, upon a relational identification. It's a wrap, the body can be removed."

Concannon emitted a humph. The medical examiner removed his rubber gloves with practiced snaps as he left the premises.

"Okay Pruitt. You can go in there. Don't touch anything! Just identify the body as that of your sister."

Pruitt was bewildered at first. His sister was sitting up against the backboard of her bed, head bent downward, to her left side, as if she has been reading only to fall asleep. As he came closer the brunt of the tragedy caught him, impression after impression seeking attention, horror upon horror. The coagulated blood spreading across her mostly white hair, the odor of copper mixed with waste, the odd and freakish tilt of her head and then as he bent down his sister's face blood smeared, her left eye swollen and closed and her tongue half out of her bloodied lips. He was close to fainting as he felt someone gently grab his arms from behind and guide him to a chair outside of the bedroom, he was assisted to the seat. "Just sit, sir," the female voice said. The voice belonged to a uniformed Rock Island police officer.

The officer asked in the gentlest of voices, "Can you identify the body as that of your sister Mister Pruitt?"

A few seconds later he said with deep sorrow, "My sister, yes."

"Just sit here for a moment, I'll be back," she said.

When she came back, she had Concannon in tow. She said, "I'm going to ask you one more time. Is the body in the bed that of your sister Agatha Pruitt?"

In an almost whisper, he said, "Yes. It is my sister, Agatha." With that, head down, he sobbed.

CHAPTER 2

A repeated problem for Bertrand McAbee was in encountering acquaintances after years of absences. An old friend named Anna had remarked, with profound clarity, that she saw him as a man with some serious issues, one in particular— aging. She had made that one comment around 20 years ago. He had mulled over it enough so that it had become weaponized in his self-reflections. She was correct – he had issues with the entire process of aging. Intellectually he understood but emotionally it was beyond him. Anna had gone on about it for a half hour, a preface to what was a three hour harangue about his deficiencies. It was a way of parting for her. She desperately needed to land blows, frustrated as she was with Bertrand's refusal to advance their relationship. But that one spear about aging penetrated his armor. She was spot on.

He, plain and simple, was not effective with the aged and or infirm. He put it down to his impatience, his ignorance, his prejudice and mostly to his own personal history. But whatever the cause Anna's parting arrow had stuck good and hard. Pruitt had called his office, managing to demand his secretary/aide, Pat Trump, to pass on his insistence on meeting Bertrand. His yelling almost caused a disconnect by her. Bertrand had read about the murder in the local paper. Unwillingly, he consented to meet with Pruitt.

All of those thoughts had raced through his head as he observed Richard Pruitt purchasing some coffee at the Panera counter. The drastic changes in Pruitt's appearance from the ten years plus since Bertrand had last run into him were of seismic proportions. His unkempt hair was now fully white, his bushy eyebrows were out of control as they almost tangled with his eyes. His cheeks were drawn; his over-generous mustache was in need of barbering. A tall man, he was stooped. McAbee felt Anna's spear about aging. He simply didn't want to deal with his old comrade. They were never close anyway. And then his mind called him out. He was himself older than Pruitt. What in God's name was he thinking? So he steeled himself and fell into line with his hectoring mind. He stood up and waved at the squinting Dr. Pruitt who walked over toward him, a slight shuffle apparent.

They small-talked for a few minutes about St. Anselm College, both getting a feel for each other before getting to the agenda.

Pruitt led. "It's kind of you to meet with me Bertrand. I was abusive to your assistant. I'm sorry about that. You know what has happened to my sister, Agatha?"

"I do in general Richard. Murdered. But I know nothing else about particulars."

"Do you know a detective by the name of Concannon? Rock Island?"

"Yes. I have had a few run-ins with him. A difficult man."

"He treated me as though I am the primary suspect. I felt I would be arrested after identifying Agatha. Very upsetting. Her death is a staggering loss to me. I am broken-hearted and he treats me as a murderer," he bent his head almost to his chest while shaking his head.

McAbee surmised that Richard was in an anger/depression valley. He went into that valley. "This must be overwhelming for you? I'm so sorry," he said consolingly.

"It is. It is. I don't know what to do, really." His hands were circulating around each other frantically. "I'm just devastated. Agatha and I are, were, very close. My other sister is in Colorado. She's unreachable. Shut down. I have no family. Never married. At long last I can finally own up to being gay, not that that means anything as I lost my guy years ago. I'm beleaguered. Lost."

"Does St. Anselm have assistance protocols?"

"They have counseling services, but I can't just open up to some invisible person on a phone. Otherwise I see nothing there of value."

"Richard, tell me about how you were notified, your experiences with Concannon and finally, and very importantly, what happened to your sister."

Five minutes later Bertrand had a good sense of how events had transpired.

"Allow me to make some observations," Bertrand said, "Concannon is known for the very approach that you have mentioned. It's of no consequence. I believe that several times in the past that his technique of bluster and accusation have enabled him to close a few investigations. Some people just waver under his belligerence. So, please put those concerns aside. You are no more a suspect that I am. When your sister's body is released after the autopsy you will need to arrange a funeral for Agatha. My assistant, Pat Trump, can help in this regard. My agency has experience in this. I will call her to alert her to a call from you if you wish. You will surmount this particular ordeal, Richard." Bertrand was pleased with himself. He had done a good job with Pruitt and was prepared to leave the man in a reasonably good place. 'To hell with you Anna' he said to his self-righteous self.

Pruitt now gazing directly into McAbee's eyes said, "All of this is very kind of you. It really helps me, Bertrand. I will call Pat."

Bertrand seeing a chance to leave said, "Stay in touch. Try to stay busy and take things by the order of the day." He began to reach for the table to use as a brace to rise from his seat. He stopped abruptly as Pruitt's right hand gripped his arm with unexpected vigor.

"Bertrand, please sit for another bit, please, please."

"Of course, Richard," Bertrand said with false equanimity.

"I want to hire you, your firm, to investigate my sister's murder."

"I'm pretty much retired Richard. Concannon, for all of his bluster, is excellent at solving crimes. Let's see what happens and then re-visit this matter," he said softly.

"Bertrand you don't understand. This was not a random killing. No money or jewels were taken. Notes were. Her PC and phone, too. You couldn't know what she was about. She was a first rate research librarian at the University of Iowa. An investigator like yourself. She was onto an old case here in Rock Island. Unsolved. I believe that's why she was murdered. Please hear me out."

CHAPTER 3

"My family grew up in Rock Island, being there several generations. There were three kids, two of them my sisters, both younger than me. My sister in Colorado became a druggie in San Francisco in the seventies. Her mind is wasted. She's in a convalescent home in Colorado. Dead to the world. Agatha and I jumped on the education train. My degree, Ph.D., is from Northwestern. English Lit. People getting that kind of degree now are in a hopeless situation as I'm sure you know. Jobs and student interest in a freefall. Trying to present a course in Shakespeare at St. Anselm is an almost suicidal effort. Deans, provosts, business managers screaming about low course numbers. No profit in a course with six students. Shame, shame."

McAbee caught a pause in Pruitt's delivery. "I know, the liberal arts are in disarray, Richard. It would be similar for me to offer a course on Plato if I was still employed there. Dead white men and all the rest of that pathetic rhetoric," McAbee said with a touch of bitterness.

"My sister Agatha took a different path altogether. She was very introverted by nature. Did you ever meet her?"

"I don't think so. But at my age and with my memory who knows? Bottom line, though, I don't remember her." As he spoke, McAbee found himself shedding some barriers about age. He located it in Pruitt, grudgingly speaking to someone in his age grouping. Since when did that bring comfort?

"She loved to dig deep into questions. A born researcher. Library science became her calling, specifically as a research librarian. She was adored at the University of Iowa. Constant accolades from professors over there. Many fields. She kept current with technology and remained important there for years until she took retirement. Some health concerns. Then she bought a house in Rock Island. She had great admiration for the Good Samaritan Home that is close to her house. She feared for her health. She was overweight, drank a bit more than she should and would sneak smokes once in awhile. But she wanted independence for as long as she could have it."

McAbee observed that Pruitt was no longer angry, caught up in his recitation. He said, "Okay Richard. Was she living with anyone?"

"No. She was the quintessential loner. Do you remember a young woman named Margaret Thode?"

McAbee was surprised. He hadn't heard that name for years. "I do. All too well, Richard. Rock Island High School. Terrible affair. Where are you going with this?"

"Margaret Thode and my sister Agatha were the closest of friends. Agatha never got over what happened to her. Ironically, a few days after she moved back to Rock Island there was a story in the *Quad City Times*. A reminiscence piece about Margaret entitled 'The Great Unsolved'. You must see Bertrand that the stars came into alignment."

"Ok, I get where this is going. Investigative research librarian prowls around the Margaret Thode case. Yes?"

"Exactly."

"What more do you know about this?"

"She called me last week. She was excited. She said that she might be onto something about Margaret. I warned her to be careful, Bertrand, I really did. She was living alone, a somewhat dark street and God knows what she might have uncovered. I never pressed her for information."

"Remind me of Margaret Thode. Particulars around her death." McAbee said, interest pricked.

"Her naked body was found at the Sunset Marina in Rock Island. She had been sexually violated and beaten savagely. Curiously, I had asked Agatha the very same question that you just asked me. That's what she said to me as well as the overwhelming fact that the murder was never solved, 45 years running. I know enough about your ACJ. Just as she was a research librarian, you're a research detective. I don't feel that Concannon would be able to deal with the nuances of what I just told you even if he becomes aware of her inquiries."

"Oh Richard. Most assuredly he will."

"I have plenty of money Bertrand. I am the sole legatee of her estate. Please undertake an investigation. Independent of Concannon."

"It's not just Concannon. The State of Illinois will be on this murder."

"So?"

"Politics. License threats. Interference. There will be a virtual fist fight between Concannon and the state cops. A privateer getting into the middle of that would be in a no man's land," McAbee speculated aloud.

"Please Bertrand."

"Let me to think about this. In the meantime if you need Pat Trump's assistance call my office. I'll alert her to your possible call. I promise to get back to you soon. Richard, I have to run."

Pruitt's head nodded. His eyes were teary, a bit of hope discernible.

CHAPTER 4

"Good morning Pat. I'm downtown. Is Augusta around by any chance? I don't want to bother her," Bertrand said.

Pat Trump had few assurances about ACJ. It was a firm with lots of crevasses. Some hostilities were deep, the mere mention of hacker Barry Fisk brought her into a state of anger. Jack Scholz did the same for Augusta Satin. Pat's disdain for him reached close to Augusta's. The point of this rumination led her to one of her certainties. Augusta always had time for Bertrand and vice versa. They were attached at the spine. She was just never sure about them as lovers, both of them very clever and secretive. She erased the thoughts about Barry Fisk and Jack Scholz. She buzzed Augusta. "Bertrand is on the phone. Put him through?"

"Sure thing Pat."

"Hi Augusta. Got some time? I'm downtown. I can walk over there in ten minutes. Be forewarned if you're not available I'm leaving in a sulk. I will stomp home."

"If you do that I'll come stomping after you. I'm more than free. I have a buzz for you."

"There Mistah," Augusta said with a smile, "That better have given you a buzz." She released him from her hug, as he stood by her office door.

"Yes. You're a supreme buzzer," he said with a smile as he looked at her appreciatively.

"So, while I totally get why a lonely man wants to seek out the company of a majestic woman such as I, I sense that there's more to your visit?"

"Your majesty is correct. There is another minor detail around my visit. A few days ago there was a murder in Rock Island."

"I read about it, Agatha Pruitt."

"Retired librarian form the University of Iowa. Single. No known enemies, I hear. But academia stores vendettas like China has stored viruses, lethal and supposedly contained. But I'm ahead of myself."

"Since when haven't you been Bertrand?" She asked tartly.

McAbee smiled. "Agatha Pruitt was the sister to a former colleague of mine at St. Anselm. He was just short of being frog-marched to the murder scene from the campus. It was his sister he said to the cops. So you're caught up with the news?"

"More or less yes. Now I await the minor concern that brings you here," Augusta said.

"So who does my previous colleague run into at the murder scene?"

"Let me guess. The head detective in Rock Island. The infamous twin of Dirty Harry? Hugh Concannon?"

"You nailed it. None other. And as is typical with Hugh he more or less accused the brother of being the murderer. Not an uncommon tactic for him. But there is a problem.

This prof is obviously very emotional about the death, needless to say, but is really furious about Hugh. We both know Hugh. Intrepid and competent. But also silly-assed and stupid."

"That just about nails him. Sorry about your old colleague. Hugh has gotten worse as he has aged. He's the Rock Island offender in chief. I came up the ranks with him. But, as you know all too well, I wasn't long for there. Rich doctors and all that jazz. Both of us married up. He caught the mayor's daughter, I caught a guy who gave me two beautiful daughters and a betrayal."

McAbee remembered this story about Augusta. Her doctor-husband fled out of town, abandoned his practice, but kept his physicians assistant, a snappy and younger version of Augusta with blonde hair. He moved to Wisconsin and declared he was not about to pay child support or alimony. Augusta came to ACJ, not very long in existence, and asked for help. McAbee fell for Augusta the minute she spoke. Things had never changed since then. The doctor was an arrogant ass. Before suggesting a lawyer and the ugly process of cross-state pursuits Bertrand spoke with Jack Scholz whom he had just recently used with stellar results on another case. Jack's analysis of the doctor was that he was a coward and that a meaningful and upfront exchange led by Jack would yield results. McAbee consented. The doc swore that he'd comply after seeing the face of menace in Jack. Bertrand thought that a touch of elegance did the trick in insuring that the doctor did in fact honor his promises. As he scurried into his Porsche and tried to accelerate forward the entire back axle separated from the vehicle. From then on Augusta never missed her compensations. However, Bertrand never disclosed to her how he got the non-compliant doctor to become compliant. To do so would have created uncertain consequences. And Jack Scholz? No. She was not a fan from the very start of her own use by ACJ. The whole affair was a corporate secret, the matter never alluded to in any documents and for all she would ever know only three parties understood the conditions under which the doctor found Jesus, as it were.

Bertrand asked, "Is Concannon still married to her? I can't see anyone buying into this guy for more than a week."

She puffed out her cheeks for a few seconds and then breathed out. "As far as I know. But you're right. He's very hard. Judgmental. For him a full glass is an empty glass. Pessimistic, suspicious, personality of a tarantula," she stopped her recital for a bit. "But at the end of the game very effective. He has broken some very famous cases across the river in Rock Island. I think that every new city manager comes in thinking that they'll fire him right off the bat. Yet no one does. You know what I mean. ACJ has had a few run-ins with him in the past."

"That's true but I always had you as a shield. Somehow you could tame him."

"I could tame him because I'm not that far from him. I'm shaped differently, I speak softer, I can smile, but at the end Bertrand I understand that guy. I'm not a fan of his tactics or the way he treats people but when we took cases together we got into sync in many ways. Do you want to know that he thinks of you?"

"This going to help me improve Augusta?"

She smiled. "Do you?"

"Okay," he said.

"He said that you are an unattached being. That everyone who worked in ACJ was doing so to provide a safety net around you. An octopus with arms. He said that if you were a crook, you'd be like Professor Moriarty in Sherlock Holmes stories. It took him awhile and some persuasion to accept you as being on the right side of justice."

Bertrand wasn't offended nor was he honored. "And you said back to him?"

"I said to him that I'm not the best judge. I love him."

"And? And?" he said.

"He never said a word. He just walked away. Your name has never come up again between us," she said with a wisp of mystery.

He thought it best to leave the matter alone. "I was hoping for your willingness to visit Hugh Concannon with me. And yes to your putative inquiry, I am taking the case."

"Of course I'll go with you. I'll call him now and see if we can get some time with him. But Bertrand, first. Are you sure you want in on this? You're in your late 70s now. I don't like you touching violent crimes." She placed her hands straight out, palms out, "No. No. I'm not trying to make any demand. Just a concern about my oldest and dearest friend. I like it better when you're dealing with investor embezzlement or nursing home neglect." She pulled her arms back from reaching out to him and placed her hands on her desk. She looked down, the very slightest of a flush on her creamed coffee complexion.

Bertrand had more or less ceded control of ACJ Investigations to Augusta. Exceptions were clear. His office was to remain intact. He'd take cases at his own discretion and avail himself of all the tools of ACJ in doing so. Power was shared between them through that filter. Their mutual love was the real hold to their contract. He perceived that Augusta may have thought that she had gone too far. Of course, she hadn't. "I see your concern. I share it. But I'm going down this road and I will stay on it until, or if, I'm bested by the difficulty of the matter." He reached across her desk and took her hand. "Thanks Augusta for caring. I'll be careful."

CHAPTER 5

Augusta made contact with Concannon on her first try. Yes, he'd see her. Bertrand noted that his name was brought up gingerly. As he pulled out of the underground garage she blew a sharp breath. Finally, she said, "Okay Bertrand drive slowly I have to say something."

He looked at her cautiously, preparing for an earthquake. He had experienced a few similar incidents with her over the many years of their marvelous relationship. He said nothing in the tense silence.

"You and I agree, actually insisted as I recall, when we found each other and realized that we were into something deep that what preceded in our lives was best kept quiet?"

"Of course I do. Unless we had to, I didn't want to hear about old boyfriends, ugly breakups and the same for you. Of course, that didn't mean I didn't want to know you, your childhood memories and the like. We shared a lot about ourselves. But, yes, there were things we edited out. Some therapists say that's unhealthy."

Augusta cut in, "We thought otherwise and I have no regrets. Once in a while something would come up and I used as light a brush as I could to open up a scab. You too, I think," she said.

"Yes," he said without elaboration. This was her agenda wherever she was going to take it.

"So, my dearest friend I have to open a past page. Please hear me out."

"Of course Augusta," he said softly as he steered the Camry toward the Centennial Bridge that would take him from Davenport, Iowa, into Illinois and Rock Island. He drove slowly.

"Before I met you I asked for your intervention with my Wisconsin escapee of a husband. I was in a very bad place emotionally, financially, and with every part of me hurting. Drinking too much. By the time I came to you I was slightly on the mend. You never met me when I was rock bottom. I even thought I would have to go back on the beat with some P.D. around here. And then, of course, my two daughters. I felt I was losing them." She stopped.

Bertrand said, "I saw pieces of that hurt when you sought our help, Augusta. But your strengths overwhelmed me. Almost love at first sight."

"If only you knew how truly scattered I was. You would have walked away."

"No. You have it wrong there. But we've been through this conversation. This isn't why you're talking is it?"

"No. We've done some business in the past with Hugh Concannon. But mostly it came through me because I was a detective in Rock Island who served with him as a partner. The two of you met a few times but it was more incidental. I kept the two of you apart because you and he are unalike in many essentials. Friction, big time, was my read on your relationship with him."

"That was okay with me. Yes. I don't care for him. He's as subtle as a two by four. Your interferences with him were appreciated. I did notice. So, this time you see a problem. I'll have to deal with him because I've taken on this case. It's okay. I'll be extra diplomatic around him. Don't worry Augusta. Thanks for the heads up." The Camry had just crossed the center point of the Centennial Bridge. They were now in Illinois, the Mississippi River to their east and west, 60 feet or so beneath them. He was not quite sure why Augusta was being so dramatic about what was pretty obvious to him. He could see her staring at him in his peripheral vision.

"Please take this exit Bertrand and turn right at the light. I want you to park at the levee for a bit. I'm not finished."

He did as asked but now he was feeling considerable discomfort as he drove onto the flood levee in downtown Rock Island.

"This is hard for me. I've weighed the matter. It's a close call but I believe it's necessary. You know I love you," she looked squarely at him, adjusting herself in her seat to do so.

"Yes, of course Augusta," he stopped the car abruptly, placing it in park.

"In those times before I met you but after my former husband had left me? I had a few relationships. Always regrettable to me now but they happened nonetheless. My center was gone. I needed affirmation."

McAbee said, "Augusta! You don't have to go to this place. We've all been there. No one gets into their twenties and thirties without significant yardage being lost in their lives."

"No, Bertrand let me finish. Hugh Concannon was one of those hookups. Bastard that he can be, he was very kind to me. We were pretty steady for a few months. His wife found out. Remember, mayor's daughter. We ended it abruptly. I still like him. No, not to sleep with, or to have dinner with, but there is a creek that runs between us. Compared to you he's nothing, but he is something otherwise. I just couldn't sit between the two of you with you ignorant of this history. I feel like that would have been a betrayal to you. I won't ever go down that previous path. Even when I told you what he thought of you I thought I was dancing on an electric wire. You see, I am a prim and proper black woman," she concluded with a soft smile.

Bertrand was confused. He quickly compartmentalized the material. This disclosure had to be very hard on Augusta. Nothing said was meant to hurt him but he was bothered by the information. Not so much that she slept with Concannon and others but that their tryst was unwillingly snapped by Concannon's wife. There were still feelings between them, a creek as it were. But he had feelings for other lovers but none of whom was snapped off by a third party. However, he had no rights over her nor she him. They were always totally free to pursue any avenue they chose. Their love was based on that premise. They wanted no holds. And yet he was thrown off stride.

"Hey Mistah. You still there? Knock, knock," she said softly.

"I'm glad you told me. Thanks. I'm a little bruised I admit. I'm stuck on the analogy. Creeks empty into rivers.

I'm threatened, I guess. And I have no excuse for that. We've always understood our freedom. Remember the date you went on some years ago? That was not easy for me to handle."

"Shoulda been. He was a loser from the word go. If anything you came out of it looking like a god," she laughed at the memory.

"So Concannon? Is he on the loose? Will there be secretive leers?"

"Bertrand. What happens to creeks when there's no rain?"

"They dry up."

"But they're still called creeks, right?

"Yeah."

"There ain't no rain in sight, mistah. Don't ever forget that."

He leaned across his seat. The seat belt snared him. He said softly, "Jesus," as he disconnected it. He kissed her deeply, hard.

When they disconnected from each other she said, "I love it when you're rough with me."

"Hah. Let's go meet this scoundrel, Hugh Concannon."

CHAPTER 6

Hugh Concannon was pissed off at Augusta. She should know better than to place ACJ into the middle of a homicide investigation. And then she said she was bringing along the owly bastard McAbee who somehow won over her affections. Wow, what a pair!

He reminisced about their torrid affair those too many years ago. She had aged well. If she gave him the chance he'd gladly try to find those times again especially as Augusta's two girls were in college. As far as he knew McAbee was still her squeeze even though the bastard was 500 years older than she. There wasn't any way to say no to her about meeting with them. But if the geezer had asked by himself he would have put him into a psychological skillet and fried the fucker. He'd see how the session would play out. Perhaps they were trying to lessen the shock for Professor Pruitt who looked like he was one step from assisted care. How those old bastards hung on at colleges and universities was beyond him. And yes, he didn't really suspect Pruitt but that wasn't to mean he didn't deserve the full Concannon playbook as he euphemistically called his shows of belligerence.

He heard Augusta's voice out in the hallway that was protected by Diane Furey. Diane wouldn't let God by her unless it had been cleared through him. He fully intended to make life difficult for the two of them even as he knew he'd have to be careful around Augusta, not wanting to terminate all hope of a future affair with her. Diane acted as instructed.

He listened closely as he could almost hear the exchanges between Furey and Satin. The stiff McAbee said nothing that he could hear. Finally, Diane buzzed him. Curtly, no other way with the former semi-driver, Diane said, "There is a woman out here Detective Concannon. She says that she has an appointment with you. She's not in the schedule book. Her name is Athena Satin and she is accompanied by a man named Brian McFee. They are both PIs from across the river. I've identified them by their cards."

"Send them back here in five minutes. Thanks," he said in barely a whisper, appreciating Furey's screwing up their names. He opened up his Facebook page and answered a few queries. There was a message on his iPhone from a nurse he had been cultivating for some action. He responded to her with a hint of seduction and then he could hear the footsteps coming his way down the hall toward his office. He braced himself.

Augusta came into the office first with a brief rap on his office door. "Hey Hugh. I'm not Athena but she was close, I guess," she said lightly.

He arose from his seat. They shook hands as he was quickly introduced to Bertrand, name also corrected by her, no handshake between the two, however.

Concannon nodded and looked away from McAbee and as he told them to sit across from his desk in the two seats that faced him.

"So good to see my old partner. You okay?" he asked as warmly as he could as he maneuvered his chair so as to face Augusta and avoid eye contact with her goddam great grandfather.

He knew she knew what he was doing, her eyes showing a bit of flame. "I'm fine. Still at ACJ and, of course, you and Bertrand have had incidental contact over the years. Appreciate the time, of course. Bertrand has taken on Dr. Pruitt as a client. As I told you on the phone that's why we're here. We'd like some help from you. Bertrand?"

Concannon turned in his chair and almost faced McAbee directly. "What exactly can I do for you? The *Times* almost had it perfectly. When I spoke with your client he seemed flustered. Upset with questions. You can assure him that he's not a prime suspect. I think he was rattled. Never been around a fresh murder scene. After all it was his sister. In no way am I clearing him but my focus will go elsewhere. What else can I help you with?" He looked back toward Augusta as he wondered about her words. She had said Bertrand took the case. Not ACJ. Not her. And didn't he hear somewhere that the buzzard was retired or something close?

McAbee said in his concise manner of speech, respectful but with a piece of steel hidden in it. "Dr. Pruitt is an old colleague from the days I taught as St. Anselm. I'm not here to console him *only* as a result of our visit. I intend to engage with the murder. I do have an Illinois license as a PI or whatever they call it nowadays. I'm hoping for some collaboration with you, Detective Concannon. It is an ACJ case. I personally will be the principal."

Concannon looked back at Augusta who was nodding her assent to what McAbee had said. In his heart he wanted nothing to do with McAbee and ACJ. Augusta? She was merely running interference for this meeting. He figured that it was now down to him and McAbee. It would be to his advantage to play McAbee along without her involvement as he was determined to keep the door open for her as a future possibility. But McAbee? He'd bury the son of a bitch as soon as they were alone. When McAbee had tossed around the word 'collaboration' it took all of Concannon's discipline to keep his mouth in check. That was just not going to happen. "Well why don't you set up a meeting with me later this week. Diane Furey has my schedule. I'll go over some of the things we've established. If I need your help, of course, I'll ask," he said through semi-gritted teeth.

"While I have you I have one particular question. Agatha Pruitt's computer, phone?"

"No," he said bluntly as he could, warning McAbee to tread carefully. "They were taken as far as we can determine." He gave a side-eye to Augusta, sure that McAbee picked up on it.

"I'd like to visit the crime scene."

"Call me tomorrow. We'll be finished in there by then. I'll see if we can make it happen. Is there anything else?"

Augusta spoke, "Do you have any suspicions?"

"Too soon. You know me. Everyone is a suspect. Both of you for that matter," he emitted the slightest of smiles. "As a favor to you Augusta I'll keep your guy here informed as long as he stays within the bounds of what a PI is obligated to do relative to an active homicide investigation." He noticed that McAbee was looking at him oddly, as if he was a specimen of sorts in a biology lab. "Well if that's it I'll stay in touch on this case. Good to see you again partner," as he gazed at Augusta and then gave a preemptory look of purposeful disdain at McAbee. When he saw them out of the building he was pleased with himself, a first-rate show on his part.

In the car going back to Iowa Augusta said, "I'm sorry Bertrand. He was being a bastard to you. It will be tough sledding for you. Let me know how it's going with him. If he's impossible I'll confront him. I've backed him down a few times over the years," she patted his shoulder.

Bertrand said nothing in response. His mind was absorbed with many things. Nothing new there.

CHAPTER 7

Barry Fisk was annoyed when McAbee's number popped up on his cell. He was irritated with him because his semi-retirement had cost Barry. Augusta Satin used him only sparingly and then so with all sorts of warnings about ethics and procedures. She was a prude. McAbee wasn't a prude but he was a hypocrite of gargantuan proportions pretending to be virtue-signaling at Barry's illegal methods yet all too ready to use anything Barry had wrested from his hacking activities. He answered the call, "Yeah."

"It's me, Bertrand. How's your short term memory, have you forgotten me?"

"Ha ha. I wish it could be that easy. A turn-off switch. What do you want from me? I'm busy," he said in exaggerated tones that concealed his secret joy at hearing from McAbee, one of the few humans he could tolerate.

"I'm taking a case. I need your help."

"My prices have gone up. Lots of clients. You'll just have to get in line." He figured that McAbee knew that this was false, not the part of more clients but that he'd ever let McAbee wait. He owed so much to him nonetheless determined as he was to make sure that he'd never disclose any of this to McAbee. No sense showing weakness to anyone, he thought.

"I know Barry. I know it all. Have you read the *Quad City Times?*"

"I get the e-edition. It gets the five minutes it deserves."

"The Agatha Pruitt murder."

"Ah, yes. A perfect case. I actually thought of you when I saw her brother taught at St. Anselm. So, you got suckered into this?"

"Yes. Suckered is probably a good word."

"Well, you are getting old," he said meanly. He reproached himself instantly. Quickly, he said, "How can I help?"

McAbee gave him everything he knew about the case, including the difficulty of working with Hugh Concannon.

Barry said, "Hugh Concannon! He's a can of Covid spit. So, specifically what can I do?"

"A complete search on Agatha Pruitt. Whatever you can dig up. She was a research librarian at Iowa. Secondly, she was privately investigating the disappearance and murder of a close friend from 45 years ago. Margaret Thode. Need everything you can find about that case. Something bothersome, Agatha's computer and phone are missing. She was brutally murdered. 'Tortured' was a used word about her. Connections between the two seem clear to me."

"Okay, I'll get on it. Is Pat Trump still at ACJ?"

"She is and I want you to behave toward her."

"Me? What about her? She fools you, you must know. She's nasty and vile. You should have fired her years ago. What does she have on you?"

Joseph A. McCaffrey

"Barry! Back off on Pat. When you've put things together call me. We'll talk."

"Okay, okay," furious at the thought of that red-headed minx who ran McAbee's life.

CHAPTER 8

Barry Fisk was puzzled as he sought information on victim Margaret Thode. The revisit by the *Times* he reasoned would resurrect the case out of the inactive inferno where it had been placed by the Rock Island Police Department. Apparently, the article had no impact in Rock Island, in Barry's judgment, the sorriest city in Illinois. But it had serious competition for that designation. The police response was probably dictated by the run of shootings and violence that the city constantly endured. It simply was a matter of a poor tax base, an over-stressed department, and too many crime-ridden neighborhoods.

What he found to be normal with that department and its IT security was its lack of security. Within minutes, he hacked the entire network of their police files. Some years ago his nefarious work was advanced when funding was provided by some federal agency for Rock Island to digitize all of their records over a 50 year period, the funding allowed for a sophisticated security system to protect all records. So much for sophisticated security as Barry was set to prowl files about the Thode case.

But first he pursued the active file that had brought McAbee into this matter, Agatha Pruitt. He anticipated problems because Hugh Concannon was the head detective on the matter. Concannon never entered anything into a computer except for some default necessities. Fisk had learned this the hard way a few years back on another query for a firm from Chicago for whom he did spec work. Concannon was paranoid about secrecy. He probably had divined that someone like Barry was lurking out there. 'Screw him,' Barry said to himself sourly as he went back to the enormous file on the murder of Margarete Thode.

Hours later he completed a quick read on the case. He was unfamiliar with the principals, likely most of them dead and gone by now. The local police were assisted by the Illinois Bureau of Investigation. However, for some reason that was not discernable from the data, the Bureau kept a distance from the case, advisory the operative word. Maybe the chief investigator on the Thode case was as fierce and protective as Concannon. His name was Abe Snider. A Google search found him dead in 1999.

Margaret Thode was an obsessive distance runner and bicyclist and at 18 years of age was quite accomplished, so much so that her parents were concerned about her mental health. Efforts were made to try to divert her, find new interests. Interviews and some hard questioning was done by Snider and his team with anyone who was involved in the effort to reorient Margaret. Snider couldn't hook any of these to her murder. The list included two high school counsellors, a Methodist Minister, several neighbors, even a few friends of Margaret who had been solicited to help dissuade her from her passion. Agatha Pruitt was on that list.

Noteworthy was Margaret Thode's brilliance as a student and her loner qualities.

Anybody who remotely resembled a vagrant was brought in and questioned harshly. All of the local police departments and county sheriff units helped with the round up in western Illinois and eastern Iowa. Three of the 57 who raised suspicions were hammered pretty hard but to no avail.

Boaters in Sunset Marina on the west side of Rock Island were interrogated but no significant leads came. The marina, which housed 49 boats, was tucked away in a Rock River estuary. Boats could work their way out into the Mississippi River from the marina. The park that edged the marina was a busy spot for cars and teens. Lead on lead generated names, questions and more questions. Yet there was no salient progress. Everything was turning up cold as the media got hotter and hotter about the 1978 killing.

Margaret's family lived five and a half miles from the spot where her body was recovered by a 12 year old boy who lived on a houseboat in the marina. The body was in a high grassy area but a boy biking along the path noticed an oddity. Her kneecap bent up just high enough to be seen and investigated by him. He fled back to his parents who were on their boat. The police were called. Clothing shredded. She had been beaten severely, and found to be sexually molested. It was an act of absolute fury, frenzied, and Detective Snider felt, but could not demonstrate, very personal. Someone who knew her. Her classmates at Rock Island High School were questioned, no one fit as a serious suspect.

She was a very quiet girl. Studious. Introverted. Scarcely, anyone failed to mention her love of running and biking.

"She could run for a half day," "I'd see her all over the city – always biking and fast too" were some of the comments.

Snider was frustrated. Days passed. But he stayed on the murder for months before his attention was taken by other cases in Rock Island. Anniversaries were ticked off.

Another detective named Bailey took a shot at it nine years later in 1987. He enlisted the media and pleaded for help. Nothing came of if it other than some false leads and memories. A few people used the new investigation as an opportunity to suggest their neighbor was involved in the murder.

Years after years came and went. Margaret's parents died, a year apart in 2002, 2003. She was an only child.

Bertrand had informed Barry that there was reason to believe that Agatha Pruitt might have discovered something somewhere. Typical McAbee, Barry thought, speculating about a speculation. That he was right sometimes did not matter to Barry. McAbee was extraordinarily intuitive, he'd give him that but there was little chance that Agatha Pruitt could dig up anything new. After all, he had scanned the whole damn file, murder book and all. Agatha may have been a proficient digger but without the murder book and all of the data he had, she couldn't succeed. Her computer was stolen because of its value, an Apple Pro. He had to be careful with how he expressed these thoughts to McAbee, who regularly accused him of misogyny. Another stupid piece of intuition by the head of ACJ.

CHAPTER 9

Barry was irate. McAbee had hit a nerve. His comment had tested Fisk's sense of superiority over others. Only he was the able one when it came to hacking into systems. Now a sullen silence had fallen across Bertrand's office. Barry expected to be appeased. After all, he had given a detailed summary about the Margaret Thode murder. Even though he was as stymied as the Rock Island police was about the killer. He could offer no new insights, no suggestions about future avenues of approach.

What caused upset was McAbee wondering if Agatha Pruitt had also managed to hack into the police networks, the insinuation that she was as gifted as Barry. Not just that but that she had seen something in the files that Barry had missed. It was merely a musing on his part but it caused Barry to take it as an insult, an assault.

In what was a rasp of sorts Fisk said, "Impossible. Hard to hack and there was nothing there. How could you even think that?"

McAbee thought that there was a slight glisten in Barry's eyes. But he wasn't going to back away from the consideration. Agatha Pruitt was no slouch when it came to research. Hacking was another issue. Would her academic experience and adherence to ethical standards preclude her from acting like Barry? Furthermore, she could have found or seen something that had no connection at all to the police files, a new datum that she unearthed in her own investigation and study of the matter. But Barry? He was no gallant knight when it came to women. In McAbee's dealings with him over the years, time after time, Barry was a repeat offender toward women – not physically but in attitude, word, and thoughts. He was a chauvinist.

"Impossible, you say. Come on Barry. Cut the posturing and the illogic. Of course she could see things that you can't. She knew some of the witnesses who were questioned by the police, herself included. That gave her a unique insider advantage. Maybe she found out something from a friend these many years later. When you use the word *impossible* I wonder about you," McAbee finished with a fist pound on his desk surface. He didn't care to confront Barry so harshly but sometimes exasperation took him to that place and predictably Barry went into a deep pout. "Do you understand my point Barry?" he said in a softened manner.

After a considerable interlude Barry barked, "Yeah, yeah, yeah. Is there anything else?"

"Not now," Bertrand said glad to see him go.

"I think I better leave before Pat comes out of her coffin," he said gruffly.

"How much trouble would it be to transfer over to me the entire file on the Thode murder?"

"No problem. I'll encrypt it and get it to you. You can print it. Over 6000 pages. You don't seriously think you'll find something, do you?"

"When I learned Greek and Latin I became a cryptographer of sorts. You never know Barry."

CHAPTER 10

McAbee was surprised when Hugh Concannon called him. He conjured a coiled snake deceitfully angling for a fatal strike. Concannon was making an effort at being cooperative. Bertrand would play along in suspended trust.

"So, we're pretty much done with our crime scene investigation. You won't find anything there. In a folder on the kitchen table, some notes. Don't take, just view. Lock code on the door is 6967. Visit today and whatever you do use latex gloves and don't remove anything. Got It?" he asked in light gruff.

"I do. Appreciate this Detective Concannon. Anything further on her computer, phone?"

"No," now in heavy gruff. "Be in touch," he disconnected.

Citizenry impatience about the murder was ticking away on Concannon. This was going to be a protracted case, Bertrand and Concannon both knew this.

Already called and prepared to accompany Bertrand was Jack Scholz. Bertrand admired Jack for his skills, his ability to cut through problem areas even though with a butcher's imprecision. It disturbed him that no one appreciated him except for Bertrand whose awe of

Jack ran up against a unified wall of disdain at ACJ. Augusta Satin, Pat Trump, and Barry Fisk were united in a strange bond of compatibility. Their spurning was based on Jack's background as a special operative for the United States Government. Any agency that used him for clandestine work had guaranteed immunity as Jack was deniable. He fostered this deniability by his isolation and his own personal paranoia. To know Jack was to know dark matter.

For some reason Jack Scholz and McAbee synced. This alone caused consternation. Augusta claimed that McAbee had lost his conscience or suspended it when he employed Jack on some of his cases. Pat averred that she could literally feel terror oozing from his skin and Barry was overwhelmed by fear and loathing indirectly accusing McAbee of being a fascist. Not from Jack himself, but from a close confidante of his, McAbee was let into some of Jack's exploits on behalf of the United States. Violence as a descriptor was an understatement. Bottom line, Jack's Irish companion in terror, Dineen, had confidentially told McAbee during a long drinking session while on a job for McAbee – Jack was a stone-cold killer. None better. But he quickly added, 'always on the right side.' By that he meant in the service of the United States. He wouldn't cut your throat except for a good and patriotic reason.

From Bertrand's point of view, he only used Jack when he was quite sure of his conclusion about someone's guilt or complicity while legally he was checked from taking any action. Into such a quagmire, Bertrand employed Jack to cut through sludges of lies and coverups. And yes, Jack did comfortably resort to torture and violence if necessary over their long relationship. Bertrand never felt guilt over using Jack. He would look the other way, even pretend not to see, but he found Jack to be a defender of truth. Augusta had seen this to be a dark trait in Bertrand.

Scholz and he drove over to Rock Island, parking outside of Agatha's house. Only a few cars dotted her street. He saw no one near the house but he thought that he might have seen a curtain move to the south of the house adjoining Agatha's place. That didn't surprise him. This quiet neighborhood had to be spooked.

He entered the code in what was the equivalent of a realtor's lock. They entered the house. It was a small ranch with a basement. On the main floor was a kitchen, a small dining room area to a corner of it, a living room, two bedrooms and a bathroom. The basement was partially finished. There was a couch, a treadmill and a television. The lighting in the finished half of the basement was ample. The other half was jammed with boxes of books, plastic cartons of papers and memorabilia, stacked willy-nilly. Agatha hadn't been there long; he was sure that she would have been occupied for a long time trying to sort everything.

After the quiet perusal of the house they entered the bedroom where Agatha Pruitt had met her violent end. He immediately was drawn to the blood-soaked sheets and pillow. There had been no cleanup.

There was an odor in the room of human waste. He wondered if Concannon had even informed Richard Pruitt that he was done and that there were services available in the Quad Cities that specialized in cleaning up scenes of terror and mayhem. Jack said nothing but was busily surveying the room. He moved back to the door of the bedroom and yanked something from atop a picture frame near the doorway.

"Camera, mic. Recent. Concannon," he whispered. "I'll look for others. We're being watched." He left the bedroom and went down the hallway. McAbee scanned the bedroom seeing a small brass lamp that served as a reading light that had fallen to the floor. A trunk that matched the width of the bed at the base of the bed's frame was opened, the lid broken on the left hinge, contents strewn haphazardly, half in, half out, of this linen storage piece. To the right of the bed was a large bureau, drawers removed and contents straddling the bureau and the wooden floor. To the left of the bed was a small closet, a similar scene – disorder. For reasons he couldn't explain, he construed that Agatha Pruitt was a meticulous woman. What was happening to her bedroom she may have witnessed before her death. He peered closely into the closet, on the top shelf there were shoe boxes. A Rock Island police tape on each box indicated that they had been searched.

Jack came back and whispered into his ear, "Two more, kitchen and basement. Left them there. Maybe more too. I'm going to probe the whole place now," he left. There was a padded seat to the left of the bed. McAbee sat as he pondered the room. This wasn't his first run as scenes such as this. He tried to void his mind of all sensation and ideas. Was there something in this scene that could speak to him at another level of understanding? What came to him were tears of anguish and redhot fury. Was it his projection or did the room speak to him about the last moments of Agatha's murder? He stood up and left the bedroom and went to take in the entire house, on two occasions crossing through Jack's field of vision. An hour later the two of them were heading back to Davenport across the Centennial Bridge. Neither of them spoke.

CHAPTER 11

"Bertrand, park by the river. I need to speak with you," Scholz said in semi-whisper.

This was nothing new for Bertrand. Jack had no trust in closed places such as Bertrand's office and, perhaps, even his car. Something was probably seen back at Agatha's house.

He parked 50 feet or so north of the river. It was a flawless spring day in Davenport, partially sunny, breezy, about 50 degrees. They left the car for a walk.

"Something queer in that house, the Rock Island police had three devices there. One in the bedroom, another in the kitchen and one in the basement. But my meter, don't ask, registered another on a different frequency. The three police ones all had a tiny Rock Island logo. Why they put three in there is speculation but I'd say they were placed in anticipation of your visit. Hugh Concannon is as trusting as I am. And yes, I know him. We don't mesh. We've had our difficulties. I'm sure he's gloating at your bringing me along with you. Accusations will fly against us both. Me? Because I was not given permission by him to be there and you because you brought me along. It's a perfecta for him. You'll have to keep him at bay on this because he's looking for a reason to get you removed. He might even try to go after your Illinois license. He's a crafty bastard but in the world I inhabit he's essentially an ass. Very beatable. A raging bull pursuing a red cape. Once in a while he gets the matador and looks good. But mostly his kind are losers."

"What else?" McAbee knew there was more to come.

"In the house itself? Whoever it was tore it apart piece by piece. Okay, I get it. Her PC and phone were taken but I think she had something else, tangible. I don't think it was found. Maybe it wasn't in the house. Did they impound her car?"

"Yes."

"When they bring it back or give it to her brother, whatever, I'd like a look."

"I'll see to it. More? The other device?"

"Yes. And this is big. Concannon missed it. That device? Movement and sound. In her living room. I wouldn't have found it unless I had a whole day with help. My meter got it at a peculiar frequency. Very different from what the cops placed in the house. My meter is still classified – highly protected. Again, don't ask. Placement of the device was extraordinary, expert. Conclusion? You're up against someone who is sharp, not Concannon."

"Can you determine the source the device is signaling back to?"

"Not sure. I have to consult. I didn't stare at it because I didn't want it known that I had taken it in. I think I was successful. So, if you go back there remember it's recording you and it ain't the cops."

"Anything else?" McAbee asked.

"The house is old. Built in 1927. Lots of cubby holes. The cops probably got everything but I'd like to hit it again with some of my guys. But I don't want Concannon showing up and arresting us."

Bertrand knew that Jack's 'guys' were almost to a man special service types. Highly trained and proficient. If something was missed by Concannon they'd find it. "I'll try to work it out with him through Augusta. You know technically it's no longer a crime scene. Richard Pruitt is in charge. Power of attorney."

"He told you that it was okay for you to go in. But did he tell you it was no longer a crime scene? Or that he was almost done? Do you see what I'm getting at? Traps. Was Augusta involved in any way?"

"Yeah. She was the medium. Concannon was in outright dismissal of me as a person. Without her, I wouldn't have gotten to first base with Concannon. I think she scares him a bit."

"Or entices?" Jack said off-handedly.

"Where did you get that from?"

"So he doesn't want to alienate her but he wants you out by your own mistakes and misunderstandings. The fact that he is using a police lock on the door tells me that it is still a crime scene."

"I'll call Richard Pruitt and then Augusta. Maybe he cleared the place with Richard."

"Doubt it. Keep your eyes open. Let me know when I can come back in there cleanly. Assume he already is cooking up a plot to get you tossed out. I'm okay here, I'll just walk. Bye." He walked away quickly.

Bertrand, driving to ACJ just a few blocks away, wondered why he was involved in the Agatha Pruitt murder. Why should he deal with characters such as Hugh Concannon? Both situations were of quicksand. He was feeling old, a bit worn down.

His mood was not helped when he came into ACJ. Pat Trump looked upset about something. He wondered whether Barry Fisk had been around the place. She said, "Did you ever watch any of the Harry Potter movies?"

"I have," he said warily.

"Do you remember a scene where his classmate is sent a 'howler' by his mother, she being furious. An owl delivers a rolled up message. When the kid opens it the letter screeches out a nasty message, mother to son. Everyone in the dining hall hears, snickering and scorning the poor kid." She stopped as she eyed him with probably sympathy.

He wasn't sure about where this was headed but there was a foreboding context. "You're being very subtle today Pat, out of character. What's up?"

"Augusta is out of the office on an assignment. So I get a call, a howler in other words, from a past adversary. He's screaming at me when I truthfully tell him that Augusta is not here. Nor are you. Amazing similarities between the message howler and Hugh Concannon. He seems to have inferred that I am a partner in ACJ and that I am aware of an egregious violation of trust committed by you. The name of Jack Scholz brought up, fury heightening. I tell him that I am merely a secretary. He concludes with a threat toward you and Jack. It was a five-minute diatribe. Augusta is to call him ASAP. Disconnect, fortunately done by cell phone otherwise I would have been permanently deafened." She scrunched her lips and corkscrewed them to one side, the slightest of smiles on her face.

"Ah Pat. Sorry about this."

"It's okay. He's theatre. He'd probably make it big time on Broadway. My *sang froid* got to him. I put my phone on speaker and lowered the volume. I remember him from a case you were dealing with some years ago. If he was willing I'd try to set him up with Barry Fisk. One or both would be out of my life forever in a few minutes. At the end of his tirade he asked 'Are you listening to me?' When I said, "Mostly" the disconnect occurred. "Am I in trouble?" she asked disingenuously.

McAbee laughed. He figured this might be close to how she handled Barry Fisk. But such an approach by her didn't always work as Barry had successfully gotten into her head and caused her to melt down on occasion. "Pat, he's an enemy pure and simple. But I have to work with Concannon no matter the conditions that haunt him. You handled him perfectly. I'm going to my office now for a bit. Augusta? Out for the day?"

"No, no. She'll be back shortly."

When Augusta came into his office an hour later she looked as tired as he felt. She sat across from him and let out a deep sigh.

McAbee said, "Is that sigh a before Concannon or an after Concannon?"

"After. Just finished with him. Bertrand, he set you up. He won't admit it but I know how he goes. He claims that you corrupted a crime scene, broke a command that you agreed to and allowed an unauthorized visitor into a scene that was off-limits. Jack Scholz does not have an investigator's license in Illinois in case you're going to assert that." She said this as gently as she could. But she was cognizant also that ten years ago when he was in his 60s, McAbee would never have missed Concannon's dirty tricks.

"What does he want?" he asked brusquely.

"Well, he wants you out of his hair. And Jack Scholz? You know this. He's on every radar of every police department in Illinois and Iowa. Yes, they can't nail him but they have the hammers, the nails, and the cross ready the minute he slips up."

"Was he yelling at you? He excoriated Pat," Bertrand said.

"He won't yell at me. I have an ace in the hole with him and he knows it. I made a deal with him…"

"Do you have to sacrifice your body?" he interrupted her harshly.

"Whoa, whoa." She held up her hands. This was a rare outburst for him. It was personal to him as a result of her admission of an affair with Concannon. She had broken through his celebrated stoicism. "Now you listen to me Mistah. I don't barter my body," she smiled trying to alleviate the tension, so unusual between them. "Just because I act like the Mata Hari sometimes don't you be assuming it here. There's nothing going on physically with him and there won't be," she looked at him, now sternly.

"I'm sorry Augusta. I feel like a fool. I walked into a trap and I'm angry with myself; I'm jealous too. The idea of him and you bothers me even though it happened before we knew each other and still and all I have no claim over you. Forgive me. I'm tired and susceptible to stupid thinking."

"I get the whole thing Bertrand. No more of this. Bottom line with Concannon, he'll back off with you. But Jack? No. He doesn't want him near this. Can you live with that? I didn't even have to play my ace, I just placed my hand near it."

"I get it. Sorry to have placed you and Pat too, into this net. If I make another mistake with Concannon, you should put me out to pasture," he said bleakly.

"Stand up and come over here," she stood and he came. She held him tight for quite a while.

CHAPTER 12

Bertrand made it to Richard Pruitt's office in Anselm Hall. On his way there, he passed through the familiar areas of classrooms, faculty offices, dusty halls, and walls that begged for a coat of paint, their current color he dubbed as shabby dirty yellow with scuff marks and stains from God knows what. The building was a problem 25 years ago when McAbee taught and had his office there. He recalled the paint crew just before he left in 1997 to open ACJ. 25 years later the fresh pale yellow had taken on the hues of a Siberian work camp. The Hall was the foundation building of the college. Its disrepair was abhorrent to him.

Except for Pruitt and a few others like him almost the entire faculty had turned over. Buyouts and a fresh set of administrators who had scant knowledge of the history of the school had decided that a 70 year old with a long record of good teaching and close student relationships was better replaced by 30 year olds who were grateful for a job in a system under decline. What did it matter if the 30 year old didn't give a damn about the school or its students as long as he or she could teach a course in literature or history? A teacher was a teacher, replaceable tires on an old car.

McAbee was aware that the school had an abysmal giving record by its alums. Anselm Hall was the iconic building; it was also emblematic of a dying heart.

"So Richard, how are you?" Bertrand asked, as he noted an office in disarray.

"Ah. I don't know, up and down. I buried Agatha privately, just a few friends. In Rock Island among my parents and a few family decedents."

"The house?"

"Maybe still a crime scene. Concannon has been reckless. I spoke to the police chief of Rock Island. He says 'soon' about Concannon and then looks down at his desk. Like he has no control over his homicide detective."

"That actually may be true," Bertrand said. "This is an important meeting for me Richard. I need you to really concentrate. I'm going to ask some questions that may seem irrelevant, off the wall."

"I understand," he replied.

"How close were you with your sister? On a scale of 1-10, with 10 as extraordinarily close."

"Six" he responded quickly. "We stayed in touch. She'd come to Davenport for dinner sometimes, maybe we'd eat out. The other way too, I'd go over there. We'd call each other two or three times a week. There's only 60 miles between the Quad Cities and Iowa City."

"Conversations?"

"Ah. Everything under the sun. Our sister in Colorado. What happened to her. What it was like to talk with her on the phone. Our parents. Our work, students, faculty. Weather. News. Covid. Retirement. How the time has passed so quickly. But we were pretty close. There'd be silences but we were comfortable with each other."

"When did she get serious about retiring from the University of Iowa?"

"She'd been talking about it for a few years. She was tired. I think the Covid scares started to focus her. She also had some health issues, high blood pressure, diabetes two, overweight and she'd smoke a bit, probably five or six a day. She sometimes drank more than she should have."

"So she retired about six months ago and heads to Rock Island. Home territory," McAbee said with a light smile. "Living at the house for about three months."

"Yes, home territory. She felt that she would eventually have to go into assisted care and she bought a house not far from where she wanted to be when her health failed. It was a health thing with her. She knew her health would be a big issue for her. But she liked the house she bought. She was pretty happy to be back here."

So far McAbee was not surprised at anything he heard. Consistent. "At Iowa City? Did she ever speak of enemies? Hostilities?"

Pruitt paused before answering, "Well not really. You know about higher ed, Bertrand. Lots of prima donnas, egos, petty politics, factions. She had to ride those waves. She was a service person. But Agatha was politically astute. She pretty much laughed at the spectacle when the negatives arose. She was great at pretending ignorance. Faculty member A slashing at B. Sarcasm or vitriol – she'd just pretend not to understand. What you're asking is would anyone act out against her. No, I don't see it. Never once did she allude to any fear of such. She would have said so."

"I got into the house, crime scene or not according to Hugh Concannon's whims. I brought along a colleague, very astute guy. His assessment? The murder was very personal, a grievance of sorts, not just a robbery gone wrong. The murderer was on a mission. Looking for something. Your sister was treated harshly..." McAbee said, purposely trying to understate what Agatha had to endure before her death. Richard was an unstable man in Bertrand's take on him. Hugh Concannon had probably already kicked him around about Agatha's last minutes.

"The neighborhood," Pruitt muttered.

"You mean that it was dark around the street?"

"Yes."

"Everything is possible, Richard. But I don't believe that the poor lighting precipitated the crime. It certainly didn't hurt to have darkness as a confederate but I think that it was an accidental, a corollary."

Pruitt said nothing in response.

"Her phone and computer were both taken from the house."

"Well good luck with that. She was scrupulous about security. She'd always preach to me. She had three levels of coding to go through including facial recognition and finger ID. If they were taken after they killed her they'd have no luck."

"You said they?"

"Just a manner of speaking," as he went to a small refrigerator and removed a bottle of water. McAbee declined when asked. McAbee looked around the office more closely. When he entered the macro impression was one of disarray. As he did a micro look he observed that there was more order in things. As Hugh Concannon would attest to Richard Pruitt was still a suspect, however remote that was. "So Richard the most likely motive? Your assessment?"

"She was head over heels on the murder of Margaret Thode."

"Head over heels. What does that mean?"

"She was fixated on it. They were the best of friends. I believe that Margaret's murder had a lifelong effect on Agatha."

"Was that a reason for coming back here?"

"If so, it was minor. *But* when she settled down in Rock Island she was struck by the article in the newspaper. The 45th anniversary of her murder. That established the groundwork for her going to war as it was. She was a world class researcher. People from the university still went to her even after her retirement."

"Would you say that she was an obsessive-compulsive?"

"Hah! That's only half of a true description of Agatha."

"So when you two spoke. What did she say about Margaret Thode?" McAbee asked as he was threading his way into what he conjectured was a likely cause of Agatha's murder.

"She was unable to get police reports. She went through channels but she hit a wall. However, she gained access to all of the newspaper reports and she was even able to interview a reporter who was close to the investigation, Kahl Home in Davenport. She also got in touch with some of Margaret's classmates. So, she was able to reconstruct some of the police approaches. A girl who was interviewed by the cops back then would remember how she was questioned. This told

Agatha how the cops were angling things. You can imagine how thorough she was."

"Must have been a bunch of potential witness deaths from so long ago," McAbee said.

"Yes. She ran into that. But there were children, for example, who would recall comments made by a deceased parent or friends."

"What kind of conclusions was she coming to?"

"Welcome to Agatha. She was leery of conclusions, at least anything she'd share with me. But some things. She thought the cops were slow, off the mark. They were not aggressive enough. The only thing that seemed to move them into action was a television story, or a newspaper article suggesting incompetency. Then they'd rise up and make noises about progress until things died down. She thought that the death of Margaret had been politicized if that makes sense. That there was some kind of wall. She was frustrated, I know that. But the more you frustrated Agatha the harder she would dig in," he smiled wistfully.

"You said wall? What does that mean Richard?"

"She'd say that she'd look at a scene, for example, a baseball field. She was a big Cubs fan by the way. Never could understand that. She'd go out to Arizona every Spring for the Cactus League. Loved spring training. An addict about it," Pruitt said in disbelief.

"How so? There are lots of people who go out there for that?" McAbee was wondering why Richard was so judgmental about his sister's love for the Chicago Cubs. Some of his best friends had that flaw in their character, he thought ruefully.

"I can't stand baseball. An insane game."

McAbee recalled baseball way back in the 1950s and 60s. He loved the game then but now grudgingly was coming to agree with Pruitt. Long game, salary absurdities, player distancing from fans and a host of other annoyances had caused him to distance himself from the sport. He remembered a time when antique stores were omnipresent in America. He thought that baseball was on a serious decline like antique stores. Was it a sport that had had its day? "You were saying. A baseball field. What about it?"

"She'd say that before the ballgame started the field was in perfect condition. Batter boxes perfect rectangles, baselines straight as an arrow, bases clean and white. Everything as it should be. She would say that the crime scene and the investigation marred the field. The field was the scene before the crime."

Bertrand was unsure about this analogy. Since when could a crime scene be compared to a baseball field before it was played on. "I'm not getting this comparison," he said to Richard.

"The comparison is this. When she looked at things she expected to see the whole field, what should have been in place should be in place. Even though she didn't have the full police reports what she should have had should be in place, the baselines, the bases – that should be there. But it was as if what should have been on the field was not there. When she looked at the case of Margaret Thode's murder things were missing that should be there. Something that should have been there was missing, as if a base was missing. That someone took it. Her vison of things was flawed not because of her eyes but because of what she was allowed to see."

He pondered what Richard said, still not quite sure what Agatha was trying to get at. "I could see her saying that if she accessed the police files. Then the analogy would make sense. It would be as if a piece of the police investigation that should have been in the file was not or that the file was unclear. Are you sure that she didn't access the police documents?"

Pruitt looked down. There was a hesitancy in his body posture as though he went into himself. He seemed smaller, contracted. He didn't answer McAbee who was waiting him out. The silence between them became a third person in the room, in effect. Finally his tired eyes found Bertrand, "She may have."

"Richard! Listen to me. You have to level with me. She can't be prosecuted. What you say to me is said to me only. Don't hold back. Once you threw that baseball diamond concept to me you told me more than you wanted to. She wouldn't be the first to gain access to the Rock Island police files. What Agatha did was illegal but I can't think of anyone better than she to study what was done. She had firsthand knowledge. She was close to Margaret Thode, questioned by the police back then in fact. So tell me more Richard."

"I'm not comfortable about this. I feel that I'm betraying her, plus she wasn't telling me that much. She would say that ignorance is a good friend sometimes. For me that is. Not for her, of course. You must understand that I had no particular interest in the murder of Margaret Thode. I felt sorry about it but the matter was not an obsession for me as it was for Agatha. She did feel great guilt about her behavior. It wasn't like her to hack. She said that things were shrouded. That the police investigation had been incompetent from the start. She wasn't sure how to proceed since she had no business accessing the file to begin with. Do you see?"

"I do. I'll try to get a better sense of this," he said, thinking that Barry Fisk might reach the same conclusion as Agatha did. However, he had no interest in sharing information about Barry and his illegal feats with Pruitt. "So Richard. Agatha basically redid portions of the police investigation on her own. On foot?"

"Sometimes. Mostly by phone or email. But she did meet a few at a coffee shop in Rock Island or downtown Davenport. Also the Kahl Home. But she was getting out there. She was trying to fill in the blanks."

"Her luck?"

"All she said was that she had filled in some blanks. But I didn't explore it with her. As I say it was not of great interest to me. I was pleased that she found things to do in her retirement. Her mind was too rich, too vibrant; she needed something like this. The fact that she hacked meant that she was onto something. The police wouldn't cooperate. So it was like her to jump the line. Will you stay on this Bertrand?"

"I will. But you have to open up to me, Richard. What you shared with me is vital for me to know. One other thing, did she ever deal with Concannon when she was trying to access the police files?"

"She mentioned him. I think it was his attitude and the way he treated her request to see the files that made her cross the line. She felt compelled to hack the files because of him."

CHAPTER 13

Barry Fisk wasn't happy. He sat in Bertrand's office, waiting for him to come back from some event. When he came back McAbee excused himself. "My meter is ticking; 25 minutes for me to get here, 15 minutes for you to be late and you are getting close to a one hour bill. It's okay with me, after all I have nothing better to do," Fisk said in faux rage.

"You know Barry. I think that you need a dog or a cat. Probably a cat."

"What?"

"Yes. I think a cat. A dog would try to win you over. That would lead to a charge of animal abuse as the dog's efforts would be futile. A cat though? No. A cat would not waste its time. Even if the inclination was there it would connect the dots immediately. It would see you for what you are."

"And what's that?"

"Ah. That's a metaphysical question. Could never be answered in scientific language. Might have to hunt in Homer's poetry for that answer. What I'm trying to say is this, don't worry about your bill. Did you bring the materials?"

"I did. On a disc. I know, I know, you like paper. But there are over 6,000 pages of material. I've re-organized it so you'll have an easy time dealing with it. Pat, your viper in residence, can run it on your printer if you insist. I'd have to get new ink and more paper," he said this cautiously as he knew Bertrand was quick to defend Pat. "I have a sense of things. It was a pretty complete investigation. They were stymied. Like they couldn't get a hold on the murder. I felt they questioned half of Rock Island."

"There's Barry the scholar and there's Barry the scanner. Which did I get from you?" McAbee asked flatly.

Barry sensed that McAbee was up to something. In reality he had not given the Rock Island police case file a strenuous read. Did he miss something? "Scan," he answered truthfully.

"There were other eyes on this file. Agatha Pruitt had also hacked into this trove of materials."

Barry was surprised. "A professional librarian just retired from a university? Hacking? Are you sure of this? Those characters holding jobs like that are ethically restrained. If she did she committed a crime."

"And? What does that mean?" Bertrand asked irritably.

"That means there are people like me who reject the very word hacking and there are others for whom the word signifies a taboo. I assume she is of the latter disposition."

"Her brother indicated that she did hack this file. She was engrossed with this case. Perhaps a long-held suspicion by her? Or a pure coincidence in that the newspaper printed a reminder of the case and that snapped her to attention. Whatever it was, she fully engaged and I think that when she focused her mind she approached the police file as would a scholar, a professional researcher."

It wasn't often that Barry had to deal with a McAbee who seemed to be looking for a fight. Something had upset him, was it that Agatha Pruitt had seen a clue that Barry had missed? He knew from two incidents over their long time tenure together that when Bertrand became exasperated with him and figurative swords were drawn that he was no match for the quick-witted man across from him. It was time to get the hell out of his office. In as mild a voice as he could muster he said, "Bertrand. I was not ordered by you to parse that police file in any kind of exhaustive way. I'll be glad to do it. A misunderstanding." He watched McAbee carefully for any sign of sword play.

"I guess I always expect the scholar in you. But I see; 6,000 plus pages is 6,000 plus pages. Agatha probably had a lot of time and her interest was keen. So, here's my plan. I personally will spend a few days with the materials but I'd like you to do so too. I'd like to be in the place where Agatha found herself. According to Richard she suspected holes in the file. That fascinates me."

Barry agreed to probe the files closely and scurried from the office, glad to be out of McAbee's glare.

McAbee placed the disc into his computer port and saw that Barry had created an index of sorts and also had arranged the file chronologically. That would be a big help. He was pleased that he restrained himself from inflicting animus into their relationship. Furthermore, Barry had not been instructed to fine comb the files, yet his adroit mind usually caught things even at the level of a scan.

CHAPTER 14

Barry Fisk studied the Rock Island police files, 6322 pages to be exact, for two full days. He was looking for the absence of something in the investigation. The information passed to Bertrand by Richard Pruitt about his dead sister's baseball field analogy uppermost in his mind. McAbee had set him on a treasure hunt. He probed the interview list, cross checking the index against the actual interview and then forward to any possible interview extension, or repeats. His best guess revolved around missing pages or changes made in the police files, yet he kept going back to missing pieces. His notes about the files were now 12 pages long and yet he saw no inconsistencies in the original Snider investigation that was reported through 5771 pages. The Bailey follow ups took up the remainder of the file. Bailey seemed to be surfing around the Snider investigation, yet unsuccessful, Barry conjectured. Concannon had yet to add to the file, perhaps deciding to keep Agatha's murder separate and distinct from the case.

On page 6320 through to a shortened page 6322 he read Bailey's take on the case, to this job of his effort at re-looking at the original murder file. It was written as follows, as Barry observed a nuanced and hedging quality in his report.

> I have reviewed this case with care but under the restraints of the current crime activity in Rock Island there were limitations imposed upon me. That said, what was done by Detective Abe Snider was quite extensive and thorough. The studious indexing of the entire police file was extremely helpful. Close to 40% of the questioned subjects are either deceased, have moved from the area, ill or simply non-reachable. Of those only three were considered to be of consequence by me. Of the remainder of the files, about 60% more or less, was randomly cross-checked by me and some witnesses interviewed by phone, mostly. Of the witnesses most relevant, five were re-interviewed, two in person. It was noted by my partner, Robert Ross, that Detective Snider would occasionally attach letters to numbers. For example on page 1341 there was a 1341a, 1341b, and1341c. I found this to be irregular and I discovered the practice in two other places 2508 a, b and 4007 a, b, c, d. There was no urgency about these additions but the use of letters allows for irregularities in the investigation. But as noted, where these practices occurred the result was of

little consequence. However-the total sum of pages (6322) does not allow for nine missing pages. I believe, in summary, that what was done by the Department holds the scrutiny of time. Perhaps sometime in the future, given the proper amount of time, there would be reason to re-open the case.

Detective Carl Bailey

Barry read Bailey's writings at least ten times, coming back to it as if drawn in by a magnet. Bailey's carefully worded comments drew blood but only into a thimble.

He hacked into the City of Rock Island Human Resources Department, curious about Bailey. Carl Bailey had retired in 2011, he had stayed in Rock Island until 2020 and had a forwarding address in Las Vegas.

He called McAbee and had to deal with the vixen, Pat Trump. He was determined to get by her without any taunts or insults just as long as she did the same.

"Is Bertrand there?" he blurted out before she could speak, the less of her the better.

"No," she answered in her usual churlish manner. "Out of town, Las Vegas," she said. He knew she knew who was asking.

"Thanks," he disconnected. He thought he had done pretty well on the diplomatic front with red headed alpha fox.

He called Bertrand. He related that Pat had outed McAbee who told him he had just entered the Paris Hotel, he'd call back in ten minutes.

Barry went onto Google and researched the name Carl Bailey. There was four listed in the greater Vegas area. He quickly ascertained that two of them had been long time residents there. The third was in a long-term care facility close to Lake Mead. The chase ended when he discovered that the fourth Carl Bailey had only been out in the greater Vegas area for two years. The Carl Bailey who was now almost assuredly the former detective from Rock Island lived two miles from the strip. The probing continued under the hand of Barry who discovered that Carl Bailey was a house detective for the Bellagio. He figured that a place like the Bellagio had a small police force of its own, security a huge issue for the Vegas crooks. By the time McAbee called back Barry had an address, a phone number, and information that Carl Bailey worked in the Bellagio on weekends, Friday-Sunday nights 6 p.m. to 6 a.m.

"What's up Barry?" McAbee said.

"Do you have some time?"

"Sure. I'm out here till tomorrow."

"This is fortuitous. I want to run some things by you about the Agatha Pruitt case. Have you had a chance to review the police files?"

"Yes, but just a scan. I'm out here on an unrelated matter. Tell me, do you have something?"

"Maybe, but I'm not sure of consequences. For sure I understand what Agatha Pruitt was speaking to. The absences of things or at least the possibility. Let me explain."

As he did so McAbee was imagining Barry's legs firing away under the table. It took him about five minutes. Barry concluded, "So, there's the real potential that some parts of the files are missing. In his report, you can read it, it's at the end of the file, Bailey was not pleased with the use of letters attached to numbers. There could be more in the files than was indicated in the page count. It was a bad practice. I felt he was upset and even, perhaps, that he was pulled off the case."

"Interesting," McAbee said.

"The files were digitized. So, things could have been pulled and either secreted away, or destroyed or placed back into the file after the digitization. Who would ever want to see the original?" Barry said.

"Anything else?" McAbee sensed there was. He didn't think that Barry would call Pat and crawl through that barbed wire unless he had more than he gave.

"I think that Carl Bailey knows more than he's saying in his summation of the case. He should be spoken to."

"I'll try to get to him when I get back. Maybe I'll bring Augusta with me. Ex-cop and all that. Alive, I hope." He sensed a trap. It was sprung.

"Guess where he is?"

"No idea."

"Vegas! And you're in luck. I have his address and phone. He works at the Bellagio of all places, on weekends. Security."

McAbee was not keen about coincidences. Augusta was, however. "Give me the stuff I have some free time."

After Barry had disconnected McAbee immediately called Augusta Satin.

"Bertrand, I've been thinking of you. How is Vegas? Hello by the way."

"Well, I had a long conversation with the attorney who did the work for Willis. I hope she calls. It's in her court. Hello to you too," he said snidely.

"Listen to you," she said airily.

"Have a question for you, back to the Pruitt case. As I told you she was researching the Thode murder, obsessively. I'm speculating that was the reason she was murdered. When I spoke with Richard, her brother, he said that she accessed some files about the original investigation. Don't ask how, I don't know." Augusta, he knew, was no fan of hacking, one of her main reasons for her disdain of Barry Fisk. He didn't dare bring his name forward in the conversation. "There was a follow-up investigation years later by a Rock Island detective named Carl Bailey. He retired from the Rock Island P.D. He's out here in Vegas working security for the Bellagio. I'd like to speak with him. Barry ran him down for me. Do you know anything about him?"

"I smell gaps in what you're telling me but I'll pass on them. Carl Bailey was a good man. Intelligent. I knew him briefly when I got on the force. He was well respected. I could call him and ease your path with him. I know he liked me."

"Who didn't?"

"Hah! Don't you give me that crap Mistah."

"I'm just jealous and insecure," he said.

"Jealous yeah, insecure baloney."

He gave her Bailey's number. She told him she'd call him back and let him know if the coast was clear for him.

McAbee moved a chair to the window that afforded him a view of the Las Vegas strip. It was 2:00 p.m. The sun was out and Las Vegas Boulevard was full of people who looked like crawling insects from his 12th story room.

CHAPTER 15

"I had to wrangle him a bit. He has turned a little grumpy. Is this the story of old men?" Augusta said airily.

"Do you think old women are any better? And by the way how old is Bailey?" McAbee asked.

"Old ladies are pretty nice and he's 71, he mentioned."

"71? He's still pretty young. He's working the Bellagio too, at that age?" McAbee added.

"Those casinos? They have more employees than customers. Their assumption? Everyone is a crook; after all that's what they are. He'll meet with you but he's very suspicious about it. He claims his memory of the matter is vague. That's pure nonsense. From the discussion I could tell that he's quite sharp and I recall that his memory was outstanding. You'll have to win him over, Bertrand."

"Do you think he called Concannon?"

"Doubt it. There was no love between them. In fact, Concannon most probably bumped him out of his job. If anything he'd like to stick it to him."

Carl Bailey rarely picked up a call anymore from a number he didn't recognize. But this one he knew to be from eastern Iowa, probably Davenport or Bettendorf, the largest cities on the Iowa side of the Quad Cities. "Yeah?" he said.

"I'm Bertrand McAbee. Davenport. I'm a PI, Iowa and Illinois. I understand that Augusta Satin spoke to you on my behalf," he stopped.

Bailey listened carefully to McAbee, a slight East Coast accent to his voice. He came across to him as respectful and careful. Satin had spoken well of him and his firm ACJ, not entirely unexpected as she worked there. "Yeah, but I can tell you now that the case details are very dim to me," he lied. The case was actually very present in his mind. His removal from the follow-up of Snider's work still festered in him. He weighed the cost/benefit outcomes of any assistance to the reasonably polite guy on the phone. He decided to give McAbee some rope.

"I can imagine. Some years ago. I'm into it because I was hired by the brother of a woman who had re-opened the case on her own. She was a retired research librarian at the University of Iowa. She moved back to Rock Island. She had been a close friend to Margaret Thode, questioned at the time by Detective Snider. Her brother said she was obsessive about the case. He thought she might have been onto something. But she was beaten, tortured and murdered. Phone and PC taken. I think there is a very likely connection."

"What are the police saying?"

"I'm dealing with Detective Concannon. Does that say anything?"

Bailey laughed. "That says a lot." He liked McAbee's straight forwardness plus the fact that Augusta certified him. He thought highly of her.

"He thinks I'm meddling. There have been problems between us."

"Well, you sure as hell are," he said lightly as he was trying to construe how McAbee would take the taunt from him.

He laughed into the phone. "Yes. I am a professional investigator. Detective Concannon was clear and distinct on his point, that meant for him, a meddler. Bottom line? We're not good with each other."

"So, to your call. What exactly do you want from me?"

"Breakfast, lunch, dinner, or afternoon tea. Anything to ask some questions. I'm paying."

"For what?" Bailey asked.

"The meal or the tea," he said with a hint of sarcasm.

"Wow! Really generous of you," Bailey said evenly.

"So that I don't lose my virtue or my money out here is today possible?"

"Boy you're very pushy. Okay, I know you're probably panting to get back to Iowa. Where are you staying"?

"Paris."

"They have the French Bistro looking out across Las Vegas Boulevard at the Bellagio fountains. I'll meet you there in an hour. What do you look like?"

"Paul Newman or Cary Grant. I know what you'll look like. I'll see you," McAbee said.

"See you then." Carl Bailey liked him; he was easy to deal with.

McAbee sat on the open deck of the restaurant, seated by the rail. He could look down at the passersby, just a few feet from him on the sidewalk. He positioned his seat so that he could see the door that opened from the inside restaurant to the deck but also gave him a viewing platform for the walkers, a great seat on a nearly perfect day, 75 degrees and sunny.

In about ten minutes Carl Bailey was stepping out on the deck, looking around. Of the 40 or so tables only three were inhabited solo, one by an older woman and the other by a black guy in his twenties. Bertrand hesitated to signal. How damaged by age was Bailey? Almost simultaneous to this thought process Bailey walked over to him. He said, in a gruff voice, "McAbee?"

Bertrand arose and held out his hand. Carl had a firm handshake. They sat. "Order whatever you want Carl. I'm paying".

Bailey picked up the menu, scanned it briefly and said, "Okay, I know what I want. What do you want from me?"

McAbee careful here. If he said that the entire investigation file was in his possession Carl might go berserk with that news. He came at it sideways, "My client's name is Richard Pruitt; he's a prof at St. Anselm. It was his sister who was murdered. I'm not positive about this," he was massaging the truth, "but I believe that this wonk of a sister might have accessed the police files, all of them."

"Jesus!"

"I know. It's very upsetting that the Rock Island police security is poor. And, as I say, I'm not positive. But she sure knew a lot about things according to her brother. Hard to figure out how without concluding that she got into the system." He peered closely at Bailey whose lips were pursed tight. Bertrand felt no guilt about his deceptiveness.

Bailey said, "Go ahead. Tell me what you think you have."

"Bottom line? I concluded that somewhere in this case there might be a cover-up. Protection?" Might as well get it out there and see how Bailey responds, he thought.

The waitress came, late 30s, tired looking, seemed like she might have been crying, orders taken, she left, not friendly, not unfriendly. Bailey ordered a bottle of wine and a steak, rare. McAbee ordered French onion soup and water. Nothing was said between them as they both peered out at the Bellagio. The fountains sprang up to a Frank Sinatra song. They watched.

Bailey said, "That's quite a leap you just made. Also if she hacked into the files she was out of bounds big time. Felony. Were the files fully digitized? They were contemplating such."

"Apparently. I don't see how else she could have read them. Can't see the P.D. letting that happen."

"You're right. They wouldn't. So, tell me again. Why are you fooling with this?"

"Her brother. He's a broken man. Loved his sister. He's convinced that his sister, Agatha, was done in because of her inquiries. I taught at St. Anselm, her brother is a former colleague."

"I understand. Assume that's correct for a minute. If someone took her out then the murderer of that girl Margaret is likely around. You're playing with fire. You're a bit old for that it seems to me," he caught McAbee's eyes with a look of curiosity.

"Wouldn't be the first time. ACJ has been around for over 25 years. We've had our share of nastiness."

The food came, then the expensive wine. Decanted, poured, Bailey sipped, and he approved. They ate as

McAbee struggled with a huge ball of cheese and bread that congealed in the liquid. Finally, Bailey spoke, "I don't know exactly what led her to that conclusion. They took me off of it. Closed the files. Threatened me, actually to stand down. Too much crime going around Rock Island to be obsessing on a murder case from ages ago, they said. Bullshit! I was finding discrepancies. I don't believe that it was Detective Snider. He was a very dogged guy. But intuition was lacking in him. He dead-ended with a lot of data, paralyzed by it. The case withered. That was the word on Snider. He was like an accountant who was good at assembling data but unable to form connective tissue one fact to another."

"If her brother had it right she might have noticed some missing pages. The purported number of pages was short by nine."

Bailey drank quickly, now deep into his second glass. "Yeah. She hacked the files if she made that conclusion. I got there too. It took me weeks. The files were collated but still sloppy by my standards. Also all of the materials from the scene itself were missing in the evidence lockers. They said it was due to lack of room. So things were being removed and destroyed. If that was true it was very selective. It was almost as though they were jumbled on purpose. I told the chief and I asked for some help. A competent secretary at the least. He said he'd think about it. A bunch of days later I was yanked off the whole thing, but not before re-assembling the file into coherency. Rock Island crime blowing up, blah, blah, blah. He was a feckless bastard. Finger out for the direction of the wind. I don't think it was his decision. Orders from somewhere higher up? The unsolved case may have really spooked someone. Things never added up, but then again Rock Island was a shooting gallery."

He was now on a third glass, just a trifle left in the dark green bottle. Half his steak was eaten, while McAbee finally subjugated the ball of cheese and bread he was down to the broth toward the end of the bowl. "I get the feeling, Carl, that you feel that you left a runner on base. That someone is out there?"

"That's what my bones were saying McAbee."

"Did you ever try to go back into the files? Secretly?"

"Nah. At the time I was under siege, being watched. I was finessed out of my job as a homicide, robbery specialist. Not right!" He tipped the remainder of the bottle and poured the wine into his glass. It was a negligible amount.

"Want another bottle?"

"If you're paying, sure."

He was down now to a few pre-cut pieces of steak.

McAbee signaled the waitress. He held up the empty bottle and pointed to it. She nodded.

It was brought over by the wine steward who repeated the process of a light pour into a new glass. Bailey sipped and nodded. The steward bowed slightly and left. Bailey filled his glass, his hand trembled slightly. "This is good stuff," he said.

McAbee did not hear any slurring. Bailey was a seasoned drinker. "Concannon?" He threw the name out as if disgusted.

"Who else? You know he married the mayor's daughter. I always looked at the mayor and Concannon as joined at the hip. Goddam mayor. He was on his seventh term when I pulled up stakes…..Rice. Name eluded me for a sec. Ed Rice. Beneath all the smiles and easy going ways was a fucker."

"His daughter? Still with Concannon?"

"I don't know. She was with him when I left. Tough cow," he looked at McAbee as he poured another glass, "You're getting into the weeds McAbee. Watch out."

"I get that, listen, I have to make a plane." He paid the bill. They shook hands. McAbee retrieved his bags. In the cab leaving the Paris he looked back at the bistro. Carl was still there looking down at the mob going by.

CHAPTER 16

He always smiled when he saw Augusta enter a restaurant, he seated at the back. Most patrons in the place would stare for a moment, some at full gawk. She had a great way about her six feet, elegant, head up, intelligent, trim – just a splendor. He didn't think that she was into it as an act of sorts. This was Augusta Satin plain and simple. She came to the table, he stood, they hugged, he whispered, "You're still stopping them dead in their tracks."

She whispered back, "Sure Mistah – what do you want?" she smiled.

They loved each other, he was sure. They talked about the weather, she surveyed the menu, they were at ease. They ordered. The waitress was pregnant, small talk led to the disclosure that the baby boy would come in mid-June. Name? Dominic Anthony. Bertrand felt sad for her. Irene, her badge said, looked exhausted.

They talked about the office, the cases that Augusta was tracking, her two daughters, even in a semi-serious way about a previous dog that Bertrand had, name of Scorpio who, as he aged, became very territorial. A white German shepherd, Scorpio did not appreciate Augusta as he growled and snapped at her on occasion. Bertrand saw it as his seeing a competitor for his affection while Augusta leaned to a racism charge. McAbee accused her of caninophobia and from there they had a regular way of jesting with each other.

"So Augusta, let me tell you about the case I'm on. There is no physical evidence in the possession of the Rock Island P.D. from the scene of Margaret Thode's murder. It was purged years ago to make room for newer crime scene evidence. So, if there was something usable it's gone. But I'm suspicious of whatever was there before the purge. I think that some materials were probably already missing."

"Whoa. That's a very cynical remark. I worked there once. I didn't see things like that. Pretty honest Department. I admit that it's a cop-world and there is always a bit of chicanery. But fooling with the evidence?"

"When I spoke with Carl Bailey I found a pretty bitter guy. Thanks to your call he opened up, a lot more than he ever would have. You must have told him how nice a guy I was…"

She held up both hands, palms outward, "Why would I ever say something so off the wall as that?" she smiled.

He grinned back and went on, "Okay. Regardless of how mean you were I softened him up. He feels that something is off base. Missing pages in the file and then he throws in the evidence locker that he said was completely emptied from that secure area." He looked closely at Augusta whose lips tightened, a frown deepening. "Too many coincidences in my book. And now the case is revived by a professional researcher and she's murdered."

"Agatha? She got into the police files didn't she? Probably not that hard for a woman of her abilities."

"Seems so," he said carefully.

"So Bertrand. Don't answer to my comment. Just listen and then we'll proceed. What I don't know I don't know nor do I want to. Knowing your admiration for Barry Fisk I am now assuming, again – don't confirm, don't deny, that he also had had his way with the official police files. I am further assuming that everything you have said has validation."

"I'd say good assumption on your part. This leads me to a new inquiry. It's not personal, Augusta."

"Go ahead," she said suspiciously.

"Right in the middle of these developments from Carl Bailey on, is Hugh Concannon. Bailey is not a fan of his."

"No. I knew that. They were not good together. Remember my time there was very limited for that observation before I left and I got married. But you're suggesting something about Hugh."

"Yeah I am."

"Let's clear up something. Does this have anything to do with my dalliance with him?"

"No. I thought that through very carefully. This isn't personal. I can see where it could be but I have systematically rooted it out of my logic. You'll have to trust me on this Augusta."

"Trust you? I would never not do that. I trust you as much as I could another human, Bertrand. So, you're asking me if it is possible for him to be a crook. My answer is yes and no. First, no, he's a very diligent cop. If he is on a case he's fierce. But can he be over the top, so task-focused that he offends anyone who gets in his way? I think that he has lost the thread in some investigations because he has infuriated people. They just shut down."

"Pretty obvious," he said.

"Could he be a crook? Dishonest? Look at it this way Bertrand. He's almost an exact copy of Jack Scholz. He operates by his own standards. If you accused him of being a crook he'd be furious, but by legal standards he could be classified as a crook. He's lawful when it is useful to a case but he's lawless when he has to be. But he'd say that he was upright and just. Just like Scholz. Both have psychopathic traits."

"I get that distinction and even the comparison. Let me be more specific. Would Concannon do a coverup? Remove pages from an investigation file? Take from the evidence locker? All of this in the name of a higher ideal? Would it have to be done for the sake of a higher ideal or would it be just an old fashioned coverup to protect someone?"

"That's a good set of questions. Let's assume the last part of your question, an old fashioned coverup. If he did that he'd re-configure the logic to make what he did a higher ideal."

"But it's not beyond possibility that he could do some twists and turns on a case. How about friendships as one of those higher ideals?"

She thought for a bit, the lunch crowd slowly left the restaurant. "Short answer Bertrand. I don't think he has any friends of that sort. He's a loner."

"His wife?"

"Don't see it. That relationship was pretty testy. I can't see him bending rules for her. Don't get upset when I remind you he's prone to be unfaithful and believe me when I tell you he'd never entertain any thoughts of fooling around with a case for a request from me."

"Did you ever ask him?"

"Wouldn't dare on two counts. It's not me, not him," she said resolutely, perhaps upset by his questioning.

"I'm not trying to impugn you. These are just hypotheticals," he said carefully aware that his best friend was breathing a bit quickly.

"Look Bertrand. It's true that through some of the time of the Bailey re-investigation Hugh Concannon was present in the P.D. He certainly had opportunity. I have been very explicit about how I see him. I can't see a higher ideal for him to latch onto to cheat an investigation on this case. I hate to say this but I do think you have crossed over to the personal. I have never known you to be jealous. Quite the contrary in fact, if you must know. I wouldn't recommend anyone to wait for you to pine over them. You're a very detached guy. Sometimes your love is a very abstract thing, like a geometry textbook. Frankly, Bertrand I think you're jealous. I think that you've been very difficult since I told you about Hugh and me."

Bertrand was stung by her comments. He reflected and weighed his feelings about Augusta against the fact of her sleeping with Concannon. He fingered his metal napkin holder. He didn't agree with her but she had some points in her comments. He shifted the discussion to an old case that they both had worked some years ago. It had exploded with the discovery of some new data. The case of Agatha Pruitt was placed to the side, perhaps it too waiting for new data and its own explosion.

It was time for them to leave. He tipped the waitress at 25%. She didn't acknowledge. She was probably dealing with some daunting concerns.

They went down the escalator in silence. At the exit to the building they bade goodbyes to each other. There was strain between them. They'd been associated with each other for almost 25 years. They'd handle it – they always did.

CHAPTER 17

McAbee looked at the 6322 page investigatory file concerning the Margaret Thode murder. His initial scan would now be replaced by strenuous scholarship. He was in for a long slog.

When he had informed Richard Pruitt that he thought the way to get at his sister's murder was by way of the Margaret Thode case he felt resistance. Richard believed that this route might take the focus from his dead sister. Bertrand defended the choice as best as he could by conceding that there were surely other possibilities. He would take these on once he could eliminate the Thode murder or at least marginalize it. He told Richard that access to the murder file had been achieved by others besides his sister but stopped at identifying those others. Reluctantly, Richard, after a prolonged silence, accepted his reasoning. What McAbee had not told him is that he'd withdraw his services if Richard tried to change his direction. He reiterated that he be very careful around Concannon. That did not meet with any resistance. Richard Pruitt despised him. Bertrand wondered again about how many cases fell through the cracks because of Concannon's abrasiveness.

He was particularly interested in Carl Bailey's work on the case because Carl had suspicions about the murder investigation itself. Agatha Pruitt appeared to be on the same track as Bailey, he stopped by an administrative intervention, she, stopped by a murder. Too many coincidences around a long ago crime.

Bailey had done a random check into the investigation. By his own admission, the case file needed a much more muscular review. Once he showed that card to the police chief he was cut off from the case. Yes, there was constant crime in Rock Island but as soon as he suggested a problem with the Thode case he was removed. Was it causality or just coincidence?

McAbee focused on pages 1341, 2508 and 4007. Bailey had concluded that letters had been used after the pagination. But the lettered pages had been removed. What became of a, b, and c after page 1341? And the others? Why, Bailey asked, would letters ever be used? And how had Bailey determined that letters had been used if they were missing in the first place? Bailey had gone out of his way to exonerate Snider, the lead detective in the original case. But then he whacked him in his concluding notes. On the other hand, Snider may have simply used a method unique to him and perhaps would never suspect that his work would be subjected to a purge of some pages. And why would he? He was a seasoned detective. Perhaps such a file deletion was unthinkable to him. McAbee would never expect someone to remove some of his sequential power points used in his lectures. Why would a detective not think the same?

He turned off his iPhone and set to work beginning on page one. He worked almost continuously for 12 hours on day one and nine hours on day two. He wrote 14 pages of personal notes.

Snider had questioned 317 people altogether. Some interviews spawned pages of notes others barely a page. Besides the vagrant roundup, many of Margaret's classmates were questioned, her relatives, her acquaintances, boat people at the marina, lovers known to frequent the marina at night and whatever leads those created. The investigation kept coming to a dead end.

Margaret Thode was admired but also shunned at her high school. Her running and biking obsession was seen to be odd and, to some, deranged. She was a brilliant student with few friends, Agatha Pruitt one of them, however.

He did find the key that was used by Carl Bailey to unlock the letters. On page 607, in a buried footnote Snider referred to pages 2508a and 2508b 'see a and b of 2508' was the notation. Similarly, on page 2012 he referred to a, b, and c on page 1341. The same pattern was found on page 4085, a referral to a, b, c, and d of page 4007. Snider left no indication of the relevance of the lettered pages. It was as if the lettering referred to some private thoughts he had, perhaps, a reminder for further research or a confirmation of something. He simply could not ascertain what was being specified in these notes. But he now knew how Carl Bailey had discovered the aberration. Bailey saw the insertion of letters as irregular. Snider was the type to get caught in a forest of detail. McAbee, never good with directions, had once been lost in a forest in the state of Washington. He was acutely aware of the potency of the analogy.

And these nine missing pages? The evidence locker with the victim's clothing, the rape kit? All missing. His mind kept coming back to Concannon. Yet he wasn't even in the police department at the time of the murder. What possible interest could he have in the matter?

Almost every interviewee had a solid alibi. Snider saw the crime as deeply personal and zeroed in on anyone Margaret might have shunned, embarrassed, or in some way hit a nerve of resentment, a powder keg awaiting a match, maybe. Margaret was not a shrinking violet; she was seen as tough, resilient, and strong.

Two of her classmates were brought back for questioning, one of them three times. Dead ends.

There was no semen and pubic hairs because Margaret had been repeatedly penetrated by an object. But at the time sophisticated screening was still distant. The loss of physical evidence was a crime itself. Who ordered that? Or was it just incompetency?

The file included xeroxed copies of articles from the local newspapers. A reporter from the *Rock Island Argus* wrote with some frequency through the first three months of the Snider investigation, 12 articles total. Her name was Gretchen Heinz, in all probability the reporter mentioned by Richard and visited by Agatha Pruitt at the Kahl Home in Davenport. He put the file and his notes aside. He went for a walk, his mind now totally engrossed with the Thode murder and its likely connection to the horrific crime committed against Agatha Pruitt.

CHAPTER 18

The next day rain came. Farmers across Iowa ended their laments about drought. He called Sister Ursula Von Hagen. She was the Director of the Kahl Home in north Davenport. She was a Carmelite nun; her Order oversaw a sprawling care facility for assisted care and nursing care for elderly residents. The facility was a huge step-up from an abandoned facility in southwest Davenport, the original site of the Kahl Home.

Von Hagen's secretary, Mary O'Brien, a phone tiger whose sole mission in life seemed to be protecting Sister Ursula from the likes of McAbee, picked up. He had engaged with the home three times over the years. Twice the matter was about contested wills and once a charge of resident abuse. Ursula had been fairly cooperative about the wills but the resident abuse matter brought out a new version of this nun. He found the charge to be bogus but during the investigation he had been subjected to nun-fury. He told Augusta that he was constantly looking over his shoulder for a face slap, a steel ruler across his knuckles or a forced chalk exercise on slate that repeated the phrase 'I'm an idiot' 50 times. Ursula's steel rimmed glasses, gray eyes, austere face and a voice that came out of her thighs was what he was expecting after Mary O'Brien forced him to a march through burning coals, before putting his call through.

"Dr. Bertrand McAbee. What a way to begin my day," Sister Urusla said flatly.

Her voice was fairly neutral. If he played it well she might pull in her claws. "Sister Ursula, thanks for taking my call. I know you've missed me."

There was a long pause. Humor, of any kind, was a treacherous ploy around her. "Your calls to me have never been taken with anything approaching joy. What can I do for you?"

She was tilting negative. He warned himself to get off the humor trolley with this 12th century scourge. "I'm investigating a case. A name has come up. She's apparently a resident under your care," he stopped.

"And?" she asked abruptly.

"I don't want to visit her if she's troubled or has issues. The last thing I want to do is unsettle people."

"Of course you wouldn't. Unsettling people in institutions is not your style, is it?" she said sarcastically.

"Glad you see that part of me Sister. Her name is Gretchen Heinz. She was a reporter for the *Argus*."

"Gretchen volunteers at our market store. She's in assisted living. She's 81. Quite capable. Smart, a bit frail. Is that what you want to know?"

McAbee was surprised. Why such cooperation? "I'd like to speak with her, privately."

"I can arrange that. But first, you're not the first. That woman in Rock Island, Agatha Pruitt, and then three days ago Detective Concannon from Rock Island. Contrary to my suspicions about you, I do know that you are able to be careful and non-threatening. I don't want her to be badgered by you. Detective Concannon brought her to tears. I won't have it here at Kahl."

"Detective Concannon is a loaded cannon Sister, I'm not that way. I hope that you told him to leave."

"You can be assured of one thing. He won't be back here again without a warrant and she won't see him without our attorney present."

McAbee enjoyed it when her venom was used on the likes of Concannon. "Thanks Sister Ursula."

"I'll connect you to Mary O'Brien. She'll take the necessary steps. Good day, hold on for Mary."

Mary put him through a bureaucratic hell for ten minutes as she made arrangements for his interview of Gretchen Heinz. Mary had to be a fan of Franz Kafka or Joseph Heller. She had all the moves.

Gretchen came into Visitor Room B. She had heard about McAbee as a reporter. They were, after all, both into crime. But she had never met him. The word on him, if memory served her right, was that he and his agency ACJ were tricky. They were not all they gave their appearance to be.

McAbee sat, his hands clasped resting on the round table. He wore glasses, balding but at the sides of his head the hair was groomed and cut short, firm jaw, slightly flattened nose, high cheekbones and, there was no other way to describe them, cunning gray/blue eyes. By the time she sat his eyes had gone from kindness, to humor, to a singular intensity, a bit of the actor in this guy, fast moving clouds.

He said, "Thanks for seeing me Ms. Heinz, I'm Bertrand McAbee. I'm a PI working on some cases."

"I feel like a debutante. Everyone wants to date me. But they don't bring me flowers. Just misery. I hope you're an exception."

"I am all of that." He reached into his satchel and brought out a large box with the name of Lagomarcino on it. He pushed it across the table. "I hope you like chocolates. I wasn't about to bring you mustard or catsup."

He had a disarming sense of humor and she appreciated the chocolates from this local sweet shop. "You make my heart flutter," she said coyly. "The next time you come how about a liter of Bushmills."

"If I have to come back I will absolutely do that. Do they allow for whiskey possession in this place?"

"That's my issue not yours."

"Sister Ursula can be pretty demanding," he said with a smirk.

"Actually, she's a very nice woman. She just has some issues with pushy men. They bring out her Germanic virtues."

"She informed me that Hugh Concannon came here," McAbee commented.

"That son of a bitch brought me to tears. At any rate, it was gratifying to see Ursula take him down. She threw him out of here. A thing of beauty!" She liked McAbee but would keep her guard up with him.

"I'm Bertrand. Can I call you Gretchen?"

"You can call me anything as long as you bring me some Bushmills."

"I take that for a yes." He said.

"I also am on Concannon's short list of suspects, apparently," she said in dismay.

"Everyone is, Gretchen," he said humorlessly. "Welcome to the club. May I ask what he wanted from you?"

"Agatha's brother told him that Agatha visited me about the Margaret Thode case. Of course, such a revelation made me a murder suspect to obnoxious Concannon. He wanted to know what she wanted from me. When I told him it was to check some facts in one of my articles way back, he called me a liar. I was covering up something and by the way where was I when Margaret Thode was murdered all those years ago. Was it a career advancement move on my part? What a jerk he is. After he gave up that approach he went after what he came for. What had Agatha turned up in her investigations? Her damn brother has a big mouth and must have been cowed by Concannon."

McAbee said, "Probably."

"So when he got around to the real purpose of his visit I was crying, yes. But I also resolved to be totally uncooperative with him. I had done business with him when I was a reporter for the *Argus*. He was always a bastard deep down. Hasn't changed. That's about the time that Ursula passed by the door and saw me. She knew. That's when Concannon met his match." She felt that she was exorcising the devil Concannon, as she spoke to McAbee, a good listener in her estimation.

"So, let me lay my cards on the table, Gretchen. I'm 80% sure that Agatha was murdered because she had connected some dots on the Thode case. Someone found out and decided that she was too dangerous."

Gretchen had wondered about the same thing but had put it aside, she repressed it if she was honest. She informed McAbee that of the three visits, on the first two Agatha had been circumspect. The first time it was about the articles themselves, a refresher, some clarifications made. The second time she had just come from an interview and was in the area. Her visit lasted no more than ten minutes. "She reported that in the interview she had taken she heard that Margaret Thode was detested by many of her classmates. She was referred to as a lesbian creep, she slept with her bike and had sex with handlebars and so on. I told her that I was aware of the fact that she was seen as peculiar, odd. I was told that she was scorned. I know how vicious high school students can be. But I didn't and I couldn't have printed anything of the sort. Her parents were devasted. This would only add to their sadness."

"Was Detective Snider a good source for you?"

"Funny thing about him. He was meticulous. Enormous mastery of detail. But he was very stubborn and stodgy. He'd give me a few things but overall I think he wasn't a very creative guy. The murder was beyond his skill set. But you know how those civil service jobs go. Hang around long enough and you'll get to the top rung." There was a window set into the door, one foot by three feet. She saw Ursula and nodded her head a fraction. She didn't think that McAbee noticed the exchange from where he sat, his back to the door.

"Ursula going to join us?" he asked.

"You're good. Very observant of you. No, you're safe."

"So," he said reflectively, "You've spoken to two of the times Agatha came over. Anything different the third time? More of the same?"

"Before I answer you. What is your role in all of this?"

"I was hired by Richard, her brother. He has no regard for Concannon who treated him a lot worse than he did you. Trust level is about zero."

"Will you go back to Concannon with anything I tell you?"

"Unless you tell me to I won't," he responded.

"Down the hall to the left is a water fountain and some cups. Will you get me a drink?"

McAbee was enchanted with Gretchen Heinz. He remembered his mother saying 'she's no one's fool' in a very laudatory way, his mother was not given to praise otherwise. There was hope for people in their 80s if Gretchen was the norm. As he re-entered the room he noticed that she had quickly put her phone away. He said, "Checking out a date for tonight?"

"Yeah, right. Codgers pounding my door down. Women, on the other hand, age much better than men. Don't you think?"

"That's a pretty laden over-generalization."

"Aren't all over-generalizations laden?" she snapped back with a smile.

"There's laden and then there's laden."

She drank off some water. "So you want to know about her third visit, the last one."

He noticed that she brushed back her thinning hair with frequency. She was petite, small, narrowing facial features. Her eyes were magnified by a pair of thick glasses. She wore a too loose blouse and a pair of slacks. She kept herself up. Proud, with a strong dose of vanity. "I didn't come here to just give you chocolates, you know."

She laughed. "First off, she was very excited. She seemed pretty stiff the first two meetings. But not the last. I said so to her. She grabbed my arm and basically said that she was on the move with the case. I asked her how so. She whispered 'police files'. I asked her which ones. She said the whole banana, 6000 plus pages. She said there was some kind of coverup, missing pages. She was a crafty woman. She was confident she could break the case. I didn't say much, in fact. She was a bundle of enthusiasm."

"Do you recall when this meeting with you occurred relative to her murder?"

"Eight days," she said sourly.

"What do you make of her murder? Related?"

"Hell yeah, it's related. She came onto something. Must have scared the bejesus out of someone," she said.

"Concannon? Think he might be buying into this?"

"No, but I almost think he might be a gatekeeper."

"Did you or Agatha know the evidence locker from this case was emptied and all the materials presumably destroyed?"

"My god, no. That's where she was going to proceed to. There had to be lots of evidence. Goddam it!" She sat up from a slouch and leaned across the table, jaw jutting out, face reddening. "Did she leave anything in her house? Computer? Phone? Notes?"

"No. Place was stripped by the murderer. Any further thoughts?"

"Not now. My memory is slipping a bit. Sometimes things come back to me. Especially in the mornings. I'm sharper then. You have a card?"

He gave her his card and said goodbye.

On his way out, he saw Sister Ursula at the door. She said, "Is she okay?"

"Yes, very."

"She say anything about a man named Bushmill?"

"She wants me to bring him if I come back."

"Good, hope you do," she turned and walked away.

CHAPTER 19

Richard Pruitt called Bertrand. Hugh Concannon had declared Agatha's house was no longer a crime scene, almost 12 days removed from the murder. Immediately, Bertrand called Jack Scholz and told him to assemble a security team for a thorough search of Agatha's house. Jack said he needed the day to mobilize a team. He asked McAbee to get Richard to change to new and double locks on the house with urgency as surely Concannon had a set of keys to the current locks. Furthermore, when he and his team came they would like Richard to be present. Knowing Concannon there was a high likelihood that he would be setting up some kind of entrapment.

By 5 p.m. all of the above had been either done or arranged. Jack would be at Agatha's house by 9 a.m. the next morning. Bertrand was welcome, of course.

When Bertrand arrived there was an Escalade parked at the curb and a Prius in the driveway. It was 9 a.m. sharp and all the players were already in motion. He wondered how Jack Scholz would strike Richard Pruitt, an oil and water combo. He tried the door; it was locked. Had to be Scholz doing that.

He rang the doorbell and Jack appeared. He motioned for Bertrand to step away from the doorstep. In a low voice he said, "We froze the P.D. videos, three of them. They have no authorization to have them in place now since it's no longer a crime scene. Maybe they won't pick up the freeze. I have three guys with me. Pros. We're going to search this place with fervor. Richard is in the kitchen. He made coffee for us; he has the *New York Times*. He's fine. Your call to him yesterday was perfect. My big concern is that other camera and I'm positive that it has a listening component. My expert already went by it and observed it without showing any interest. We're in a bit of a bind. We want to know everything about it but only if we can do it without notice. That way it can be turned to our advantage. Besides that we're going to take this place apart. If she had something of importance we'll find it. You okay keeping Pruitt in one place?"

"Sure."

He followed Jack into the house. He noticed that Jack double locked the front door again. Richard was seated at the kitchen table. In varied locations were three men, all of them in black clothing. Each of them eyed McAbee, as he did them.

Jack said, "This is our boss, Bertrand McAbee. He'll be present for our time here." All three nodded but said nothing.

Bertrand instinctively drew upon Aristotle's predicaments or categories as they were sometimes called. *Quantity* – one of them was overweight by a good 40 pounds. He dubbed him fatboy. This was not a time for political correctness. Another had a *Quality* – a full moustache ending across his upper lip and downward by an inch or so.

He dubbed him Zorro. The third was tall, wiry. He wore a gold chain. *Equipment* or *adornment* in the Aristotelian list of nine accidents besides substance, they all had substance, of course. He christened him Goldilocks. There were six other categories that he didn't employ, unnecessary. He recalled teaching a seminar on Aristotle's logic ages ago while at St. Anselm. It was still a useful technique for quick classification.

In a whisper, Jack said, "Please be careful what you say. I believe that we are encountering a listening device of possibly extraordinary capacity." He motioned to the three to step outside the house with him. Bertrand stayed behind with Richard who said, "We've been here since 8:30. He called me last night. They've already prowled around the place. A look-see. He's quite a character. I think he could run circles around Concannon."

Bertrand nodded as he poured himself a cup of coffee and sat across from Pruitt. "So, Richard, how are you faring?"

"Up and down. I don't like being here. I feel her spirit, restless and angry. I know, I know, you're a rationalist. You don't believe in that stuff. Nor did I. But sitting here I do. Hard to explain. I know what you'll say – a projection on my part. Maybe it is but, then again, maybe it isn't."

"Richard, I'm a rationalist but I'm also a skeptic. There's no finality for me in most of my judgments. You may be very correct. I'm sorry that you have to be here."

"I need to be. Even as I feel her anger I believe that she's living here that we're in some kind of communion."

"Did you say any of this to Jack?"

"My God no. I'm sure he's a good man when he's on your side, doing a particular task. But he's most assuredly a black box full of very set judgments. There is a lot of darkness emanating from him. I would never bring up a feeling about an angry sister's presence in this house. He's not someone you say those things around."

"I think that's a wise course for you to take. He's not into metaphysics."

Jack and his team re-entered the house. Then they spread out without a word. Bertrand had brought along his iPad that had the digitized file of the police reports on the murder of Margaret Thode. He began, again, to read it. It would be the fourth time for him.

At 3:35 p.m. Richard Pruitt was told to lock up the house. The three men left for the Escalade where they just sat. Richard drove away. Jack asked Bertrand to walk with him.

"Here's the deal Bertrand. We have pictures of the device. Remember the tall guy? He's as techie as could be. Straight out of the NSA. Came in from Washington last night. It's Israeli and it's state of the art. I could get one through my network but it's not an easy get even for me. It's video and audio and it's super-sensitive. It's the feed that he will work on. Where's it going to. He believes that he can do it. Questions?"

"It's still on?"

"Oh. Of course. I took down the three Rock Island ones. They're on the bathroom counter. Concannon has no authority to keep them here. He'll find out and he'll be pissed off big time. If asked, you know nothing. I don't mind him knowing that he was screwed and if he thinks it was me, good. I want him to know that he's stupid. I'm sure he has no idea about this Israeli one. He'd never find it."

"If the device is that sophisticated what does that tell you about whom we're up against?"

"That's a worry. A bridge to be crossed. But I'm sure that's not a local police thing. This is someone with high access."

"What else?" Bertrand asked.

"There is not an inch of the place that wasn't scrutinized and searched by us. When you and Pruitt went to lunch we did the kitchen." He removed a ziplock baggie from his jacket. He handed it to Bertrand. In the baggie was a folded note and bracelet. "We found this in her freezer, folded into a half-eaten bag of fish sticks. Almost unseeable. But my guys don't miss anything. In my judgment, this is some kind of smoking gun Bertrand and it's the only find that relates to the murder of Margaret Thode. It's pretty clear. Agatha Pruitt was onto something. How she managed to acquire this, where she looked? Don't know but I'll tell you this. I'd hire her in a second. No criminal would be safe if Agatha set out against him. She's a match to that little bastard Fisk."

Bertrand let the comment slide. The bad blood between Jack Scholz and Barry Fisk was built into the very essence of ACJ. It would never cease. If the likes of Jack took over the country, Barry Fisk would be drawn and quartered in the blink of an eye. But it was two-way. Fisk would see to it that Scholz was dismembered piece by piece. But they were essential to the success of ACJ. "What's the best way to proceed Jack?"

"I think we should get out of Rock Island now. What we discovered is self-evident as you'll see. You might be able to put things together when you run things against the police file. In the meantime, we'll run down the device in the house. Pruitt gave me a set of keys if I need them. I've got to get the NSA guy back to the airport."

"Got it. Thanks Jack and to your people too."

"They know that," he said as he walked to the Escalade.

McAbee entered his car and sat in it for a bit. He looked back at Agatha's house. He was spooked for a second. He could have sworn that he saw a curtain in Agatha's house move ever so slightly. He put it down to fatigue. He drove back to Davenport and the offices of ACJ. He was fascinated by the ziplock in his pocket and what Scholz thought to be a smoking gun.

CHAPTER 20

"I'll be in my office for a bit," he said to Pat at almost 4 p.m.

He had a small refrigerator in his office. He took out a Diet Coke, poured a bit into a glass and sat at his desk. He placed the ziplock on his desk eyeing the contents of it. There was a folded note, unreadable until he'd spread it out. In addition, there were several layers of tissue wrapped around some kind of object. He stared at them a bit. To Jack these were important and if *he* thought so, it was to Bertrand too as Jack was rarely wrong. He shook the bag, it was light but it had enough heft to announce weight.

He unzipped the bag and took out the note. When he opened it full on his desk it was an unlined standard typing page. The handwriting was meticulous, tiny and unhurried. The message was lengthy.

> If this is found it was so because I have been encumbered. Hopefully, I can live to talk about this ziplock. If not, I am hopeful that it has fallen into good hands. Since there is no possible way to know the future I can assure you that what matters in this note is

true. I am gay, always have been. But I have always been discreet. A few relationships over my lifetime. My happiness has been found in my professional life. My first infatuation, really my first love, was with a classmate at Rock Island High School. Her name was Margaret Thode. We were connected in every way possible, including physical intimacy. She was my first and greatest lover. Just about everyone knows how she was murdered. I don't wish to pursue that in this letter. Thinking about that is emotionally brutal. Her murder is unsolved for all these years. Upon my retirement I have dedicated myself to solving that murder. When her body was found those years back one item was missing. It was a secret between us. No one knew about it. She would always wear it when on her bicycle, a reminder of our love. The police reports made no mention of it, all 6000 pages plus. But it was gone from her. I personally had explored the area of the killing many times as a teenager to no avail. The only conclusion is that the bracelet was stolen from her. My fear of our secret love becoming public caused me to withhold this fact from the police. The detective was simply not nice, offensive. There are only a few antique shops within 100 miles circumference of the Quad Cities. Most of them trade in junk. But there are three that trade in jewelry, primarily. The first two I went to had nothing pertinent to Margaret. It was a needle in a haystack search, after all. But it was the third shop that stopped me in my tracks. I was about to call Detective Concannon. I had the break. But then I concluded that he would cause harm to me. Personally, when in the store I was careful not to obsess on the object. I created a story about having one in high school. He said that what I saw was a keepsake piece for someone. I told him it looked liked mine. I had lost it ages ago. He let me study it. Simply put, this was the one that I gave to Margaret on her 16th birthday. My heart throbbed. I asked about a price. He quoted me $125. Hah! He knew that he had me. But I did knock him down to $100. I would have traded my house for it. I asked him when and how it came to his store, in Muscatine, Iowa. He was the son of the original owner. To the best of his knowledge it was an item in the store that he inherited from his father and mother. That was 19 years ago, 2003. It was just a quiet piece among many. He brought the drawer (probably had 75 assorted items in it) to antique shows. Ugly ducklings is how he described them. His father is dead but his mother is still alive. She lives in Muscatine. I will visit her. She's elderly.

Bertrand withdrew the bracelet from its surrounding tissue paper. It was a charm bracelet, probably pewter. It had four charms on it, a heart with tiny lettering that read 'I love you,' a diploma that was inscribed 'college,' a bicycle built for two but no inscription, and a double heart inscribed with 'me, you.' The store on a business card was listed on Main Street in downtown Muscatine. It was called Jewels of the Past. His name, Sonny Azdbo, mother, Irina.

He sat back, rubbed his eyes. He was concerned that in some manner her discovery of the bracelet may have doomed her. But he wondered how A connected to G, so many transit points.

CHAPTER 21

"Agatha's murder was professionally sloppy. I think that the disorder at the crime scene was meant to mislead. To make it look like a robbery gone bad. The search was done quite professionally and the insertion of the device itself says professional." Jack looked sideways at McAbee as they walked along the path a few feet from the Mississippi River.

The outdoor setting was a clear sign that Jack was going to deal with super-sensitive information. Added to that was his fear that they were being taped in any indoor setting. He spoke quietly, too, just in case. "The device?" McAbee said.

"Top of the line. Israeli. CIA and FBI have each ordered a pretty big supply. Extraordinary visual feed and acoustics. I don't think it could hear a pin drop but it might hear the flapping of a butterfly's wings. The view we got was adequate. Almost positive it was placed the night of her murder. So, you can figure everything in that house on the main floor was heard. Whoever placed it knows that you and I are involved in the case."

"Who has access to such advanced equipment? Can't buy that stuff at Best Buy."

"Precisely. Plus the question is where is the feed going to, then you might begin to break the case."

"And?" McAbee asked.

"My NSA guy says that they have the capability but it is rarely used. Only in very special operations and only with a secret judicial approval. We can't get there through that path. Not even a ghost of a chance."

McAbee observed some barges crossing under the Centennial Bridge. If ever there was a seal on the death of winter barge traffic was it. He heard in Jack's statement, though, that there was more to come. "You said that our connections through your contacts at the NSA and others are dead ends. But you referred to that as a path. Any other paths?"

"I'm down some rabbit holes. How good is the midget?" He said rancorously.

Jack Scholz wasn't going to change neither was Barry Fisk. So, when Barry referred to Jack as a Nazi or an S.S. Officer the comment flew by him virtually unheard. But he would never use the disparaging descriptions when speaking back to Scholz or Fisk. "Barry is as good as they get. Awesome skill set. Like yours Jack. I don't know if he trades in this kind of sleuthing but he's a quick study and loves challenges. Do you recommend him for this?"

"I wouldn't recommend him to clean toilets. But that's me. You're another story. I'm going to give you an envelope with all of the information we have about the device. It's super sensitive. If this information was discovered in his possession, it could lead back to my guy. It has to be burnt after he masters it. Is he good for that?"

Without the slightest hesitation, Bertrand said, "Yes."

"I'm going to be honest with you. I don't like the feel of this. The device suggests the taste of ruthlessness, money, power, and access. Do you still make every effort *not* to pack a weapon?"

Jack had hit on the one thing that united his dysfunctional team. They all, including Pat Trump, castigated Bertrand for his refusal to regularly carry a firearm. A month ago Pat had at him with a remark that went, 'Do you think that Scorpio is still around and is going to protect you? Really?'

"I'll think about it, Jack. I certainly get your point. Now let me review what I understand turned up in that packet you found." He went on to narrate the information on Agatha's note, including her trip to the antique store in Muscatine. He noticed that Jack was impressed as he nodded throughout his recital, he had probably already read it.

Jack said, "Hard to figure that out. Hard to believe that there is a possible trail back to the Thode murder. Is that old lady in Muscatine sane?"

"Good question. I'm going to visit her. Wouldn't it be something if she could recall some details about that bracelet?"

"You know I always believe that there is a loose end in every event. That there is something out there, a connection. Many times we're not smart enough or lucky enough to catch its trail. But I have to say we have a chance on this one. Arm yourself, Bertrand." He turned and walked away after he slid an envelope into Bertrand's hand.

Unusual for McAbee, he called Barry and told him he was going to drop off some information for his immediate attention. He disconnected before Barry could say no.

At Barry's house, he explained the advancement of the case to him and made the request for him to prowl around for the source of the device in Agatha's house. Barry was visually reluctant to handle the envelope because it came through the hands of a Nazi. But the excited swinging of his legs told another story.

CHAPTER 22

Bertrand asked Augusta to come to Muscatine with him. They would be given the opportunity to interview Irina as long as Sonny was present. Sonny was corpulent, had a stained white shirt and an unshaven face. Jack would call him a fat slob, Bertand merely observed. His store was closing at 5 p.m. Bertrand introduced Augusta. Sonny told them to follow him to the Kentucky Fried Chicken restaurant. He was going to pick up dinner for his mother. That done, they followed him out of town on a rural route for eight minutes. They pulled off the road and drove into the driveway of a typical farmhouse. There were no cars present as they took a half circle and parked behind him. He waved them forward, waiting for them to come up to him.

The kitchen was to the left of the entrance, to the right was the living room. He laid the chicken meal on the kitchen table, still in the bag. Sonny brought them into the living room where a loud TV blared the local ABC news. The weatherman was overjoyed with the April weather that eastern Iowa and western Illinois was having.

"Mom!" He yelled.

"Jesus!" A screeched reply came back as the TV was muted. "Did you bring that creep from Davenport with you?" He Looked at McAbee and Augusta and shrugged. Loudly, he said, "Yes he's with me. He heard you call him a creep. And he has another friend with him."

"Two creeps."

Both Bertrand and Augusta stifled a laugh.

Irena's son was gladdened to see their response as he threw a guarded smile at them. He wound his index finger near his temple a few times, signifying to them that his mother was not all there. "I brought you a chicken meal, mashed potatoes, coleslaw, and a corn muffin."

"You brought that the last three nights, or four, or five. Can't remember. No other place open in that decrepit downtown area?"

"I thought this was special to you mom," he said defensively, still in a scream of sorts.

"Okay, okay. What do these characters want?"

He pointed to McAbee and swirled his arm forward signaling McAbee to come around her chair and face his mother.

McAbee did so and faced a heavyset woman buried in a huge lounger under a comforter. Her round face was dimpled, her hair colored to a burnt orange. She had a drawn mouth, if she had natural teeth, she was down to a few and/or was dealing with ill-fitting dentures, not a pleasant sight. She was chewing on something. He didn't want to know. He said, "Thanks for seeing…"

"Speak up you jerk!"

McAbee looked across at Augusta who hadn't moved since they came into the room. She had a handkerchief cuffed to her mouth, strangling a laugh.

McAbee now in lecture mode told the story of the charm bracelet. He watched her closely as he did so, her eyes going up and to the right. She was listening and calculating. Was she sharp? Was it possible for her to remember such an obscure bracelet? He concluded by saying that a murder had been committed and that this bracelet had a tale to tell. Only she could deliver some information, in his judgment.

She looked downward when he completed his recitation, eyes closed. He thought that she had fallen asleep. He cleared his throat very loudly hoping to arouse her.

She screamed, "Holy good Jesus! Let me think you idiot. Did you ever do such a thing as thinking?" Eyes now wide open with a stare manufactured from somewhere in her bowels.

McAbee did not need to look at Augusta who was enmeshed in a state of *schadenfreude* that he knew all too well. She had an underground sadism in her that only someone as far out as Irina could reach. But the same went for his hidden masochism when the likes of Irina were romping around the edges of his personhood. He imagined that in the car going back to Davenport their mutual laughter would have few bounds.

"What was the number? The tag? Can't tell you anything without that knowledge, by the way, did you say your name was Bertrand?"

"Yes."

"Well you don't look French to me. Your mother give you that curse?"

"You're right, I'm not French. Yes, my mother gave me that name. Wasn't a curse to her."

"Beat you up on the playground?"

"Always one step ahead of the bastards!" He took a chance with her, maybe he could lighten her up.

"I'm sure. The only way a Bertrand could survive! Now give me the numbers and letters or get lost."

"P-78-10-21-DFG, J.P" he said in the hopes that the code could be deciphered by her.

"Sonny," she said to her son. "Go down to the basement and dig out the 1978 register. You know where they are. Hurry, goddam it. I'm hungry."

He left for the kitchen. McAbee heard a creaky door open and descending steps to the basement.

Irina said, "So who's with you. Bring him out so I can see him."

Augusta came forward and said, "Hello Irina."

There was a long interlude before Irina spoke. "You know. You're the first black woman to have ever come into this house while I've been here. Born here by the way. I'm 87. My parents told me that this was a rescue house for escaped slaves, underground railroad. Records are somewhere. Great grandparents knew about the whole thing. Course the place was renovated over the years. But you're welcome here. But this guy you're with I don't know about him. Should be in a rocking chair if you ask me."

Augusta emitted a grand smile. "I keep telling him about rocking chairs but he won't listen. Says that if I bring him one he won't talk to me again."

"If that's the case I'd buy him one in an instant."

McAbee was being pummeled by these two. He wanted to return fire but held back as Sonny now came into the living room, blowing debris off a large rectangular black ledger book. He gave it to his mother.

Immediately before he could back away from the battlefield she yelled, "Glasses, glasses." He retrieved them, gave them to her and sidled away, behind her chair, out of sight.

"We were the greatest record keepers. Had to. In those days we had a pawn shop section in our store. Had to be very careful. Cops, you know. Fencing stolen goods a dangerous charge. The IRS. Goddam police state. Okay, simple enough. Pawned item. 1978, October, $21. Davenport Fair Grounds. Used to have a big merchandise fair down there. Jake Petersmith made the deal. Never paid for by the pawner. We had a bunch of these in a glass case that we'd carry to shows. It was an old maid. Never sold it. Normally we keep the tags when they're sold. But old Sonny here is sloppy. What else you want to know?"

"Jake Petersmith? Still alive?" McAbee asked.

"Yup. Lives in Moline. Has a small antique store there last I heard. He'll talk your head off. But he's one sharp bastard. Used to be at any rate. Haven't seen him in a good ten years. But that's it. Can't help you anymore. I want to eat. Sonny warm up that crap in the mike." She looked to Bertrand and Augusta, her last words, "Now get lost. That's enough from the two of you."

Bertrand thanked Sonny who said as he and Augusta were leaving the house, "You probably won't believe this but she was very well behaved toward you two."

On their way back to Davenport, laughter filled the car. Augusta said, "You should have seen your face when she set out on you. Happy you have such a good sense of humor."

"And you? Choking into that handkerchief as she blistered me. Enjoying every minute of it."

"The whole thing was Comedy Central. Sonny is frightened to death of her. I'll bet she carries her will in her purse. One false move on his part and he's disowned," she said.

As they neared downtown Davenport he said, "I'll try to run down Petersmith tomorrow. I think I've caught up with Agatha, maybe ahead of her. But somewhere she stepped on a trip wire."

"Be careful Bertrand. If you did actually catch up with her then you're in danger."

He dropped her at her car. They kissed and he drove off.

CHAPTER 23

Irina was correct about Jake Petersmith. He was a talker. It took McAbee a good five minutes to get a few short sentences in asking about his availability for a meeting. He was fine with that; he was on Fifth Avenue in downtown Moline. Bertrand arrived at 9:30 a.m.

Jake's place was called 'Jake's Antiques.' He wondered how many stores had that assignation in America. He found a parking place right outside the storefront. Downtown Moline was not a magnet for commerce. Of the 15 or so storefronts on this street, five had for sale or for rent signs. He was preparing himself for the coming cascade from Petersmith. The lengthy entryway to the front door was flanked by two parallel display windows. He noticed on the right display window some old railroad and construction equipment. On his left there were displays of animal heads, a moose, a bear and some kind of larger cat, perhaps a mountain lion. There was camping equipment spread across the floor of that display.

A sign on the door displayed the times of operation. McAbee was in luck as the store was only open on Tuesday and Thursday, 9 a.m. to 3 p.m. He speculated that Jake just needed to stay busy and the rent was low.

A bell jingled when he opened the door. The store was long, about 80 feet but quite narrow, maybe 20 feet. Jake specialized in outdoor merchandise. There was no sign of jewelry. A feminine touch was not in sight. As he looked back to the back wall of the store he saw a door to the right, it said bathroom. There was no sign of Petersmith. He heard a clomping behind him, footsteps. The store had a cellar. It was to the right of the entrance. Bertrand had missed seeing it as it was blocked by a cabinet.

"You McAbee?"

"Yes. Jake Petersmith?"

"You got it. Irina called me a bit ago. Nice to hear the old bitch after so many years. Hasn't changed. She said you had a question about an item that I bought for her store. Is that about right?"

Irina spoke about his loquaciousness but had not mentioned his machine gun speed of speech and his loudness. The man needed a cathedral to contain his volume. Bertrand resolved to escape from this irritable man as soon as possible. He said, "I might have to come back. Do you mind if I call you Jake? My name is Bertrand. I'm a PI and I am working a case from ages ago. May I show you the item? Irina was right, I'm trying to shake your memory. She said you were a legend in the memory business." He was talking fast and tried not to allow Jake any space for comments. He withdrew the baggie and took out the bracelet.

Petersmith, a man in his 80s it seemed, didn't wear glasses. He had a full head of white hair, very much in need of a trim. He was a small man, very thin, bad stoop. His eyes, however, were keen and observant. "Ah. A bracelet. Irina made it sound like you were some kind of goof. But to be honest with you she's never met a human being who wasn't a goof. Most judgmental bitch I ever met. Let me tell you a few stories about her."

Bertrand feared this and interrupted Petersmith. "Jake I have to be back in Davenport right away. When I come back we'll have coffee and I'll want to hear about her," he counted four outright lies in his brief comment. It just had to be that way with the likes of Jake Petersmith otherwise he'd be cemented in the store until closing time.

"I understand." He looked at McAbee in a way that said he knew that Bertrand had lied to him. He reached for the bracelet as he sat on a nearby stool. "There's a magnifying glass over there," he pointed across the aisle to another showcase, on its top was a large magnifier. "Thanks," he said to Bertrand when he handed it to him.

Bertrand watched him as he studied the tag and then very carefully the bracelet. After a rather lengthy time Bertrand said, "Pretty unusual?"

Jake looked at him as if he had been struck. "You want me to remember this buy? This was 45 years ago. You are a bit pushy you know. Why don't you look around the store for a bit."

"Sure. Sorry," McAbee said lamely. For some reason Jake Petersmith reminded him of a rabbi studying the Talmud; Bertrand once again reminded that people needed time.

"Okay Bertrand. I'll be short for you, as I know you have to leave for Davenport," he caught Bertrand's eye as he emitted a look of irony or was it, anger? "When I worked for Irina, and make no mistake, it was her who ran that store not her dim-witted husband or poor stupid Sonny. Every other Sunday in Davenport there was an open market. The fairgrounds. For about ten years I went over there. Selling some stuff from the store in Muscatine but we also operated a pawn business there too. That's how we got this piece. Funny thing about me. I have a fantastic memory for anything I ever bought or sold. Yet sometimes I get lost driving home more than I care to say. But things like this bracelet I remember like it was yesterday. So, Irina was right, my memory is good. Here's what I can tell you. A guy, late teens, druggie-looking, came over. He said that he bought this bracelet," Jake picked it up and looked at it again, "but couldn't make the payments. But he really wanted it back. How much could he get? He also said that the clasp was broken. I remember that distinctly. Easy repair for someone like me. He was very edgy, scared? I was concerned that it was stolen and because of the unique arrangement of the charms it could easily be identified. Irina was always nervous about cops. Always worried about hot items, fencing. I bought it after some serious consideration. Really hadn't done any business there the whole day. Now it's your turn. Why the hell are you interested? Won't tell you anything else till you come clean with me."

Bertrand thought that he was running into his fair share of old sharpies. He said, "The bracelet was a love token for a murdered girl. The case was never solved. The giver of the bracelet, the lover, found it in Muscatine a few weeks ago. Sonny sold it to her. However, the purchaser was murdered but commented in a note that this could be a way to discovering a murderer. That's why this is so important Jake."

"Ah. The seller, all those years back. He was apprehensive, furtive. Handsome guy. Blonde hair, blue eyes about six feet. But a bit broken. Educated. Smart. Rich, I thought. High class kid gone bad. That's why I didn't think it was stolen. But something was fishy."

"Do you think you could re-construct the face of that guy?"

"Sure. I can kind of see him in my mind as we speak."

"As I told you I have to leave. If I came back with an artist would you be willing?"

"Yup. Wouldn't mind the company. If you know what I mean McAbee."

Again the look as if he could see right through Bertrand and his false statements. "I'll be in touch. Thank you so much." Petersmith bowed his head slightly.

CHAPTER 24

Bertrand was at his office trying to get his mind back to the case of Agatha Pruitt. Someone was shaken about her investigation into the murder of her soulmate from those many years ago. The key to the puzzle went back to 18 year old Margaret Thode. The murderer was so hateful that he violated her while alive and then went after her corpse, almost as a maniac, if not one. Both Margaret and Agatha would be around 62 years of age in current time.

Was Margaret's murderer a contemporary in age or an older man? Every year going beyond age 62 was broaching the Social Security network. Agatha had not been sexually violated but any inference from that was useless. Someone was scared and whoever that was had access to very classified surveillance equipment. Jake Petersmith identified the charm bracelet back to a contemporary of Margaret. Could Petersmith's memory be trusted?

He called Barry Fisk getting from him the usual snarly "Yeah!"

"Yeah back to you Barry. Can you talk for a few minutes?"

"Clock's ticking," he said gruffly.

"Rock Island High School," Bertrand said with purposeful vagueness.

"It's in Rock Island," he countered, clearly looking for a skirmish with McAbee.

"Good work Barry. Don't know what I'd do without your skill set."

"Okay, okay. What do you want Bertrand?"

"I want to know about every graduate from there between 1975 and 1979."

"What?"

"Hear me out," McAbee said edgily as he realized that Barry was not in the mood to be teased. "I want to know about anyone who is a success either financially and/or famous, that has something to lose from those years. It would also have to be someone who is connected to sources with access to secret government programs used for surveillance. Ironically, sometimes a crime like this can only be solved at a distance. Only when all the cards in a deck have been played. I think the deck has been fully played out. Best guess algorithms. This narrow enough?"

A different version of Barry came back, without the snarl. "That's a big N, five years. But then again it's Rock Island High School. Lots of losers right off the bat."

McAbee shook his head. Barry had a hate dart for almost any population on this earth. He added, "Barry. This is getting serious. There's momentum going for me. Please put a rush on this," he said while hoping to avert a tirade from Fisk.

"Well if you think you have momentum I'll get on it. I'll go wide and then narrow it down. It'll take some time as you know."

Bertrand went on to explain the latest features of the investigation, especially about Jake Petersmith, the bracelet, and some tentative identity features of the bracelet's seller.

CHAPTER 25

Bertrand met Alice Riggens at Biaggi's Restaurant in Davenport. He was delivering some bad news to her. ACJ was unable to recover some $60,000 that had been scammed from her by an operation out of Nigeria. Barry had tried his best to reverse the game but was not able to. She left, anger with herself in full flower. He paid the bill. He was about to leave Biaggi's when a shout flew across the bar area. He immediately recognized the voice that had rendered the name McAbee as a sort of incoming missile. It was none other than Sebastian Stratmann, the brilliant and untamed bomb thrower who was unceremoniously fired from St. Anselm College years back. McAbee had a love/hate relationship with this man who was by far one of the most learned men he had ever encountered. He hesitated as he weighed the front door distance, 30 feet or so, against the voice from the dark end of the bar, also about 30 feet. A graceful escape was not in the cards. Stratmann was moving toward him at rapid speed. After Alice, he didn't need Stratmann, who in ten minutes could deconstruct Western civilization. He thought that if Augusta was with him she'd say how come

Bertrand didn't hire Stratmann into ACJ, thus completing a trinity with Barry Fisk and Jack Scholz.

Stratmann was of average height but he carried at least 300 pounds of weight. He thought him a brilliant Falstaff. As he looked at him he saw an unkempt man, thinning white hair, blue eyes that still had fire; but his teeth were yellow, his mustache ungroomed and his clothes very worn and ill fitting. In itself this did not mean that he was poor as he remembered him as having come from money.

"So, you lousy Irish bastard. I saw you looking at the door," he laughed and smacked McAbee's left shoulder that threw him about six inches from his position by this 60ish outsized character. He now grabbed McAbee's right wrist and said, "Sit with me. I'll buy whatever you want." He allowed Sebastian to drag him back to where he was sitting. A part of Bertrand was happy to see him as a verbal gunfight was probably in the making.

"I'm not drinking. I'll sit with you for 15 minutes. I'm dealing with some heavy stuff and I don't need your rambling insanity at this time," Bertrand said.

Stratmann laughed. "Would you like me to speak about Russia and Ukraine. The LGBTQ community. The Trump phenomenon. You name it and we fight."

"We're not getting into any of that you fat rat. I just want to know what has become of you after you got up in the middle of the opening mass of the semester and shouted that Jesus Christ was not only not God but was a nasty cantankerous Jew."

"Ah yes, one of my better moments, 30 years ago when I was shy and withdrawn."

"Not before or since has that College moved so quickly in its decision-making, your defense of academic freedom fell on deaf ears. Really Sebastian!"

"If I had to do it over I would also excoriate the Virgin Mary and her fornicating husband Joseph. But when the high and mighty bishop's face went to blood red I worried that I might cause the sorry bastard to have a stroke. So, I just strutted out into a goddam thunderstorm. I'm sure all of the devout bastards and bitches were hoping for a lightening bolt right up my ass!" He laughed heartily.

So did McAbee who asked, "What has become of you? I thought you fled to Seattle. Why are you back here? Are you happy that the Theology Department of St. Anselm more or less agrees with you as the current bishop, college president and the Vatican look on hopelessly?"

"Hah! No. I'm here because my aunt died. My only good memory of my childhood was she. I'm still in Seattle. Filthy rich. Who isn't out there? But don't worry I'll be gone shortly. And you McAbee?"

Bertrand gave him a short summary of his career at St. Anselm and the creation of ACJ, he concluded, "I'm on a bad case, That's why I have to go."

"ACJ, great name. Christian mythology, marvelous. Saints Anthony, Christopher, and Jude! You're ahead of your time. Give America another 20 years to see the wisdom of that name. I know you have to go. But I want to say something to you, your support back then? You were the only one to try to soothe things. I'll always remember that. Foolish of you but quite brave. There's a part of me in you McAbee. You know that."

Bertrand got up from his stool as did Stratmann. They hugged. Anyone watching the scene, McAbee thought, would sense great sadness – a lost age, a lost world.

He left the restaurant at 9:15 p.m. By that time the place was virtually empty. This was not unusual on weekdays in Davenport where by 9 p.m. most places were either shut or close to. He heard complaints about that often through the years as he would hear about Italians or Spaniards just now starting to eat.

His Camry was parked to the south of Biaggi's. The parking lot was dark and empty except for about five cars accenting the vacancy. He walked to his car carefully, always fearful of a trip. He heard movements behind him, startled. He half turned when he felt a searing pain in the area of his right knee. He was shoved and he fell as another blow was delivered to his stomach, with the comment "Back off fucker." He looked up and saw two brawny, masked characters, who were just getting started. The employee door to the south side of the restaurant opened and some significant light was shed close to the area where he was trying to scramble away from the two thugs. He yelled, "Help!"

One of the thugs, said, "Tha," as the other was winding up with a baseball bat to hit McAbee.

He didn't succeed as one of three waiters crashed into him and sent him sprawling. The other thug went after that waiter as the waitress was on her phone with the police and the other waiter was yelling as loud as he could. Within 30 seconds a black vehicle, lights off sped out of the lot.

Only then did McAbee confront the pain. His right knee screamed at him, he felt it, his hand dealing with a lump the size of a baseball. He vomited up his salad and whatever else was parked in his gut. If it wasn't for those three employees he wondered just how badly he would have been damaged.

The cops came, an ambulance was called. The waiter who had butted the one had been hit hard on his jaw, some loose teeth. Sebastian waddled out. He was upset but he was cheered when McAbee told him that his conversation with him might have saved his life because it allowed for the wait staff to happen out when they did. As he was being loaded into the ambulance he asked Sebastian to reward the three employees. "How much?" He said $100 apiece and any treatment for the one who had been hit, that he'd cover the expenses Sebastian nodded and said, "Got it. It's on me Bertrand. Get better."

While in the ambulance he called Augusta. She'd be at Unity Point Hospital immediately, it was just a few blocks south.

CHAPTER 26

During the night Augusta had been busy after she heard that ice was the primary way to treat his knee. Secondary to that was a ten pill regimen of Oxycontin. His stomach area was purple but no permanent damage was noted after x-rays and a scan was done. She helped McAbee get into his condo, got him to undress and he conked out in seconds. She stayed and slept on his couch but not before calling Jack Scholz, Barry Fisk, and Pat Trump. "There's going to be a come-to-Jesus meeting with this man and I want all of you to be on the same page." She then went on to articulate her intentions. "Food?" Pat asked. "Yes, a tray of bagels from Hy-Vee. Cream cheese." Fisk asked, "What the hell can I do?" She said, "Be gentle and nice, that shock might cure him of his problem." Her comment wasn't friendly. Fisk disconnected. Scholz said, "It's about time. He needs a kick in the ass, I'll be there."

The meeting at Bertrand's condo was set for 11 a.m. It was 1:26 a.m. when Augusta sat on the couch. She was crying. Her night was fretful as she checked on Bertrand hourly, his frequent groans penetrating heavy sleep.

She realized that behind her sadness and fear there was a stab of boiling anger that she'd have to control in the morning.

Bertrand was up by 9:30 a.m. He was urinating a pinkish blood stream, his mid-section would spasm in pain and his knee stabbed at him with agonizing regularity. In the shower he dropped the bar of soap but was unable to pick it up. He stood under the water for at least ten minutes. The hot water didn't alleviate the pain but it did force a counter sensation to battle the pain, a distraction at the very least. He dried off as well as he could when Augusta knocked at the half-open door. He welcomed her help for drying and leaned on her shoulder as he crossed over into his bedroom and sat on his bed. "Ah Augusta. Thanks. I got the hell beaten out of me. So sore. The pain comes out of nowhere."

"I'm going to get a pill for you. It should help. Then you are going to the living room in a bathrobe, over there." She pointed to a recliner about 15 feet from the bed. "I'm going to make you some toast and coffee," she said this is a commanding way.

For a second he thought that this was his house and why was she giving him orders? But he kept his feelings in check.

She went on, "I've invited a few people here, to go over things with you."

"I can't handle a meeting Augusta. My mind is in a swamp. What meeting? In this condo? I'm going to need a few days."

"All is taken care of. The meeting will be short. Pat is coming."

"Good. You notified Pat, thanks."

"Yes. Yes. ACJ is under control."

At that moment, and only then, did he sense something was off key. He wasn't used to her issuing orders, drying him off, serving as a crutch, demanding his bathrobe to be worn, in fact, how did she even know where to find it. He hadn't worn it in years and wasn't sure where in his place it was. It wasn't part of her to snoop. There were some borders after all, he thought in a guarded sulk as she handed him a glass of water and a pill. There was an overwhelming fact, however. He was at her mercy and she knew that damn well.

The toast and coffee went down easily. Another cup, another piece, please. His doorbell rang a few times close to 11 a.m. She answered it and showed whoever it was into his study that was in a hallway out of his line of sight. He noted that each entry was in silence. Twice, he heard the partition to the study roll to an open and close. The pill was helping with the pain as he brought his attention to what possibly could occur at 11 a.m. Perhaps it was his doctor. That would make sense but as he thought about it he was skeptical. Doctors coming to a house?

Augusta came back from the last of the doorbell affairs. Brusquely she said, "Are you ready?"

With a bit of bite in his words, he said, "What's the big mystery?"

"Lean on me," she said, all charm long gone.

He noticed that several chairs to his dining room set were missing. He limped along holding her arm as she slid the partition open to his office. And there they sat, Jack Scholz, Pat Trump and Barry Fisk. Pat turned pale a bit, Jack had daggers in his eyes and Barry Fisk looked at his watch and shook his head once. Augusta eased him down on a chair as she sat beside him and facing him. They almost formed a circle around a small rectangular table. There were several towels on it with an object of sorts under them.

He returned the stares of each of them, puzzled as he was about this meeting.

Augusta said, "I called this meeting, Bertrand. Let me say we all feel terrible about what happened to you. We all feel this is about your case, Agatha Pruitt. That you have crossed into dangerous waters and you are up against very violent people. Before you got up this morning I spoke with a man by the name of Sebastian Stratmann. He told me about last night. Bottom line – you're lucky to be alive and/or not brain dead."

Barry Fisk squirmed in his chair and said, "Well, he's brain dead if you think about it. I don't know how often you've been warned to carry a weapon. Sheer stupidity. I had things to report to you about the Agatha case but to what end? Giving it to you will probably get you murdered," he said legs kicking wildly.

Jack Scholz weighed in next. "I rarely agree with that character," he pointed across to Fisk, "but this time I do. You're outlandish. You get into a game such as private investigations, run cases overflowing with danger and you're unarmed. My advice on this is scorned by you. It's as if one of the goddam ACJ saints is going to protect you? For an old man you need to grow up or get out."

McAbee heard about confrontation sessions with drug addicts or alcoholics. Relatives and friends could pile on and force the offender to get help. This is what this session was about. What did they want? Should he carry a sub-machine gun?

Pat looked at him with a few tears in her eyes. "Bertrand. This isn't the first time you've heard this. Surely not this harshly but you've heard this. Much to my regret I have to say that I agree with them. Your luck almost ran out. My heart almost broke when Augusta called me last night. That is all I'll say. You're too smart not to get the point and hopefully, you're smart enough to heed this advice."

"And just in case you don't understand my position," Augusta said gently but with determination, "I concur with everyone here."

Lamely, he said, "Okay. I get the message. I'll try to be better."

Jack stood up and tore the towels off of the object on the table. It was McAbee's Glock, holster, and a small wooden box of bullets. Years ago Bertrand had bought these after he was almost killed. He could hear his assassinated brother, Bill, saying, "Goddam idiot." Jack now pointing down to the cache said in a voice that Bertrand had only heard rarely, "No! No! I'll try to do better is not sufficient. We all insist that from now on you are going to wear this. You're licensed, you know how to use it and I've purchased sessions at Castle's shooting range for you to refresh yourself." He retrieved from his pocket a small card, "There's $300 on this pre-paid."

"We're not leaving here Bertrand, until you agree to this," Augusta said.

"This isn't a fair fight," he said defensively.

"Fairness?" Fisk scoffed.

McAbee slumped down. He loved all four of these people. He knew, in his heart, that they were right. But due to his inherent stubbornness and self-centeredness bucked at being ordered to do this. He recalled Epictetus, the Greek slave to Roman masters. He was a great stoic philosopher who argued in the treatise called *The Enchiridion*, there are things we control and things that we don't. Live a life only absorbed by those things that we control. Ultimately carrying a weapon was in his control even though the demand came from those beyond his control.

He looked at their stern faces and said, "Okay, you win. Thanks for caring. You're right I have been pressing my luck I would feel a lot better today if I had planted a slug or two in the knees of those bastards."

They all laughed, except for Barry, who stared at McAbee in a weighing manner.

Augusta declared the meeting over. Jack and Pat left. Barry said, "I have some information about your request about Rock Island High School. Interested?"

Bertrand saw that Barry's legs were shaking at high speed.

CHAPTER 27

Barry Fisk stared at him. Augusta sat closely by him.

"So, Barry. You did Rock Island High School. Five years," Bertrand said. His sharp pains were in a temporary cessation, even though the ache was still agonizing.

"Are you sure you're up to this?"

Augusta said, "As long as you get to the point, he'll be okay."

Bertrand did not remember ever hearing Augusta so tightly wound, so demanding, almost belligerent.

Barry said, "That'll be easy. I don't want to hang around here anyway."

Augusta and Barry were not friends, their mutual animus usually under wraps. She didn't bite on Barry's gibe. Bertrand said, "Okay Barry I'm listening." He noted that Barry's legs had become still unlike the encounter session minutes ago. This did not portend well he thought glumly.

"There were 935 grads during those years. I didn't include all of the students who passed through the place in those years, drop-outs, moves and so on. I concentrated on the graduates. It helped that you called about Jake Petersmith's memory. I'm assuming that the bracelet seller either knew something or was the actual killer. Otherwise this was a pretty hopeless task. This whole dimension was an angle that the Rock Island P.D. never pursued. Agatha should have said something way back then about her love for Margaret and the bracelet. But she didn't so what can you do?"

Bertrand noticed that there was a small tremor beginning to show on Barry's small legs. He had something, after all.

"Of the 935 grads 483 were girls, 452 boys. This is before the times when we started counting LGBTQRF creatures." He curled his lips and looked at Augusta in particular, perhaps awaiting a pushback. When none occurred he went on. "Of the 452 boys 192 are either known dead or have disappeared. So, we have 260, too big a number. When I started my probe I was looking for someone with a lot to lose, access to top secret gadgetry and super smart, at least in the top 25% of their class at the very least," as his legs were starting to pick up steam. "Now I'm down to 32 people, some remote as possible others more interesting. I know there are holes in my logic but this isn't the FBI that throws 500 bozos on this. Just lonely me so, now what?"

"Don't know," Bertrand said into a spasm of pain. He hoped that Augusta didn't notice now that she decided to command him.

"So," he continued with increasing pedantry, "I looked very closely at those 32. Eleven of them are medicos, dentists or doctors. Yes, they have something to lose but I didn't see them accessing secret military devices. So I'm down to 21. Of these, five of them are retired living in Florida, Arizona, and Utah. Down to 16. Seven of them did not go to college, some successful yes, but no college. That gets me to nine. Following?"

"You'd make a great CPA, Barry," McAbee said in some irritation.

"Three of them have had lifetime disabilities. These were serious enough for me to exclude them given the physical prowess of a conditioned athlete such as Margaret Thode. Now I have six. Manageable for tight scrutiny. So, I go back to Jake Petersmith. Assuming that he's as good as advertised to compare the physical description of the seller of the bracelet to those six. Not even a close match on four. Now I have two," his legs were now competing for a tryout on the Rockettes, McAbee thought.

Augusta cut in, "Lot of logic leaps to get to two."

He snarled, "I know. As I told you this isn't the FBI. And your boss there respects my logic."

McAbee didn't appreciate being the third person in the room. Fisk and Satin were in a stare down. They were both right in what they said but antipathy got in the way of a useful discussion. Some sharp wedges of pain slammed into him. Finally, he said, "Barry, I understand the constraints that I put on you and I agree you're not the FBI. If you ever became that my regard for you would be diminished. So, understanding that you had to take leaps of logic, tell me about the two you hit on," he said this in the hope of piercing the stalemate between the two.

"Here are the two. They both meet the criteria that I set up, especially access to that one spy device. The first is a man named Forrest Graham. He was a classmate of Margaret Thode. Family owned an appliance distributorship. Mother from Omaha. Piles of money, she a graduate from Smith.

Yearbook photo fits to some degree with what Petersmith said. Have you set up that sketch session with him? Family of much wealth back to the lumber business in the 19th century."

"Not yet. Keep going."

"Well, Forrest Graham is with the CIA. Had to really dig in to determine this. Secretive bastards. He's high up, very high up. Director of Operations in South and Central America. Lots to lose, of course. Access to devices a given. Agree?"

McAbee was impressed as he quickly looked over to Augusta. She was nodding. "Second one?"

"This was a bit more of a reach. I wanted to exclude him but every time I was about to I couldn't. Even now I hesitate to bring him up. Intuitional rather than logical." His legs were still kicking out.

"Go ahead Barry. I know that you're on a high wire," Bertrand said as he noticed Augusta was nodding in agreement with his comments.

"The second guy owns a string of restaurants all through the Midwest. Loaded with money. Lives among the high and mighty. Part owner of the Kansas City Chiefs and the Kansas City Royals. I cannot determine how much he's worth but I'd say the lower billions. But with a debt structure you never really know what he's worth. He fits Petersmith's description of the bracelet seller too."

"Why were you so hesitant about including him?"

"Disability and access to advanced devices."

"Disability?"

"Has only one arm. Unless he farmed the job out I think he'd have had a hard time with Agatha. Not impossible though. And then there's Margaret Thode."

"What if he did farm out the job?"

"That's another cause of my hesitation. Would you trust anyone in the world to do this? Open yourself to blackmail? He has a reputation for shrewdness and obsessiveness for detail. He has a home in the Quad Cities. I cannot not keep him off the list. All sorts of women problems."

"Name?"

"Roger Smalley."

McAbee was taken aback. He was a noted benefactor in the community. He faintly remembered an incident from years ago. Had Smalley been in some kind of fight? He had no idea that Smalley was a graduate of Rock Island High School. "When did he lose the arm?"

"When he was three. Very traumatic. Two pit bulls attacked him. Almost killed him."

"Petersmith never mentioned a one-armed guy."

"I understand. Also would he be able to access the listening device? That's why I hesitated."

"Was his name mentioned in the police files?" McAbee asked.

"No."

"So it's an outside chance but it sounds like we should take a run at him."

Augusta said to Barry, "You eliminated all women right off the top?"

McAbee said, "So did the cops. They questioned some women but only to get a sense of Margaret Thode as a person. Should Barry have done otherwise?"

She responded, "Well, yes and no. I understand that he's trying to find a needle in the haystack. But I'm not sure that you can be so set about it. After all, she had a sexual relationship with a female. Were there any traces of semen at Margaret's murder scene?"

'No. Violation galore but no semen. But it was the 1970s and what we know now about murder scenes is categorically different from then," McAbee said.

"Just a thought you guys. Don't underestimate what some women can do in a state of hate."

McAbee put aside her observation on the basis of it as unlikely and not fitting into Petersmith's comments. He said nothing else to Barry except telling him to go all out on the two he fingered. He was exhausted, his pain was gathering for another assault.

He went back to his bedroom, unrobed and went to bed. Augusta brought him another OxyContin. He told her to leave; he'd call. He was asleep in minutes.

CHAPTER 28

Bertrand awoke two hours later. No one was in the house. Augusta left a note that indicated her almost instant availability should he call. The pain was endured as a constant; but the spasms that flashed through him caused him to groan.

Beside his recliner were two folders left by Barry. He sat and opened one of them. It detailed information about Roger Smalley. Left arm, missing as it was, did not impair his ability at racquetball and subsequently pickleball that had gone on to seemingly replace the former. He was in the A class skill-set. His picture showed a light haired man with a long, thin face, his ears pinned back, nose thin, chin inclining to a point, intense and weighing eyes. McAbee wondered if his facial muscles could contract for a smile. He had a wolfish look.

His history as a businessman was impressive even if he was born on third base. His wealth exploded through the decades. He was well known for his philanthropic efforts, colossal in the eyes of a poor man but negligible for the kind of wealth he had garnered.

He was known for his fast temper and had been sued on six different occasions by beaten-up people. One case he lost, one he won, and four were settled out of court.

In his four-story building in downtown Bettendorf he had been named in a seemingly continuous series of sexual harassment suits. Apparently his right hand was in the A class for fondling, grabbing, and caressing, McAbee concluded. Never once had ACJ been involved with any of these matters. He was a man on the periphery of McAbee's knowledge. This he found to be unusual.

Relative to the Margaret Thode murder case he had never been questioned by the Rock Island Police. Apparently there were no known connections to him. Barry had squirreled himself into the high school records that had all been digitized. McAbee was surprised at how much of Rock Island was in the cloud. If Barry was God the whole damn city would probably disappear into the clouds. It came out that Roger Smalley, as a student, was in Barry's estimation, 'a pain in the ass,' constantly sent to study hall for bad behavior, especially toward girls and minorities.

He went on to Ohio State University in Columbus and majored in finance. He grew his family's wealth into a mountain. But it was clear that his behaviors were swollen with arrogance.

He did fit all of the categories that Barry used to flit through five years of high school graduates. Even the terrible violence inflicted upon both Margaret Thode and Agatha Pruitt was possible though the logistics of how he might do it were daunting to his imagination.

McAbee put that folder aside. He realized that he might have to enter that tiger's cage himself. Not something he relished.

The other file was about Forrest Graham of the CIA. He was a very different man when contrasted to Smalley. McAbee thought of Plutarch, a second century C.E. savant, who wrote and contrasted the lives of famous Roman and Greek personages. He would have cherished the contrast in the instance of these two as it was so stark.

Graham was from a blue blood family from Davenport. Their wealth was generational, originating when lumber was sent down from the North and through the untamed rapids of the Mississippi River in the Quad City area. The family was Presbyterian to the core. It thus was penetrated by some severe Calvinistic qualities such as abstemiousness, disjunctive and absolutist thinking, and most of all that their success was a sign of God's favor.

He was a brilliant student, who ended up at Yale and was recruited directly into the CIA upon graduation. McAbee backtracked. How had Graham ended up at Rock Island High School given his roots in Davenport? He noticed a small asterisk on page two that he had missed probably due to a pain spasm. On the back of this page he saw that Barry had anticipated McAbee. There was a divorce. All files closed forever. Barry couldn't get near them. What he did determine is that Forrest Graham became an inhabitant of Rock Island, living with his mother in a 12 story aberration in Rock Island but famed for the wealth that occupied the building.

Barry was displeased by the apparent lack of sin and perfidy in Forrest's regard. He was never associated with Margaret Thode, never questioned, never the slightest tinge of scandal around him. From the scant information available he fleshed out that Graham had married and had risen up in the CIA apparatus. He was unable to breach much information about him and feared any effort at trying to penetrate CIA files was too dangerous.

All of that said, he met all of the criteria that he had posited for a possible murderer of Margaret Thode and Agatha Pruitt.

At the end of the file he showed two pictures, one from the yearbook of Rock Island High School and the other a picture from a hearing before a committee from the U.S. Senate that was investigating an incident from the first Obama presidency concerning events in the country of Columbia and their drug trade. Graham had been identified by the *Washington Post*. This time McAbee caught another asterisk and turned over the page.

Forrest Graham aging was very true to his picture as a senior in high school. Light haired, kind eyes, high browed with a squared face. He wasn't handsome but it didn't surprise McAbee that he had a presence about him, self-assuredness, stolid, and honest-looking. Was this a good disguise in an organization such as the CIA that was built upon the edifice of deceit and game-playing?

He wondered whether the *Washington Post* had been chastised for releasing his name, probably not, as he thought that all the arcane rules in Washington were well-known to the editors of the *Post*.

Yet for all the purity around this man Barry had fingered him as suspect one. Bertrand understood that Graham had checked all of the boxes and yet he seemed to be beyond suspicion. He considered the matter and thought that Forrest Graham was worth looking into but he doubted anything would come of it.

CHAPTER 29

Jane Cullen had taught at St. Anselm for ages as an art professor. She retired a few years ago. She was a marvelous sketcher, some of her work found its way into several museums in the Midwest. McAbee decided to call her after a stern rebuff from the Davenport P.D. whose Chief was currently engaged in an all-out non-cooperation war with ACJ. The two had never been as estranged as they were now as McAbee's last big case with Russian overtones had snapped the Chief's patience. Even Augusta who had a positive relation with him was unable to secure a peace treaty. McAbee was in police hell, not for the first time.

"Jane, Bertrand McAbee. Been ages but I hope all is well," he said cautiously to this sensitive soul.

"Ah. Yes. I'm okay. And yourself?"

"Hanging in there. I realize that we haven't seen or talked to each other in ages."

"True enough," she said warily.

"I need your help, or at least, your advice."

"Well I knew you weren't calling for old time's sake," she said suspiciously.

McAbee winced, Jane was not a sarcastic woman. "Jane I've lost contact with so many people since I left St. Anselm. Different worlds. It doesn't mean that I don't have a high regard for you."

There was a lengthy pause. Finally, she said, "Ditto Bertrand. What do you want?" This said with a touch of disdain.

He explained his need for a sketch artist. It involved a case he was working on.

"I'll do it. Get me out of the house."

"Charge?"

"Do you have any money? I heard you had some pretty lucrative cases," she said mirthfully.

"I have vaults of money, Jane. How's $500?"

"It's a deal," she said cheerfully.

After the logistics were set up by Pat Trump, Bertrand found himself outside of Jake's Antiques in Moline. Finally, some rain came to the Quad City area. He stood in the doorway looking at a sign that read, 'Closed.' Within a minute the 'Closed' sign was changed over to 'Open' and at the same time Jane was walking toward the front door of the store.

Jane, always thin, and of medium height, had aged poorly. Her sensitive face was acutely lined and pouched. Her formerly rod-like posture was stooped badly. But she showed a smile and her green eyes still exhibited kindness. He wondered how he registered in her eyes after all these years. He didn't pursue that woeful path.

After introductions inside the store and 20 minutes of rapid-fire reminiscences and questioning of Jane by Petersmith she got down to business as she withdrew a sketch pad from a carrying case, set up a small easel and asked Jake to close his eyes. She was as able as ever as she cranked out his memories beginning with the hairline of the bracelet seller. And then they meshed nicely as a pair – his extraordinary memory and her extraordinary sketching skills.

After 20 minutes she turned the easel toward Petersmith. He looked at it for a bit and said, "That's damn good. Couldn't have been better. That's the guy."

Jane smiled, the affirmation of her work by Jake pleased her. Bertrand slid across an envelope for her. It was a check for $500. She tore off the sheet from the sketchpad and looked at Bertrand said, "Let's get some coffee sometimes. Catch up," she started to walk away.

McAbee said, "Thanks Jane. Absolutely about the coffee." Did he notice a slight shrug in her bent shoulders? Correctly, he thought, it probably would not happen. He knew very well that his ghosting behaviors were accelerating as he grew older.

Petermith interrupted his chain of thought. "That's quite a woman. Reminds me of a girl I used to date in high school. I…"

McAbee put his left hand out as a stop sign. "Jake. Please look at this picture. Is there anything else? Ear lobes, mouth, teeth, freckles?" He knew that Petersmith saw through McAbee's ghosting behaviors, that he didn't like them and thus didn't like McAbee who had no intention of listening to Jake recount his life story. They were on two different continents.

Tersely now, Jake said, "Nope. Nothing else. Closing up now."

McAbee thanked him and left, the rain picking up as he paced quickly to his car.

He arrived at his office. The new six lane I-74 bridge, between Moline and Bettendorf was a pleasure to drive. It took ages for the old bridge to be replaced, a tight four-lane menace that some refused to use out of fear. The new bridge was a seven-year project that caused multiple delays, accidents and road rage in the Quad City area. An engineer client of his had argued that the Chinese would have had it all done in one year. He went on to assert that was the reason America would soon be subject to that nation. Bertrand didn't argue with him. But in his view China wasn't necessary for America to collapse. Americans would do it to themselves if they kept up the prevailing nonsense that was noosed around so many necks.

In his office he brought up the recent pictures of Smalley and Graham. Other than the light hair they were facially very dissimilar. He then studied the sketch made by Jane and tried to bend that to their current ages. He was having no luck in finding a match. He asked Pat and Augusta to come into his office for their take. Pat, quick about things like this, said "Inconclusive. Could be either. But if I was forced to choose I'd say Graham but I'm not convinced either way with the two."

Augusta said, "Can't see either of these guys being the one in the sketch. But we all know that aging is a twisted business."

It wasn't conclusive that Graham or Smalley were innocent. The sketched face could have been another kid who had somehow come into possession of the bracelet, perhaps lost by either Graham or Smalley. Too many possible scenarios. Yet there was an accurate sketch of someone pawning that bracelet. If he attended Rock Island High School someone could identify him. This sketched kid may not have been the murderer but he knew something.

CHAPTER 30

Just about every school has someone with a long history in it and with an equally long memory. The task was to find this person. The principal of Rock Island High School during the 1970s was dead. Barry's search for a knowledgeable person from the 1975-1979 years came up with three possibilities. Unfortunately one of them had Alzheimer's, the other lived in Toronto ('Don't ask why Bertrand') and the third was in Cambridge, Illinois, in Henry County. It is a small farmer-centered town of about 2200, some 45 minutes southeast of the Quad Cities. His name was Stan Fullbright. He was 84 years old, he seemed to live by himself, presumably able-bodied and of able mind, Barry reported.

Bertrand set out on the drive. The farm fields were fully plowed and surely some planted given the good weather that prevailed into late April. But he knew farmers and their fear of a possible late freeze even into May. So, *some* were planted.

Cambridge was a neatly kept town. Most lawns were cut by now, the downtown with its proverbial square and courthouse had energy and commerce. He hadn't called ahead, a decision he weighed as 50:50 for outcomes. In fact, still hurting, he brooded that the whole trip was at 50:50 odds.

Fullbright's house had a ramp neat and fresh looking, angling up to a front door that was flat to the cement. McAbee rang the bell and instantly he heard the bark of a dog, a big one. It was at the front door snarling and growling. This dog was no puppy.

Seconds later he heard a "Yeah?" through the door. Bertrand explained his visit concluding with a plea for entry into the house.

Fullbright said, "Wait a minute. I have to put Groucho into my laundry room."

A bit later he heard Fullbright telling him to come in. The door was open.

Bertrand inferred that Groucho obviated the need to lock doors. When inside he noticed that Stan's electric wheelchair was going backwards, ending up in his kitchen that had a small circular dining table with two chairs at its end. The arrangement made easy routes possible for the wheelchair.

"Take one of those chairs over there," he pointed to the beginnings of a living room. McAbee did as told. Stan said, "I don't eat out here much anymore. I watch the tube, eat there," pointing again toward the living room. "Sit down, please."

Fullbright was fragile, perhaps 100 pounds in weight. His short sleeve shirt showed arms with multiple bruises. Bertrand thought his entire body was probably encased in bruises and scars. His face was thin, a hatchet-like nose his most prominent feature. He wore a cap emblazoned with 'Vietnam Vet'. His voice was like a razor being scraped across glass. Yet he had friendly eyes and appeared happy to have company. Stan said, "I'll help if I can. You know I was a newly named Assistant Principal at Rock Island High in 1973. Fresh out of the hatchery of other minor posts. In those days I was pretty dynamic, got to know a lot of kids. Now," he peered at Bertrand, "I'm on the road to death. They give me six months. Supposedly I have four conditions that are working in concert to kill me," he smiled wistfully.

McAbee liked him instantly. "What kind of dog is that behind that door?" pointing to an area at the far end of the kitchen.

"Ah. The love of my late life. He's an Akita. Seven years old. One man dog and I'm the man," he smiled.

"Groucho?"

"When I got him he had some markings on his snout. I thought of Groucho Marx. He's a great dog. I'm trying to get my neighbor to adopt him when I go. So far, they have not bonded. But I hope."

"A little more about my mission." He elaborated on the bracelet, the sale of it in Davenport, the memory of Jake Petersmith, and its connection to Margaret Thode.

"You know that murder broke my heart. Margaret Thode was a singularly obsessive girl. Very regimented. Very private. Few friends. Getting a smile out of her was an obstacle course. If someone took her bike it would be like someone stealing my dog, Groucho. But I really liked her spunk. Would have made a great Marine, her."

"Friends?"

"A few if I recall right. She wasn't into boys. They knew it too. Some of them gave her a hard time."

"Fight back?"

"Oh yeah. She had a long middle finger if you know what I mean," a vague smile on his face.

155

Bertrand told him about Agatha Pruitt.

"I sort of remember her. Very bright. Are you saying there is a connection to Margaret's murder? I read about Agatha in the paper. Long time between those murders. I never thought of any tie-in."

"Tell me more about Agatha Pruitt."

"Well," he was fingering his chin, "first off I don't remember anything between the two girls. I don't remember ever seeing them together but they wouldn't show that anyway. They did have one thing in common though."

"What's that?" Bertrand asked.

"There was a loner quality in both of them. Introverts. Agatha and I had little contact."

Bertrand was torn about throwing out the names of Smalley and Graham to him. He decided to go after the sketch first so as to not prejudice Fullbright. "I'm going to show you this sketch. Perhaps you can identify this guy. I'm not even sure that he had any connection to Rock Island High School. But I'd sure like to speak with him. I think that he might know something that he doesn't know he knows."

"Interesting take. That's what the interrogators in Nam would say before questioning prisoners."

Bertrand withdrew the sketch made by Jane Cullen and placed it on the table in front of Stan. "Ever see this guy?"

He lowered his glasses toward the tip of his nose and bent over. He studied the picture for a few seconds. He looked up toward Bertrand and said, "I'll be damned. That's Scooter. Scooter Benson, I'm sure of it. Sad story there. Got tossed from Rock Island High School not long, a few years at best, after I got there. Drug sales and possession. Flaky kid, his father was a doctor as I recall. That sketch? Where did you get it?"

"I told you about Petersmith and his memory. Well I hired an old friend to sketch off of his memory. Freshly done."

"Well it's perfect. I'll say that," Fullbright said.

"Can you tell me more about Scooter?"

"He just didn't belong. He'd disappear from classes, come late. Teachers were up in arms about him. You know how it is, the more they got on him the more defiant he became. Because he was a doctor's kid the principal gave him a lot of rope. Finally, he went too far. Cops got involved. I believe he was a senior, probably about 17 or 18 when it all got sorted in the principal's office. Essentially, as long as Scooter disappeared all would be forgotten. The only one who was happy about that solution was Scooter himself. Case closed."

"Did he have any friends?"

"Sure. Any kid who was using drugs. Scooter was selling but we never caught him red-handed. But what is a friend? A user?"

"Do you know what became of him?"

"Sorry, no. But my guess is that he was on a road that few can come back from. A bad road. But who knows? Life is a trickster."

"First name?"

"Larry," Fullbright said.

"Can you tell me more about him?"

"The big thing about him is that he never thought about consequences. In my day, they were really nailing down attention deficit behaviors. I think that was a basic part of him, like he'd do something stupid, get caught, and then repeat the same behavior the next day. Not that he was stupid, *per se,* just this defect. Someone probably ran him in the drug selling business. If the cops knew they never disclosed it in my presence, at any rate."

"Was he a user?" Bertrand asked.

"Almost positive. His behaviors certainly suggested that."

"Please understand Stan I'm asking a lot of questions. All sorts of names came up. Recently two in particular besides Scooter," McAbee was trying to be very diplomatic at this juncture. "They are Forrest Graham and Roger Smalley. Remember them? Any connections to Scooter?"

Fullbright did not hesitate in his response, his memory admired by McAbee who would frequently question his own adequacy in this regard. Stan said, "Forrest Graham, first off. No way would he be seen with the likes of Scooter. Scooter skulked around, Graham strutted around. Graham was a peacock in love with his feathers of virtue. If they had any contact with each other it would have been a closely kept secret. Just don't see it. But high school is a strange environment. Never say never. By the way would you like to meet Groucho? He knows you're not dangerous from the tone of our voices," his eyes had plead in them.

Bertrand was in a dilemma of sorts. He had no reason to trust a seven year old Akita who was probably looking for the slightest sign of an aggressive tell from McAbee. Nerves? Dislike? Fear? God only knew how Groucho's mind was wired. On the other hand he did not know exactly how to say no to this marvelous old man. "Sure" he said with false cheerfulness.

Wheels in motion Stan moved to the utility room door. He opened it and told Groucho to sit and stay. He obeyed but that didn't stop his alert eyes from giving McAbee a thoughtful stare. Stan grabbed his collar and slowly the two started their move toward Bertrand whose paranoia about the entire spectacle was on a rapid ascent. Stan brought Groucho up to him as McAbee stayed stock still, his right hand on his knee and his left hand staying quite proximate to his groin.

In a soothing voice Stan said, "Groucho, this is Bertrand. He's a friend, it's okay." To Bertrand he said, "Just put your hand down vertically and let him sniff. Don't worry he'd never do anything to you. By the way, you're already one up on my neighbor."

McAbee did as told and Groucho was released by Stan. The Akita sniffed around McAbee's personage. McAbee patted him and all went well as Groucho eventually went down on his haunches and monitored the remainder of his time with Stan Fullbright.

Stan said, "You asked about Roger Smalley too. First off, I don't know if Smalley and Graham ever were in touch with each other, night and day there. But you want to know about Smalley and Scooter. Let me say this. Smalley was a wise ass. If I had to say who'd know Scooter, hands down it would be Roger Smalley. But that said, I don't recall them ever being together."

"Tell me more about Smalley. Characteristics?"

"Well, you surely know about his missing arm. In my estimation this dictated his entire personality. A major compensation going on there. He was in his share of fights.

God help the girl or guy who stared at his missing arm area. He was a taunter too."

"Someone said that he was a pain in the ass."

He laughed gently. "Well that's for sure, as a starter. Just an over the top kid. Full of himself."

"Would you be surprised if I told you that he and Scooter were in cahoots? By the way," Bertrand added hurriedly, "I have no evidence of such. Just thinking about compatibility."

"Compatibility? Absolutely," Stan said. Groucho picked up on Stan's intensity, ears up, on alert.

"Now the big question here is this. Any connections between five kids at Rock Island High School? Roger Smalley, Forrest Graham, Scooter Benson, Margaret Thode, and Agatha Pruitt," McAbee said.

"Wow! That's quite a bundle. Talk about complexities of personality. This reminds me of my favorite author." He pointed to a two-shelf bookcase. McAbee looked back. All of the books, it appeared, were by Charles Dickens.

McAbee laughed. "Yeah. It's looking like that isn't it?"

"One thing about Dickens is his ability to link so many characters in so many ways and make it believable. I think that we'd need Dickens himself to connect those five," Fullbright said.

"I didn't mean to suggest that they were a secret gang," Bertrand said through a smile, "but I'm very interested in the two girls *vis-à-vis* the three guys."

"I get that. Hey," he clicked his fingers, "hold on. Have some time?"

"Sure."

Fullbright rolled back a bit and sat near a small end table. Apparently, he never ended his relationship to a rotary phone. He started the old dial turning that brought back memories to Bertrand. He said, "Hi Hilda. Stan. You okay?"

There was some chatter from the other end.

"Have a favor to ask. I have a man here who's looking into the killings of Margaret Thode..."

Chatter.

"I know. Ages ago. But also Agatha Pruitt, a few weeks ago..."

Chatter.

"First off do you remember any give and take between them as students?"

Chatter, prolonged.

"I see. Didn't know that. Sure?"

Chatter.

"That positive. Boy, I never saw that or heard about it."

Chatter.

"Next. Any give or take between three guys in particular? Scooter Benson, Forrest Graham and Roger Smalley. And importantly any connectivity between the three guys and two gals?"

Chatter on steroids, McAbee thought.

"Thanks dear. Come over to see Groucho sometime. He likes you."

Chatter.

Stan laughed gently and hung up and then he looked at McAbee and said, "Well you're in a bit of luck, Hilda was a counselor at Rocky High. First off, she did not deal very much with any of the five except for Scooter who frequently told her to go to hell. No love affair there between Hilda and

Scooter. So she said that she is not under any confidentiality codes. That said, she was in the know about things. By the way," he stopped and stroked Groucho who leaned his head into Stan's knee, "she's my age. A sharp cracker, she. So, unbeknownst to me she suspected that both Agatha and Margaret were gay. She offered that up without any prodding from me. As you heard, I didn't lead her into any of this. Give her a name and boom, out comes an answer. She used to be so guarded and secretive. Different now with her. She knew of no contact between Forrest Graham with the two guys, Scooter and Roger Smalley. Unlikely, she thought. She said that Forrest acted like an old 80 year old ultra right Republican. Prim and proper. The two girls, if anything, he would probably have held them in low regard. But Scooter and Smalley? She suggested that Smalley was probably into drugs and therefore Scooter would be in the picture if that was true. Lastly, if either of those two suspected that either girl was a lesbian there would be no holds barred for ridicule and abuse. Now, Bertrand, you've been kind and I appreciate your work but I'm exhausted. Let me show you out. Call again if you need me but I'm pretty sure that's all I can provide for you."

On the drive home, he wondered about the interlocking pieces and the reliability of information and insights from over 45 years ago.

CHAPTER 31

The search for the whereabouts of Scooter Benson caused Barry Fisk a headache. Two days of intense online activity had yielded little. Even as he had secured a social security number for Benson it only led to an issued motorcycle license in South Dakota in 1983. Then it was as though he dropped out of the human race. Barry chased down arrest records, change of names, foreign countries but could find nothing on the former student of Rock Island High School.

His father, Dr. Benson, had legally disowned Scooter in 1981. His gathering assumption was that Scooter was buried somewhere in the west of the country. A troublemaker, probably prone to run into bad company, had simply been disappeared. A motorcycle gang? Who knew?

He understood that his lack of success would disappoint McAbee. One of Bertrand's oddities was his supreme trust in Barry. Secretly, Barry was uncomfortable with McAbee's seeming belief in his omniscience. He knew the limits to his craft all too well, even as Bertrand was too much of a believer in him. Because of these considerations he was hesitant to report about Scooter.

Simmering in his unconscious was his cursory background check into Scooter's father and mother. As a last resort he drove onto that road. Was it possible that an outlier such as Scooter got into some groups who barely had intercourse with the greater society? He doubted it but he wanted to run some kind of check on such groups, given what he had discovered. Dr. Benson's wife Clarissa had been a Mormon. Probably not practicing, but a Mormon nonetheless. Dr. Benson was prominent in the Methodist Church in downtown Rock Island. From old records kept in the church history he noticed that some hefty contributions had been left to the church in the name of both of the Bensons. This was a sign, but not dispositive, that Clarissa had become a Methodist. Barry was thrilled about getting into the records of the Mormon Church as they had cultivated, in his mind, a severe psychosis about genealogy and salvation. Such beliefs had caused the Mormon Church to obsess over immigration, baptism, birth records, and just about anything that related to a person's existence on this earth.

Clarissa Benson was born as Clarissa Smith. Great name for a Mormon. Disaster for a researcher into their history. She was born in 1930 in Keokuk, Iowa. He found out that her family had not gone on the famous trek to Utah but had stayed in this southeastern city of Iowa. However, the family did trace back to Nauvoo, Illinois, and the celebrated flight from there in 1846 across the Mississippi River and onwards to the West.

Barry knew that Joseph Smith, the founder of Mormonism, was murdered in 1844 in Carthage, Illinois, not all that far from Nauvoo. The meticulous records kept by the Mormon Church in Salt Lake City traced a genetic connection to Clarissa from none other than Joseph Smith himself.

Barry had the long held conviction that Jews were Jews, Catholics were Catholics Mormons were Mormons and so on. That somehow their DNA was altered. Accordingly, as he traversed Clarissa's connections, he assumed that Scooter, a defective bastard, had Mormon juices in him. And so he pursued that angle, the final stab before telling McAbee that he was beaten by Scooter's disappearance.

The Mormon Church believed in bigamy from the outset. Brigham Young, Joseph Smith and a host of early Mormons had their legions of wives, to Barry, concubines. They formally disavowed that tenet of their religion in 1890 but not without schisms from those who celebrated the idea and dug in to protect the practice. To Barry, the ultimate loner and misogynist, the idea of having four or five whining bitches hanging around his house was tantamount to a global disaster that would make Covid look like cutting one's nails.

So he thought hard about the connective tissue of Nauvoo, Joseph Smith, Clarissa Smith, and Scooter Benson. Was it possible that a varmint like Scooter would revert back to his roots? If so, there was probably no better place to lose one's identity than among the screwballs living along the Arizona and Utah border where polygamy was openly practiced and older lechers could obscure the tracks of a needy lecher with ease.

After two days of frustration the idea was seen as feasible. Thus Barry did a full scale inquiry into Hildale, Utah, and Colorado City in Arizona. These were considered the epicenters for the Fundamentalist Church of Jesus Christ of Latter Day Saints (FLDS). He started his research into Colorado City in Arizona. Essentially it was owned and controlled by this Fundamentalist group. The town had a population of about 2500. Polygamy was openly encouraged, the women garbed in 19th century clothing with long skirts, a bonnet on the head, and a heads down posture when out in public.

Colorado City had a very contentious history with the State of Arizona. In one famous incident Warren Jeffs was arrested for having 24 wives, one of them aged 12. He was given a life sentence currently being served in a hell-hole called Palestine, Texas.

Warren Jeffs was considered to be a prophet by these fundamentalist Mormons. He exerted extraordinary influence in the city, one time expelling a large number of teenagers from the city. He was accused of eliminating competition for the women in the community. Barry gave him credit for being an astute forecaster. Another time he ridded the town of the mayor and other officials and then disposed of their property and wives to his in-group. Property and wives a distinction without a difference. The more Barry read the more he felt he was doing a gaper's delay, a term used in Chicago for traffic delays caused by drivers who could not resist slowing down to gape at an accident. Barry thought of himself as a full time gaper, amazed by the absurdity of places such as Colorado City. He couldn't take his eyes off of his screen.

Back to the Bensons he observed that Dr. Benson died in 1985. Clarissa moved to St. George, Utah, a fast-growing community in south Utah with a huge Mormon presence. But the population was of the main congregation. The Church of the Latter Day Saints was centered in Salt Lake City, unlike the breakaway heretics in Colorado City. However, the move to Utah suggested that Clarissa was backtracking to her roots. Was there some kind of awkward connection to Scooter? Was she a repressed Mormon all the while comforting her Methodist and socially prominent husband? He stopped his ruminations, went to his couch, and slept for two hours. He was on thin ice, he knew. Nonetheless, it was ice.

Back on the prowl he found that Clarissa had died in 2011 in St. George. No mention had ever been made in the Quad City papers. The entirety of her probated will was left to the Mormon Church in Salt Lake City. There was no Scooter.

The Moore Funeral Home in St. George had opened a webpage that allowed for condolences and memories for Clarissa. Fisk scoured them for any sign of Larry (Scooter) Benson. There were 73 notices. He scrolled through them quickly. The 64th stopped him cold. Almost to the letter the mentions were the usual pap. 'Sorry to see you go, such a wonderful person', 'May the Lord reward you for your kindness', 'I remember when you helped that desperate family in need those years back.' Barry became bored and complacent and then came 64. 'I get it that you missed your train and caused the travails that came thereof. You have much to reconcile in your future life.' Signed with a 'S'. Fisk knew that comments about the dead were scrutinized by the funeral home's staff. Negatives did not make the cut. In one case Bertrand showed him what a Davenport mortician had removed from the remembrances of a particularly nasty character: 'May you rest in hell you son of a bitch;' 'Even as you're finally dead I don't want to be in the same room with you;' 'I curse you to eternal damnation you fucker;' and so on. About 37 were taken down by the mortician.

But the comment about Clarissa maintained through the scrutiny because it was vague enough. Allowed for interpretations, Barry supposed. The anomaly in the case was that the solitary 'S' was allowed in the face of all the other comments that ended with a signed name. There was no way to track the source of the comment. But it was there knife-like and given to an interpretation of vindictiveness.

The twin sister, as it were to Colorado City in Arizona, was Hildale in Utah. They were twins from the same egg. He studied their histories, their origin stories almost identical. Both the states of Utah and Arizona went after them with waxing and waning hostility. Finally, the denouement was the capture of Warren Jeffs in Nevada. He was on the run from the cops. Taking a 12 year old girl as a wife was a bit too far for the authorities. Ultimately, it was found that he had 78 wives, 24 of whom were under 17 years of age. Barry figured that even the most licentious Ottoman sultans would be impressed. Jeffs simply replaced the word harem with the word compound.

According to some reliable sources it was estimated that there were still about 10,000 faithful adherents in the sect.

But the central question was this. Could Scooter successfully hide himself in such a group?

Barry looked for pictures of residents in both of the cities in Utah and Arizona. He had purchased sophisticated facial recognition software from the dark web that he had obtained illegally from a Russian source. ACJ bore much of the cost. He had only used it once in an investigation several years back. He respected its accuracy. His research into the two controversial cities not only obtained still pictures but also some film made by a Salt Lake City TV station and also one in Phoenix. Various faces were run through the software off of the sketch that he had of Scooter Benson created by Jane Cullen. The entire enterprise, in his judgment, was a long shot. He was reminded of a comment made by Bertrand when the Kentucky Derby was won by Rich Strike in 2022, at 80-1 odds. McAbee said, "That's why they run races. Long shots win sometimes."

The software wobbled a few times over a few male pictures. Finally, toward the end of his inquiry the picture froze as a green light flashed on and off. There was a hit! Could this be Scooter Benson? Full beard, long hair, thin-faced and a gaze from his eyes that were somewhat hypnotic. There was no other captures from the software.

Barry was exultant. He would continue to be seen by McAbee as omniscient! And given what he had just pulled off? Why not!

CHAPTER 32

Bertrand's call into Roger Smalley's office in downtown Bettendorf felt like an absurdist saga. The secretary who answered the phone acted as if she had been goosed by one-armed Smalley himself. She sounded as though she was a resurrected Marilyn Monroe. But the real Marilyn was no idiot. This one? McAbee withheld judgment as he tried to find a voice suited to a 12 year old.

McAbee tried to explain why he was trying to visit with Roger Smalley. As soon as he intoned the word "murder" she said, almost in a shriek, that McAbee would have to wait for her to connect him with Smalley's personal secretary, Claudia. He chose not to speculate about the woman's purpose in the Smalley's enterprise.

The contrast between the Marilyn copycat and this new voice was stark. Her tone was mordant. She would truck no nonsense, a multi headed Cerberus guarding the king himself.

"What's this about?" she said in a growly voice.

"I'm Bertrand McAbee. I head the ACJ Investigation firm in Davenport. I have a case that…"

"Wait. Does Mr. Smalley know you or of you?"

"He doesn't know me personally but of me I don't know."

"You said the word murder to Ginny?"

"I did." Marilyn's real name presumably.

"Give me your name again, spell it, and your agency. ACJ? Is that right?"

He did as asked.

"I need a name relative to the murder."

"Margaret Thode." He spelled the last name. "She was…"

Cerberus disconnected.

Claudia Reiser immediately googled ACJ and Bertrand McAbee. The agency had been in Davenport for over 25 years. The name had sounded familiar to her as she took in the fairly copious material around ACJ. She ascertained quickly that the agency was secretive, perhaps a bit nefarious. She called a secretary from the security firm used by Smalley.

"Hi Pamela. Claudia. Questions," she went on, not interested for a bit, about charm or manners. "Had a call from a man calling himself Bertrand McAbee. PI. Runs an outfit called ACJ. What do you know about him and it?" Claudia was no fan of Pamela. She thought her a bit of a bitch.

"Rotten gang. We've had our problems with them for years. Don't ever turn your back on them. Unscrupulous and underhanded. The boss is a former professor, classics, I think. He'll tell you all about Aristotle as he puts a noose around your neck. Whatever are you doing bumming around that scum?"

Pamela, in Claudia's estimation, was probably worried about her firm's lucrative contract with the Smalley group. Even still, the bitch was no slouch. "Have you ever met him, McAbee that is?"

"Twice. Hangs around with a Black thing. She's a goddam Amazon. Don't like either one of them. Cagey. He's always looking around like he's casing the place for a future break-in. She? Like she's trying to figure out the fastest way to kill you. Spooky pair. Hope you're not doing any business with them. Like stepping in quicksand. Why do you want to know?"

"Anything else?" Claudia asked softly.

"No. That's about it. I can go back into our files."

"Do that. If you find something else that I should know call. Bye!"

Claudia rapped her fingers on her desk. Roger Smalley was an obsessive. She would have to tell him of McAbee's call and his agenda. She googled Margaret Thode anticipating some questions from Roger. She read some of the stories about her murder. Even with the steel that she had forged over her many years with Smalley she shuddered. She did not like the idea of going into see Roger. It was a no-win agenda. But ruefully she thought that maybe McAbee and Smalley deserved each other. She banished the thought before it had a chance of being nurtured by her.

Claudia entered Roger Smalley's office after two brief knocks and a five second wait, a studied minuet between them.

He was studying some legal treatise, marking it in red, eyes knitted. She didn't recognize what he was working on. She sat and said nothing, best to match him from her experiences with him. He was an excruciatingly difficult man whom she neither liked nor disliked. To work for him was like riding the rapids somewhere out West, never sure where the next boulder was. And yet they co-existed for over 23 years. He paid quite well but she worked hard for every penny of it. She oversaw a staff of five secretaries with different responsibilities. Lots of them quit because of his invasive arm that was led on to search for the private parts of these women. Lawsuits and private settlements were all too common even as new women kept applying for jobs. On occasion, she would hire a woman whose plainness was apparent. In no uncertain terms she was warned off that approach. The offices demanded beauty she was told. The last time she tried to work around him, with the intention of protecting him from his predatory arm, she hired a young woman who had left an Amish community in Bloomfield, Iowa. She was innocence trebled, her modesty and bearing would have had her on an A-list for a Carmelite Monastery. Claudia's head was on the block that day. It was the last time she ever attempted to assuage the roving arm of Roger Smalley. The poor woman fled back to Bloomfield within the week. Handmaids were not acceptable to Roger, his desires went for qualities that stood out. Tits and ass.

Finally he looked up. "Yeah?" he said curtly.

"A call this morning. Ginny wisely transferred it over to me," she said.

"Ginny? The one at reception?"

"Yes."

"Wisely. A bit of an oxymoron no?"

She didn't bite on his acid comment that suggested that he had sized up Ginny and had probably already noted her tangible assets which were significant by any account. "There's a private investigator by the name of Bertrand McAbee. He wants to interview you about a murder case from years back. Margaret Thode." She observed his dark eyes narrow.

"I've heard the name McAbee before. Barney Thompson had some trouble with him. Also, do you remember that woman who was here, the one who was murdered a month ago or so, in Rock Island? Agatha. Last name? I spoke with her for about five minutes. Kooky bitch."

"Oh, Agatha Pruitt. Rock Island High School. I didn't know that she was asking about Margaret Thode. She said that she was doing a story about your class. You said okay."

"Well she lied. She was up to no good. I got rid of her. You were at lunch. Don't need to have all that crap brought up again especially as she was murdered. You know how things can get balled up. MLB, NFL. Above reproach. I have enough trouble with all these vamps around here falsely accusing me. Touch a shoulder and you're accused of rape for God's sake. Make sure that you keep warning them that I'm a touchy, feely guy. Tell this McAbee that I'm not interested. Barely knew Margaret Thode. Regrets and all that and goodbye."

She snapped her steno pad closed and left. There seldom was a doubt about what he felt about a decision.

She saw Ginny leaving the women's bathroom. She wondered when touchy-feely's one arm would crawl around that stacked girl.

At 2 p.m., the same day of his curious experience with Smalley's duet of secretaries, he was called. She identified herself as Claudia, now, for the first time. Brusquely she said, "Mr. Smalley will not meet with you about your investigation. Agatha Pruitt was enough when she visited."

McAbee was prepared for this and had already armed himself with a rejoinder. "Tell Roger Smalley that I have some information about Scooter Benson. He might be interested. The Thode case has been re-opened by my firm. Please ask him to re-consider his refusal. It is in his interest to do so." He disconnected. That was rude by his standards but he felt that he was in the middle of corporate game-playing in the small city of Bettendorf, Iowa. He surmised that Roger Smalley needed to be very careful around this issue. The huge takeaway in Bertrand was the disclosure that Agatha Pruitt had met with him and, by implication, had been brushed off as some kind of a nosey heathen. To this point of his investigation he had yet to hear one good word about Smalley.

CHAPTER 33

Jack Scholz was listening to Bertrand with curiosity as he asked himself how this man fell into so many testy situations. The latest, now, Scooter Benson who had been tentatively identified by the morose little cripple Barry Fisk. And of all places, Colorado City, Arizona, in the middle of nowhere supported by some theological absurdities justifying lechery. Over the years of his service in the variety of wet work assignments that he did in the service of the American government little surprised him. McAbee ended his summation of Fisk's work with a question. Jack was not at all surprised by it.

"So, Jack, is there any way we can penetrate this community and run down Scooter if in fact he's really there?"

"I'm sure there's a way in but I'll have to send out feelers. There's a very slight chance that one of my men from years back could be there. He was a bit odd but quite good with a knife. Mormon. But not your ordinary Mormon. He was at odds with one of my team members who was a Salt Lake Mormon. Lot of arguments. This was 30 years or more ago. I'll go back into my records. What exactly do you want from this Scooter if he's there? The mission."

"The bracelet. The murder. His relationship with Smalley, perhaps with Forrest Graham. He knows something."

"This could get very expensive. Is Pruitt good for this?"

"Supposedly. He teaches at St. Anselm so I assume that he's not rich. I think they pay English teachers like Walmart employees, a buyer's market for the school. I informed him that this whole thing could end up nowhere and with a hefty bill at the end. He didn't hesitate for me to go forward. Money from his dead sister. I take it that you've not had luck on the device in Agatha's home."

"Not yet. Lots of feelers out there. Disconcerting. But it just takes one crack of the door. Did you ever get through to one-armed Smalley?" He knew that Bertrand didn't like his tendency to label enemies or potential enemies in derogatory terms. Bertrand had a slight tendency to be politically correct. But at least Jack had gotten him past the heavy frowning. Just a gaze now. McAbee, when all was said and done, would always be a working project. Why this strange man had ever thought he was suitable to be a PI was the mystery.

McAbee responded to his question. "Roger Smalley is a big fish. Not yet."

After he left McAbee along the bike path adjoining the Mississippi River he went back to his place on the outskirts of Davenport. He instinctively checked his phone for any intrusions on his property, about an acre and a half. The land was wired with sophisticated equipment. Anyone coming onto it unbidden was in instant danger. There were no intrusions.

Jack had his entire files stored in the cloud, but still preferred the feel of paper. He remembered the mission when the two Mormons served under his command. Kuwait in the early 90s. He shook his head in dismay over the quick passage of time.

There were 33 men on the mission. All returned safely except for one shot that found the arm of one of the men. He was upset at the memory. The two Mormons were Josiah Fellow and Richard Cumming. Fellow was the oddball, his look was that of a dead stare through blackened eyes and a horsey face. When he first saw him he wanted to feed him a carrot or an apple. His characterizations helped his memory.

Anyone who went into service under him had one quality that he took for granted. In fact, the slightest waver would find that guy or gal out on their ass in an instant. It was fidelity to him, the mission and his comrades. This didn't mean that there weren't arguments and sometimes brawls but at the end of things issues were resolved in a manly way. Over the years Jack had remained loyal to all who had served under him. This accounted for his ability to summon help from multiple contacts, only rarely was he refused and that with full apology. Just once was he outrightly and rudely rejected. It still bothered him to this day. He kept his network as up to date as he could. As expected bad things had occurred in the lives of some of them. It was life. His contact list was at 661.

He decided to call Richard Cumming. He was now considered a bishop in the Church of the Latter Day Saints. He lived in Salt Lake City. A bank vice president on the side.

"Jack. Wonderful to hear from you," he said cheerfully.

From that they spoke of old times, guardedly, but with joy at the remembrances of the past. The unforgettable experience of bonding and purpose.

"Rich, I need some information."

"Jack, I'll help, of course."

"You remember Joshua?"

"Yes," he answered in careful manner, was it warily.

"What became of him?" Jack asked.

"Unfortunately, he's not among the brethren. He has chosen to retreat back into the past. He almost came over to us but we lost him. Last I heard he was in Arizona, Colorado City. Polygamy was the dividing line for him. Even here in Salt Lake we have some doing this. In the bushes as it were. I mended my ways with him after the mission. Good man overall, but terribly flawed. I have a number in my rolodex. Need it?"

"Ah...yeah. I'm going to call him. How can I go wrong with him?"

Cumming laughed as he said, "Don't break up his family."

Scholz hit a voice machine after two rings into the number provided by Richard. The somber and leaden voice said, 'This is Josiah. Leave a number and a name.' "Jack Scholz. Call me back." He gave his number and disconnected. Three minutes later Jack was getting a call from Arizona, no I.D. Taking a chance he said, "Josiah, Jack here."

"My friend from the past."

They chatted briefly about past exploits, in a circular fashion. Jack was glad that Josiah adhered to regs. He was a taciturn as usual but friendly by his standards.

"You're not calling to pass the time of the day, Jack" he said with a slight touch of humor.

"I hear that you're in Colorado City."

"I am."

"I have a few questions. If you can't be honest in answering tell me now," Jack said in his commanding type of voice.

"Of course I'll be honest with you, of all people," he said as though he was upset about the alternative.

"Your community? Does it ever disappear people?"

There was hesitation. "I won't ever lie to you Jack. But I need to know something. This about crime?"

"Not sure. Probably unlikely. A case over 45 years ago. A witness thing in my judgment. Has nothing to do with Colorado City per se. Need to speak with him. Think he's among you. Won't compromise you or your community."

"Why do you think he's among us?"

"Recognition software. Mormon mother." Jack would not lie to him. Because Joshua understood that quality in Jack, neither would he.

"Suggests that he's been here for some time?"

"I think so. Perhaps in the 80s or 90s," Jack said.

"That helps. Have a name?"

"Larry Benson, Scooter nickname," Jack said in low pitch.

"Not sure on this. I'll call you back."

He figured that there was a blanket of hiddenness out there. Joshua might have to make a number of inquiries. Twenty minutes later he picked up the phone atop his desk, Arizona, no ID.

"Joshua," Jack said.

"This is what I found out. He's here. Secretive. Not liked but observant. Name is Howard Smith. Has a small compound high walled. Wives and children."

"How does he make a living?"

"State of Arizona. Child welfare. Since the state doesn't recognize plural marriage he gets state money for each woman, each child. Enough to conduct a life. Not uncommon here. Not my style in case you're curious."

"Think he'd speak with me or someone who went out there?"

"No way. Just don't see it."

"Address?"

"Public record. Larry Smith. Only one here. Probes are getting too hot for me Jack."

"Got it. Thanks Joshua. Bye."

Jack was appreciative. Their bond maintained throughout that very difficult session for Joshua.

He called Bertrand and gave him the information. For the moment, at any rate, it was now in McAbee's court.

CHAPTER 34

Bertrand took in the information provided by Jack Scholz. The house on Richard Street in Colorado City that he zeroed in on with Google Maps was of medium size, surrounded on every side with sand, and shrubs. It seemed to be built in the dead center of the walls surrounding the complex. There were two entry points, a small archway gate and then a larger entry that would allow for a car or truck.

He called Barry Fisk and received back the usual snarly, "Yeah?"

"Question," Bertrand said tersely. "Your make on Scooter Benson? How sure are you on it? Right man?"

Bertrand waited during a long pause. Barry, casting aside the disgruntled act said, "I'm not positive, not 100% on it. But I've done more with the picture. Removed the beard, reversed the aging, zeroed in on the eyes, my conclusion? 95% sure. Best I can do. But it is off of a sketch."

"And it was a great piece of work Barry. I have to make a decision on this, just wanted your degree of certitude." Bertrand disconnected.

His next call was for Jack. A meeting was set for the pathway under the Centennial Bridge, near the baseball stadium that housed the Quad City River Bandits, a single A baseball team.

They met and started to walk westward along the path. There were users – runners, walkers and cyclists as they went. Bertrand was unsure about how to proceed with Colorado City and its probable citizen Scooter Benson.

Jack finally said, into the silence, "So, Bertrand. Did you just call me out here for a nice stroll? My charming company?"

He noted that the last comment was as close to humor from Jack that he would ever get. "Besides noting your amazing charm I'm not sure about how to proceed. We don't have 100% assuredness on this guy. I know that that is pretty much your standard for intrusion."

"Always hoped for," he said briskly.

"95% certainty. Could be an error in the works," Bertrand said.

Jack looked over at him and stopped. "First off how important is this guy to you?"

"Very."

"I can arrange a capture on him but I want to hear from you, directly and forthrightly that you're asking me to do it. Understand that we may be acting on an error. Also, it'll probably require some rough treatment on this guy. With 100% assuredness, I have no problem. Don't need your okay. But 95% there is no escaping for you."

Bertrand felt the hidden anger in Jack's answer. It was no secret for either of them that McAbee was prone to look the other way when Jack used his forceful ways, a nod to false innocence when he knew well what Jack was up to. He always appreciated the information from Jack but pretended not to see, ingenuous. It was a trait within him that he abhorred as it was generated by his desire to appease Augusta and Pat who detested Jack's methods. He was ethically compromised. His brother Bill who ran a global investigation firm and who, was himself, a virtual twin of Jack when it came to brutality would bark at Bertrand to understand the world that he, Bill and Jack inhabited. There were few rules when facing down evil, no back doors, viciousness against viciousness.

"I get it Jack. But 95% is good enough for me in this instance. Scooter knows something even if he was innocent of the murder of Margaret Thode. Go after him but don't kill him."

"It'll be done. Lots of cost here but we've been through that."

They turned around and headed back toward the ballpark. Bertrand withdrew from his pocket a sheet of paper. "These are the questions that need answering. Call me if something further is required from me." He handed the paper to Jack.

They parted. Nothing further was said between them.

Jack Scholz flew into Salt Lake City the next day. He was met by Ginger Adams and Trevor Bowlsby. Both of them were hardened under Jack on three missions. When he called them they assented immediately. To what? They didn't know and didn't care. If the matter was an issue for Jack it was an issue for them. That was the way of this brotherhood and sisterhood. On the drive south to St. George via I-15 he briefed them on the mission. Jack had already gathered some significant information about Colorado City, Richard Street and Scooter, either as Smith or Benson. The plan the next day was for Ginger to bike into Colorado City and hopefully gain the attention of Scooter, who was perceived to be a lascivious creep. Ginger, at 43 years, was still an eyeful. Tanned body, muscular, five feet five inches, strawberry blonde, about 135 pounds. She could do the innocent act better than any actress Jack had ever seen. But under the innocence was a malevolent killer if provoked.

The following day, about ten minutes outside of Colorado City, Route 59, they took a rented racing bike from the back of the van. She would be thirsty, hurt, and lost as she entered the city. At Richard Street she would try to gain entry into the compound. She was sent on her way. They had rented a cabin outside St. George, only about 50 miles from Colorado City. If and when Scooter was taken they would do the interrogation in that cabin. Jack thought she could lure a saintly monk into depravity with a shake of her goods and her innocent voice.

Trevor was a muscle builder. He had won his share of contests as such. Touching his body was like touching a rock. He had once managed to lift the front end of a jeep in the rescue of one of Jack's team members. People generally walked to the other side of the street when they saw his six feet, six inch, body coming their way. He was perceived as pure trouble even though Jack had seen in him a kind and generous man.

Jack and Trevor were two miles west of the city. They pulled into a dirt road and waited for news from the wired Ginger.

It took three hours to now hear a conversation between her and some man who said, "Are you seeking sustenance and the truth Miss?"

"Always am. But I'm terribly thirsty and my hamstring is pulled. Is there a hotel in this city? I'm just exhausted."

"If you wish you can enter my compound and stay the night."

As Jack listened he couldn't believe his ears. Ginger was the ultimate con.

"I'm Ginger."

"My name is Elder Smith, you're very welcome here but on one condition."

"What would that be Elder?"

Jack puzzled that no one that innocent sounding could ever be so goddam violent and crafty.

"You'll have to listen to me pronounce the truth of my faith and community."

"Well sure. That'd be a supreme pleasure. But I have to let my driver know that I don't need him for tonight and maybe, if you'd have me, for more. There's something about you that I find engrossing."

"I have the truth sister. Please call him and let him know. In the meantime I will get you some of my well water." Under her breath she said, "This is the guy. He's menacing." Loudly she said into her phone, "I need my bag. I'm staying here on Richard Street." She disconnected. He heard Ginger say, "He's right near us. He's been looking for me. My dang phone was off. He'll bring my clothes and be off," she disconnected her wiring switch.

Minutes later Jack pulled up to the archway in the van. Trevor was in the back of the van ready with a taser. Jack exited the vehicle with a forced smile.

"Looking all over for you Ginger. You're always getting lost. Anyway I've got to get back to St. George. Already late for an appointment." He looked over at Benson who didn't seem to catch the danger he was in. "Do you want me to take the bike?" he asked Ginger.

"No, just need my bag. I'll stay here for a few days and I seem to have also aggravated my hamstring again. Elder Smith has been so kind. When I get better I can bike back to St. George. Now don't you worry."

"Okay, your bag is in the back. You shouldn't be lifting it with the hamstring injury," Jack said squeezing out as much sympathy as he could.

"I'll help," Smith said as he came to the back of the van that had its side window slightly open thus allowing Trevor to overhear from inside of the van.

Jack, a limping Ginger, and Elder Smith proceeded to the back of the van. Jack made some effort to show Smith that the door latch was jammed, a further warning to Trevor to prepare. Finally he pulled the door open as Ginger now behind Smith pushed him into the van and Trevor tased him and pulled him beside him. Next came the bike and then Jack and Ginger entered the van and off they went to the cabin outside of St. George. By the time they arrived at the cabin Smith/Benson was thoroughly trussed, mouth taped, and his head covered with a heavy black hood. After thrashing for a bit he calmed down as Trevor's strength was used to turn him and then lift him up. This expression of strength caused him to sink into silence. He'd been had.

Smith was seated in the middle of a darkened room. His arms were tied downwards and his legs attached to chair legs. The mask was taken off and the tape around his mouth also.

He looked about him and his native cunning decided on silence. He knew that he had no leverage.

"My name is Jack. If you answer all of my questions you will be returned home unharmed. No one in your community will be any the wiser. Answer me before I proceed. Do you understand?"

"The Lord will punish you beyond anything you can imagine."

"You didn't answer my question. We all need to go home. You too. You heard what I said. Let me now give you the alternative. We will be here for as long as it takes. You *will* answer every question I have but you will undergo terrible pain and eventually you will lose parts of your body in the process. In several ways you will be a lesser man. Now answer me."

He looked at Jack defiantly.

Jack caught Trevor's eye and nodded to him. Trevor said, "Will you help me with some of that wood by the driveway? It's cold in here. Ginger, we'll be back in a minute." They left.

Ginger took a chair and brought it up in front of him. She sat. "Elder Smith you were kind to me. Because of that I'm going to warn you about that man, Jack. He has questioned a lot of people. He has never failed. I have personally seen him do some vicious things. I really think you should comply with his wishes. Once he starts, his sadism takes control of him. He has killed many times in the service of America."

Smith spoke. "Why did you fool me?"

"Oh, I work for him. This isn't the first time for us. The other guy? He's nuttier than Jack. You're in a no-win situation. A few years ago, a drug lord from Mexico, Jack chopped his penis off. Nasty business. He got what he wanted and then he murdered him. But he had good reason. Please make it easy on yourself. He meant it about bringing you home. Unharmed."

The door opened. Jack and Trevor had some logs in their hands. Trevor attended to the fireplace as Jack came back. Ginger, now behind the Elder's back, did an arm forward as if welcoming someone into a house. Jack would know that she had performed her act of solicitude on the subject. She knew that he was hesitant to proceed to torture because he was not 100% sure of the man's identity.

Interestingly everything she had told Smith was true. The drug lord had sold Fentanyl into the Atlanta area. Three of the brotherhood had sons, in effect, murdered by him. There was no issuance of any mercy toward him as there might be in this case.

She watched Jack step into his role. Consent by Smith would happen now or he'd be sorry for the rest of his former lascivious span of life.

"I understand. What do you want?" Smith intoned, a defeated man.

"Who are you? Name?"

"Elder Larry Smith of the Fundamentalist Church of the Latter Day Saints."

"How many wives do you have?"

"Eight"

"Children?"

"Nineteen."

"When did you come to Colorado City?"

Smith hesitated over the question. Then he answered, "1989."

"Where were you born? Before you answer this question I know a lot about you. If you lie to me you'll feel very regretful."

"Illinois."

"Big state. Where exactly?" Jack said as he caught Smith in full glare.

The fire sputtered in the fireplace. The room began to warm up.

"Rock Island."

From the briefing that Jack had given to her and Trevor on the way to St. George she was aware that Smith was at a turning point. The correct name would bring the matter to a 100% identification. Not a good situation for Smith as truth would expose an unyielding Jack if he tried to lie his way out of the situation when Jack pressed.

"What was your real name at birth?"

The hesitation came. Jack waited him out. Finally he said, "Benson."

"Nickname Scooter."

Smith, now Benson, jerked his head back as if Jack had hit him.

"Yes. How did you know this? Why is this of concern to you? A past life before the truth unfolded."

"I'm not interested in the unfolded truth. My concern is with you during your folded truth phase. I want you to head back to Rock Island High School. In those days you were a drug dealer. Remember?"

"Yes," he answered warily, probably trying to calculate where this was going.

"Some names. Forrest Graham!"

"Smug. Tight. I didn't sell him anything. He peered down at me."

"Roger Smalley."

"He used. Tough guy. One arm. I don't know anything about those two. I got kicked out of Rocky High and never saw them again, either one. Are they up for some type of top secret clearance? Is this a background check? For a government post?"

"Nope. Do you remember a girl name Agatha Pruitt?"

"Ugh. Not really. Smart. She didn't use. Maybe gay."

"Good. So far you're doing fine Scooter. Now stay in the Scooter frame of mind as the next set of questions are very important, but truth more so. Much of this is confirmation of what I already know."

Ginger went back behind Jack and gave a brief knowing nod toward Benson. This was, of course, all part of the game.

"Now tell me about Margaret Thode. All of it."

Benson slouched in his chair and let out a long breath. Ginger noticed a line of moisture had appeared on his forehead. "That was a long time ago. She was murdered. I had nothing to do with her. I think she was of the wrong sex. Should have been a man. She was no druggie."

"You're mightily connected to her. Mightily. Why did you murder her?"

"No! No! That's not true! I never touched her. I have never killed anyone. This is not true." The steam behind his denial seemed authentic to her.

"Be careful here Scooter. You're in very dangerous waters. Tell me how you got a hold of a piece of jewelry and what was it, just so we're on the same page."

"I can't believe this is coming back at me." He stopped and asked for a glass of water. The refrigerator was shut off. Ginger went out to the van and returned with a bottle of tepid water. Benson drank off half of the bottle. "Sunset Marina was a selling station for me. Lots of deals down there. I heard a few screams off in the distance, a couple of hundred feet. I was a full time user besides a seller. I shrugged them off, under the influence. But from that same direction I heard a really loud squeal of tires. Loud enough for me to go over in that direction. Took a few minutes maybe for me to get there. Groggy, slow walking. I saw the scene. Had to puke, ran down to the water, a few times, heaving. I went back. I saw a bracelet on the ground. I took it. I ran."

"Why didn't you call the cops?"

"No, no way. Already been on notice with them. Figured they'd hang me for it. No."

"What did you do with the bracelet?"

"Pawned it. Evidence. Sold it in Davenport, pawnbroker, Fairgrounds. It took me years to get over the sight. But I didn't touch her. If you think I did you're wrong," now a man pleading.

"What do you mean a loud noise?"

Be specific.

"Kind of like from an explosion. Too much acceleration at the start of a car or a motorcycle."

"That's not uncommon," Jack said quickly.

"No. But that and the scream was."

"Why were you disavowed by your father? Mother too, I guess."

"That has nothing to do with Margaret Thode," Benson said with conviction.

"If you comment one more time about my questions you'll regret it." Quiet settled in the room.

"My father was a doctor. He was in the ER when an overdose came in. A girl, 15, she died. The cops told him that I was probably the seller. He asked me. I should never have admitted it. But I did. He started the proceedings the next day. With his connections the whole thing didn't take long. My mother, as usual, said nothing. You could shoot her and she'd not say anything."

"The obit from the Moore Funeral Home? Number 64. Signed with an S. You?"

"You know everything don't you? Yes."

"The murder? Who would do that? Surely you thought about it."

"A bunch of us conceivably. We were not nice to her. We saw her as a stuck-up bitch. A dyke too. Gave her a hard time. But murder? I don't think it would ever happen in that crowd."

"Roger Smalley?"

"Roger Smalley was something else. Tough bastard. Dangerous. Maybe. But I don't see it. Very ambitious. He'd back away in light of the risk of being caught. There was a shrewdness to him."

"Other names?"

"Willy Forbes. But he's dead, Again, I don't see it. He'd be too scared. A weakling. Only brave when around us."

"I need more on this," Jack said. His tone had lightened, Ginger noticed.

"There's nothing else really. I have no reason to lie to you. You pretty much know everything about me." He fell into silence.

"Keep thinking. The reason I'm here is to find out who murdered her. We think that there's an association with it to another murder just over a month ago. Agatha Pruitt."

"What? Do you know why I'm in Colorado City? I have found the truth. I've told you…wait, wait. Margaret Thode. It wasn't just us – guys. There was a gang of girls. Witches, pretenders, lesbos. They had at her too as well as some jocks. Margaret Thode drew hatred, believe me. The more she received the more she gave back. She was not a wallflower. Agatha Pruitt, I just don't remember her."

"What were the girls about? Names? Sweeties or toughies."

"Tough. Three of them. Smokers, drinkers, users. I sold to them, two of them anyway. Tattoos on two, same two. Blackened eyes, the whole trip. Biker gang material. Don't know their names. Just too long ago. They were in our grade. I know that."

Jack went in front of him. He sat in the chair that Ginger had used. He looked sternly at Scooter. He said, "I think that you've been honest with me. We're going to drive you home." He extended a card to Benson who took it but didn't read it. "Call the number on that card if you think of anything related to what we've questioned you about. One other thing. If it turns out you've lied I will have a sharpshooter on the hills above your compound. He will shoot to kill you. You're advised to never leave your compound and your house if you know you lied and I find out. Understood?'

"Yes," came a timid and defeated response.

Jack retrieved the sheet that McAbee had given him. He had asked most of the questions. A few remained. He did as asked and then Elder Smith was returned to Colorado City. There were three cars parked outside his compound. He sent Smith on his way, three blocks down on Richard Street. He did not want to entangle himself with the crazies down the street.

CHAPTER 35

Bertrand arrived back in his office after a lengthy walk by the Mississippi River. Jack had much to say. He concluded with, "It was all very calm; 90% psychological. What he gave us? About 90% true there too. He has my number just in case his memory snares a thought. He doesn't want to see me again. I'm keeping tabs on the bill."

"No worries. Thanks Jack."

He sat down in his lounger and thought. Minutes later Pat messaged him. "There's a pretty aggressive character on the phone. He's the one you told me about. You called him a week ago. Roger Smalley. Put him through?"

"No. I'm busy. Tell him to try later."

He knew that he was playing a game of chicken with him. But his comment about Scooter Benson to Smalley's secretary had to have caused some *angst*. He went back to thinking. Jack had said he had no information on the sensitive device that had been placed in Agatha's house, presumably the night of the murder. Another buzz form Pat. "Detective Concannon on the phone. Interested?"

"Send it through," she did, he said, "Detective."

"When's the last time you were at Pruitt's house?'

"Let's see. About seven days ago."

"Are you sure? Not last night?"

"Let me repeat, about seven days ago," McAbee said sharply.

"I hope for your sake your memory is accurate," Concannon now in full rancor.

"Why are you asking me?"

"A break in. Professional, but we caught it. Camera on the neighbor's tree. In and out. Whoever came left 58 seconds later. Nothing was taken as far as I can see. By the way, we had cameras in place. They were taken down. You have anything to do with that?"

"Why did you have cameras there? Dr. Pruitt never told me anything about being asked."

"Fuck you McAbee," he disconnected.

Bertrand called Jack Scholz. "Jack, a second. The Agatha house. Remember that ear-eye thing? Think it was stolen last night. Break-in there," he said obliquely.

Jack went silent. "Okay. I have a set of keys. I'll check." Disconnect.

Causal or coincidental with Jack's visit to Scooter? Because of his belief in Jack he decided that it had to be coincidental, probably because Agatha's house had nothing else to reveal. But he speculated about the oddity of calls from two belligerent characters within 15 minutes of each other. One of those days!

Fifteen minutes later Pat buzzed, "Smalley is on the line again. Spitting fury at me and you."

"Send him through." Connected, Bertrand said, "Thanks for calling Mr. Smalley. I'm Bertrand McAbee with ACJ."

"What the fuck do you want with me? Margaret Thode? Scooter? Who the hell do you think you are? Don't you ever bother me again."

Bertrand waited for the disconnect but it didn't come. He said, "I've found some interesting developments around her case. Some involving Scooter. Still alive by the way. Your name kept coming up Mr. Smalley. Just trying to be fair with you." Bertrand was keeping a steady and calm voice with him. He stopped, positive that Smalley was listening closely with curiosity.

"Can you come over here today? I'll talk with you, you talk with me and then I hope you get lost forever."

"Time?"

"3 p.m."

"I'll be there," call ends. Bertrand's assessment – Smalley throws hard balls at the head. If that doesn't work he walks off the mound. Classic bully.

The Smalley Enterprises building was a four story refurbished bank building. Lots of glass, marble, ebony, tilting to glitz but short of it. It was impressive. He was stopped just inside the entrance by a 30ish security guard who'd been around the block, professional and formally courteous. Not to be messed with. He was armed as well. McAbee was expected and told to go to the fourth floor. The elevator was noiseless and fast. He came out to a bright anteroom, a large secretarial desk, behind which was a sweeping stainless steel lettering that read Smalley Enterprises. After the last 's' there was a one-armed, clenched fist serving as an exclamation point. Smalley couldn't hold off on the glitz.

A smiling woman of about 20 looked at him. She was beautiful. Blonde, good smile, extended eye lashes, red lipstick. She had to be the same woman he had spoken with. It would be inappropriate to speak to her as a 12 year old as was his wont when he called Smalley's offices days ago. She was a stunner.

"Hi. I'm expected by Mr. Smalley at this time."

"Oh yes. Dr. McAbee. They told me to call you that," she smiled innocently, voice, though, high pitched, more like that of a teenager.

"And you are?"

"Ginny. I'll call Claudia. She's Mr. Smalley's private secretary. She'll escort you."

"Thanks Ginny." He took a seat gazing at Ginny surreptitiously. He figured that this woman might end up breaking a lot of hearts with, perhaps, no knowledge of having done so.

A minute or so transpired before a 60ish, white hair in a bun, slender woman appeared from a door to the left of Ginny. She looked at McAbee with curiosity. Maybe disdain too. She said, "Follow me." He went through the door from which she came. There were about 15 people in an open pod, surrounded by doored offices tracing the contours of a square building. He thought the woman rude and figured that Claudia had developed a persona of frigidity. She walked quickly, legs tight together. He wondered whether she had chafed inner thighs as he prepared himself to meet the one-armed bully.

Two knocks, a hesitation, she opened the door. "Dr. McAbee is here."

"Show him in." She did, she left.

The tone of his voice presaged unpleasantness and posturing from Smalley. McAbee didn't look at him. The office was large and lush. It sat at the southeast corner of the building. The view was extraordinary. To the south the Mississippi River and across from it Moline, Illinois. To the east a full view of a boring downtown Bettendorf. Smalley's desk was huge, larger even than that of the Davenport Police Chief whose public service desk was scandalous.

He saw that Smalley was looking at him as Bertrand finally caught his stare. He still had a bullet head, a long thin face, angry, piercing eyes. Bertrand figured that their relationship was doomed. In such cases he said that for all of his life he had never met the man and that he was reasonably happy. Simply, Roger Smalley was insignificant to Bertrand's existence. He would keep it that way.

"Do you want my secretary to give you a guided tour of my office?" he growled sarcastically at the observing Bertrand.

"No. That's not necessary."

"What do you want from me?"

"How about inviting me to sit?"

"A wise guy. Yeah, sit! So?"

Bertrand sat. "Did you hear that a classmate of yours from high school was murdered a month ago?"

"You're not telling me what you want. Get with it or get the hell out of here."

Bertrand laughed gently. He stared at the space on Smalley's coat sleeve that should have held a left arm. "If I get up now and leave it will be a detriment to you. You'll regret it. I already told your secretary of my agenda. The murder of Margaret Thode. If you want me to leave just say so. Just so you know Scooter Benson did *not* send his regards." He made a motion as if to get up from the chair he was sitting on. He felt that he was in a poker game with the one-armed groper, intense dislike rising in him.

He was studying Bertrand, his narrow eyes in full focus. "Tough guy too besides being a smart ass. I should have you thrown out of here or call the cops. Intimidation. Blackmail. They do whatever I ask them to."

McAbee knew the Bettendorf Police Chief as a straight arrow who ran a strict and fair department. He wasn't buying the bluff. The poker game would continue. "I'm busy. You're busy. If things end this way then they end this way. Your call," McAbee said.

"If you know something then spit it out."

"I'll spit out a lot of things but only after you answer some elemental questions. Take it or leave it," McAbee sensing that Smalley was breaking a bit, he, again, made a small motion as if he might be getting up.

As much as a man with his baggage could, he relented. "Go ahead ask your questions."

"You're aware of Agatha Pruitt, her murder over a month ago?"

"I am. I didn't really know her. Just a faint memory from Rocky High."

"She left the University of Iowa recently. Research librarian there. Extraordinary talent I take it. There was an article in the *Times* soon after she moved to Rock Island. It was all about Margaret Thode, murdered 45 years ago. They had been very close in high school." McAbee kept a close eye on Smalley. He showed nothing. "She devoted her skills to re-opening that case, unsolved for over 45 years. Margaret Thode? Remember her?"

He stared at McAbee for seconds. Hard to read. "Talk to me about Scooter. What did he say, if anything?"

"I'm getting there. The question was about Margaret Thode."

"When this is all over and you're out of here and driving home? Remember one thing. In my eyes you're a son of a bitch."

McAbee laughed. "The line starts at the river. Your perception of me is irrelevant. Back to Margaret Thode."

"Queer bitch! Autistic! Screwball! Wouldn't piss on her," he said angrily.

"I've had a few people look at this case, anew. You're a suspect and you're certainly not saying anything to refute that suspicion."

He continued to look at Bertrand. Finally he said, "Scooter?"

"Scooter is a flawed person," Bertrand said.

A mean laugh from Smalley.

"Among other things, he said you taunted her. A few others too."

"Is that right? Did he tell you that half the goddam school taunted that bitch?"

"No. He focused on his group. Thus you. Said you were a user of what he sold."

"Whatever I *was* is long past," some defensiveness in his voice.

"He mentioned three girls from your class. Witches, I think before Goth and witches came into vogue. Do you recall them?"

"Hah. More weirdos. The waywards! I don't know this but I assume they had at Thode too. Rocky High did Shakespeare – Macbeth. People said the three witches stewing over the cauldron inflamed those wackos and they became haunted by them. Acting like them at Rocky. I could give a damn. But a nasty trio. Look McAbee I didn't murder Pruitt or Thode. Get over it."

"Well I'll give you credit for one thing."

"What's that?"

"At least you finally started to act and speak like a human being."

"Are you done?"

"For the moment at least."

"Good, get the fuck out of here!"

"One more thing? The three girls, you know their names?"

"Sure, Creep 1, Creep 2, Creep 3. You're the detective!" he snarled.

When he left Smalley's office he was escorted to Ginny's reception area. Claudia closed the door noisily as she returned to the main offices.

He looked at Ginny who was smiling. He said, "This is a crazy place, isn't it?"

She looked at him for a few seconds, innocence seeping from her, "You never know Dr. McAbee." She then flipped him a pronounced wink from her left eye.

When he went down the elevator he was perplexed. Ginny was not as she appeared, his conclusion.

CHAPTER 36

The next morning found Bertrand heading back to Cambridge, Illinois, to visit with Stan Fullbright. Small towns such as Cambridge submit to change grudgingly. All was as before as he knocked and heard the Akita set up his defense of Stan and the house. His bark sounded even louder than a week ago as he pawed at the door.

"Groucho!" Stan yelled. "Heel."

The barking and growling ceased immediately. A few seconds later he heard, "Yeah."

"Stan. I'm back. Bertrand McAbee. I need a few minutes."

The hesitation in response bothered Bertrand. Perhaps he should have called. "Okay, wait a minute."

Bertrand heard a few mutters from Stan and then the closing of a door. Groucho let out one bark, a protest? "Come on in. Door's open."

Bertrand entered through the kitchen. Some plates were on the counter and there was a build-up of dishes in the sink. He didn't see it as a good sign, certainly not something that he'd associate with his perception of Stan Fullbright.

Stan had already camped out in the same place as before. He pointed toward the seat that McAbee had sat on previously. As Bertrand was sitting, Stan said, "Just a little today, sir. I'm pretty ill. Things are catching up to me. Concentration is blown."

"I'll be quick, Stan. Sorry to hear this about your health. I found Scooter. Arizona, breakaway Mormon group. Wives. Lots of kids. Keep that to yourself by the way. Got some leads that I hope you can help with. Or Hilda? Your friend."

Stan shook his head at the mention of Scooter. Disgust? Told you so? He said nothing.

"I spoke with Roger Smalley. Essentially he says that he knows nothing. Doesn't care for me and has bad memories of Margaret Thode. Didn't expect anything different. We'll never be friends."

There was a thin smile on Stan's lips, he nodded.

"I'm here because of something Scooter said. Probably a deflection but I need some light from you." He paused, Stan was very quiet. "He mentioned that Margaret was a punching bag for a lot of kids at Rocky High. I guess that's pretty much a given. She was an unusual girl in a world of *usuality*," Stan winced at the word, McAbee thought it appropriate. "Not a useful trait in teenager doings. Scooter hit very hard on three girls whom he said had it in for her, steroidal in hate indices, he insinuated."

Stan learned forward, his interest peaked. "Keep going, Bertrand."

"They were classmates. I infer that their oddness of character excelled beyond anything that Margaret Thode manifested. You're familiar with the word Goths or Gothic in appearance?"

He nodded.

"I think that before people started emulating that look and appearance these three girls were ensconced in it. Witch-like. Ring a bell?"

He thought for a bit. Then, he said, "Scooter may have been deflecting. But, yes, I remember the three of them. They were lethal. Throwing curses at kids in the hall, shrieks in classes. Detention slips off the wall. Messed up but I pitied them. Lost souls. Drugs suspected but they were never caught. Principal was concerned about their appearance at the graduation. Fact was they never came. I don't think that they were violent, lot of bluff. But we were all happy when we could pull their entrance cards to the building."

"Names?"

"I'll call Hilda. My memory for exact names and facts is waning quickly," as he moved his wheelchair to his rotary phone, hesitated, and asked "Like to see Groucho?"

Not as fearful as last time Bertrand said, "Of course."

Groucho was brought out of the utility room by Stan. He took in McAbee as if looking for an Al-Qaida terrorist. He went to Bertrand, sniffed around, and laid his head on Bertrand's knee.

Stan was delighted. "Boy you two are pretty compatible."

Stan wouldn't ask, Bertrand was sure, but he really wanted someone to take this beautiful animal who now wandered over to Stan who was dialing Hilda.

"Hi Hilda."

Chatter.

"You too dear. Listen I have that PI back. Question. Do you recall the three girls, classmates of Margaret Thode, who dressed in black, wore satanic symbols, and made themselves up in black cosmetics?"

Lots of chatter.

Stan said, "I'm having a very bad day Hilda. Would you mind talking with Bertrand McAbee? Today?"

Chatter.

Hanging up he said, "She lives now in Galva, Illinois. Not that far from here." He wrote down the address. "Just take 82 south and 34 east." He handed the street address to Bertrand. His eyes pleaded for McAbee to leave. Sadness was overwhelming in the house.

As he was leaving, Bertrand looked back and saw Stan's head down and hands tight to the arms of his wheelchair. Groucho looked at McAbee quizzically. Bertrand sat in his Camry for at least five minutes before starting for Galva. Grief came over him in waves.

Hilda Pederson was glad to see him. She was cheerful as she welcomed him into a house architecturally not very dissimilar to Stan's. He saw she had cooked a batch of chocolate chip cookies. He sat in her living room, on a couch. He knew the cookies were in his future as well as coffee.

She was in her 80s, this from Stan. She was heavy, about five feet, two inches, a round face, too red, and a head of curly white hair. The contrast with Stan was stark on many accounts.

"So, you're the guy who's resurrecting some interesting times. The murder of Margaret Thode? I hope you nail the fucker! But I think 45 years is probably way too long. How do you take your coffee and how many freshly baked chocolate chip cookies can you eat? I saw you gazing at them when you came in." She smiled as she looked at him.

McAbee was now being placed in a box he kept to himself, a quirk in his behavior that Augusta smiled at but some were offended by. He didn't wish to be served food by anyone and didn't care for home-cooked anything except from his own doings.

He said, "A small cup of coffee, cream or milk whatever, and a spoonful of sugar. Two cookies would be great. My waist keeps growing."

She had been turning to the kitchen as he spoke. She swung around abruptly and gaped at him, not unfriendly, but more one of wonderment. She said, "Your waist? You must have better excuses that that since you really don't have a waist to speak of," she left with a slight laugh and a shrug of her shoulders.

The cookies were still warm, quite tasty. He said, "So Hilda you seem to have a great memory, a trait that I don't have. Yes, I am re-working the case of Margaret Thode and the collateral murder of Agatha Pruitt, which I believe to be associated. I have found a thread. Let me brief you. But you must promise to keep what I tell you as confidential."

Then the perpetual smile on her face fell dark. "When I tell you yes that's it. What you say will be held as a secret. I was a counselor at Rocky High. I have many secrets in me," darkness moving to the light.

McAbee briefed her on many aspects of the case. She listened closely. He concluded, "What I am trying to run down is, as Stan mentioned, the three Goth girls. Names, perceptions?"

Her cheerful face took on an air of sadness. "Two of them, I'm afraid, were lost souls. By the time they were graduating they were already hurling their bodies at a motorcycle gang. Very rarely, in my experience, does anyone come back from that. Now they're up in age, if not long dead. You want names?"

"Yes, if you'd be so kind," he chomped into the second cookie thinking that Hilda was an accomplished baker. "By the way, the cookies are great. Thanks."

"Maureen Blong and Angela Diaz. Tough, tough pair. I have no idea what happened to them. If you told me they were in a prison, they were dead, they were street people in L.A., nothing would surprise me."

"I'll run some checks. The other?"

"If you see a girl in a wheelchair playing in a professional basketball league you'd say it was incongruous, an anomaly, shouldn't be or couldn't be. The third of these was really out of place. I could not sync her presence with them. It offended my senses. Samantha Ogden. She was the daughter of two profs at Augustana College in Rock Island. Bright as a star. Suddenly, after a summer, now as a senior, she's best of pals with Maureen and Angela. Black clothes, makeup everything. But she's even more obnoxious than the other two. What do they say? Converts are the worst! She was. But she didn't go biker like the other two. Her parents were going through a protracted divorce. Acting out was my take. Toward the end of her senior year, late Spring, I noticed a slight separation between her and the other two. Nothing explicit, just very subtle. Have no idea what became of her but I don't think you'll find her in Frisco or L.A. on the street."

"Sexual orientation?"

"Good question. Angela and Maureen were probably switch hitters. I think they'd fuck a dog. Samantha? She was probably gay. The boys stayed clear of them but especially her. Quite a girl, attractive even when doing her Goth act."

"Did you see any interplay between them and Margaret Thode?" Bertrand asked.

"They'd have at her. They probably saw a kindred spirit in her. Odd seeking odd. But I don't know anything else in that regard."

"Hilda, here's a speculative question. Of all the individuals mentioned, including the boys. Murder? Could any one of them do it?"

She went into herself, contemplating. "If I had to guess, sure. Scooter Benson, Roger Smalley, Angela Diaz, and Maureen Blong. Forget Forrest Graham and I think, also, Samantha Ogden."

Bertrand drove away from Galva, another farm town, similar to Cambridge. He thought that both towns would have a survival fight in front of them in the next decade.

CHAPTER 37

In 1987, the State of Iowa closed down 207 outlets that controlled all hard liquor sales in the state. This was controversial given that a nearby state, Kansas, was towing the line – no hard liquor that we can't control – virtue signaling on the rampage. Nowadays liquor was easily obtainable throughout Iowa. The state forced every county to comply; it would be a wet state. McAbee remembered going into one of the state stores back in the seventies. The clerks had developed high-strung muscles around their eyelids that always seemed to raise and express horror at an order of hard liquor. Purchases were scandalizing these public servants. Occasionally, he thought, most of them were alcoholics. Many residents of Scott County that was proximate to the Mississippi River would simply drive across to neighboring Illinois where liquor was cheaper, on display, and not hidden in some back storage area away from public eyes as was the case in Iowa.

In December of every year before 1987 when residents of Davenport, Scott County, would drive to Illinois for cases of liquor to fuel parties there would be at least one public arrest of an Iowan for crossing state lines with alcohol. The liquor would be seized at the border and a hefty fine given to the unfortunate exemplar of a high crime. The news outlets would be notified and public shaming would commence. The dutiful Iowa Liquor Authority was on the watch; taxes belonged in Iowa.

McAbee entered the Hy-Vee grocery on Devils Glen Road and went into the richly stocked shelves on the lookout for a bottle of Bushmills Irish Whiskey. He found it, bought it and started his drive across Veteran's Parkway to the Kahl Home. A visit to Gretchen Heinz was in order.

He entered the home at 3 p.m., not a good time to visit an assisted care facility, when sleep fell on many residents. Mary O'Brien, Irish truculence written across her florid face, asked him what he wanted.

"Gretchen Heinz, and good afternoon to you," he said in exasperation. This woman should not be dealing with visitors.

She looked at him as though he had slapped her. Her redress? Sister Ursula Von Hagan appeared out of nowhere, it seemed. Probably some silent alarm that good old Mary would press when being assaulted by bad men like McAbee.

Mary said, "I needn't say more, Sister. I'm not comfortable with this man," she said in false anguish.

He wondered why he and Mary O'Brien were in such a hellish relationship. He remembered a psychiatrist who argued that the people we dislike have a feature of themselves in them that we hate in ourselves. He hoped this was wrong because Mary O'Brien was a harridan.

Sister Ursula stepped between them. She turned to Mary and said, "Mary, I understand I'll take it from here." She turned to Bertrand and said sternly, "Follow me please."

He tried to figure out the context of her remarks. What was meant by 'I'll take it from here' and what exactly did the good sister 'understand'. Someone once opined that one of the worst combinations of combatants was where Germans and Irish fought. A future exploration for him.

In Sister Ursula's modest office, a sign to him that she was probably a devoted nun, she turned and said, "I see that you and Mary are not a suitable couple. Well fortunately you don't come here often. You seem to bring out the worst in her. Gretchen?"

"Yes. That's all. I didn't come here to do combat with your cheerful receptionist."

"Of that I am quite sure," she said as lightly as her personality would allow. "I hope for your sake that you brought Mr. Bushmill with you?"

"In my bag."

"Let's see if she's awake. Not the best time to come. But you know that don't you?" No answer required.

They proceeded to the wing where Gretchen was housed. At her door Sister Ursula held up a hand and whispered to McAbee, "I'll check on her." He waited in the hallway. A minute later she came out of the room and said to McAbee. "She's ready for you. But don't take too much time. She's not as healthy as you might think. On your way out do *not* say goodbye to Mary." She left.

He entered the room. Nothing had changed, including the chair Gretchen sat in. "I brought a friend with me Gretchen as you requested."

"Ah. I have only one friend I need to see today and it's not you. Did you bring some Bushmills?"

"I did, of course," McAbee said as cheerfully as he could.

"Not that I don't trust you but let's see it," she said while looking at McAbee as though he was a thief of sorts. "Show me the liquor!" she said smilingly.

He showed it to her. A liter. He got a crooked smile from her. "Why don't you trust me Gretchen?"

She said, "Trust? Here? Now while you're standing there. Go to the sink over there and in the cabinet below are small paper cups. Pour me a half a cup, no water. Then I want you to hide the bottle deep into that area behind the cups. Can you do all of that McAbee?"

"I can," as he obeyed her commands and finally, brought the cup to her.

She took a small sip and said, "Jesus, now there's a good medicine. Thanks."

"Why are you hiding it? Ursula knows you're into it."

"It's not her. It's the goddam attendants. I had a bottle a few months ago. Big son of a bitch plants his wide as a barge torso, blocking me out, and tips his fat head back and I swear he drank off a quarter of the bottle. Bastard!"

"Didn't you say anything to Ursula," he asked.

"I did. She fired him. But he still damaged my supply lines. Like the goddam Russians in Ukraine. You're not here to listen to me complain. Tell me how you're doing with the Thode case."

With some edits he gave her a summary of things. He ended up, "So Gretchen," he saw her take a bigger sip this time, she coughed a few times, "I need you to go back. You were aware of the abuse at Rocky toward Margaret Thode. She was a target. In the United States we seem to almost encourage teens to slaughter each other, verbally, huge aggression besides all the micro ones. You said you didn't want to report these because of her parents. Too hurtful."

"That's true. And I was right. Both of them dead years later. Broken hearts. I couldn't have lived with myself if I had gone down that road."

"I get that and you didn't. However, you were on that road in your investigations. Try to remember some things said to you. Egregious things relative to abuse and hurt."

"McAbee! Why are you raising this up again?"

"You know damn well Gretchen. It's not just Margaret Thode it's also Agatha Pruitt. I've been hired by Agatha's brother to fathom what happened to her but to find that answer I'm back on Margaret, there's a connection there."

Another sip was taken by Gretchen. "Okay, okay. There was bad and there was bad. Some cliques were particularly vile. She didn't seem to have any protectors. Because she was a loner on the bicycle or running she was ever present. Kids drive cars. Taunting, veering into her as if they were going to hit her with their cars. That's what I found out."

"Always boys?"

"There were some girls from what I was told. One clique of athletes, Bertrand, runners, softball. Another? A group of psychos, motorcycle types. Some lesbians. Margaret was quite attractive in her own way. Amelia Earhart type of girl. But as I say I would never print anything like this. I don't know if the cops even worked this stuff or if they did how deep," she ended as she sipped again.

"They did to an extent. Guys. Never saw anything about women, girls."

"Doesn't surprise me. Girls wouldn't do that kind of crime, I think," Gretchen said somberly.

"Anything else on the girls? The motorcycle ones?"

"No. Just heard it. Not even sure where or from whom? I think they pretended to be witches or something like that."

"You have my card. If you think of something please call me. I believe I've been here longer than I was allowed. I don't want Ursula clawing at me."

She laughed, "Ah. Ursula. Latin. The bear. Clever McAbee. Very clever. Thanks for the Bushmills. Bring me another sometime."

He left the home, avoiding Mary's baleful look.

CHAPTER 38

Bertrand called a meeting in his office. Attending it was Augusta, Jack, and Barry. There was noticeable discomfort among all three. He felt comfort, however, with all three. Each of them affected him oddly, but at the end of his consideration was a deeply-held respect for each of them. Augusta, of course, was at a different level, his love for her with few boundaries. He summarized the case as he saw it, loose ends, and all.

Jack, speaking in code, was first to report. He had confirmed that indeed, Agatha Pruitt's home had been entered and that an object had been removed. He gave a brief nod to Bertrand. They all knew what that object was, the sophisticated device created by the Israelis. Bertrand would have preferred speaking with him by the river, alone, when Jack would be more explicit than he would in Bertrand's office. Jack held up a piece of paper with the name Forrest Graham on it, printed in large black letters. "I ran this name through a bunch of contacts. He is perceived to be a tight-assed professional. Beyond reproach. Would surely have had access to the object but there is no connection with either victim." He looked over at Barry Fisk and said disdainfully, "Maybe a hacker can dig up more."

Barry sat back as though he was struck by Scholz. Collecting himself he said, "Yes it will come back to me, of course. It's that way so we can avoid murdering or torturing the problem," he looked at Jack defiantly.

Jack was about to say something but Bertrand jumped into the short void saying, "Barry dig as deep as you can on him. I always wonder about people who are so clean that they are beyond reproach, myself, of course, the exception," he said with a smile, trying to avert a war between the two. Silence reigned but only Augusta smiled. Fisk and Scholz not known for their sense of humor stayed true to form.

Bertrand informed the group about the potential of the three goth girls. He handed across their names to Barry and asked him to run them down, especially Samantha Ogden, the girl who only converted to the coven in her senior year.

Barry remarked that the facial recognition software might be a help on this matter.

"One more request Barry. In the murder book Detective Snider spent only three pages, mostly inconsequential, on Margaret Thode's parents. Both of them are now dead, 15-20 years ago. Will you also work on that angle? What happened? Relatives?"

Barry interjected, "I have other clients, too, you know."

Jack hissed and Augusta showed a frown from hell.

Bertrand said, "I know that you do Barry. But your work is invaluable. Give me all you've got, I think there is someone out there who is scared and the missiles we have in the air are to our advantage."

Augusta, silent for all the meeting said, "Bertrand. Even if it seems that we're at odds we will all help wherever possible. But, personally, I'm concerned that this case is draining you a bit. We don't want to visit you again at your home. Every missile you send up is also a message to the killer that you're sending it up. In more ways than one there's danger in the air," she said with finality.

He spread his coat apart. He was armed. He smiled and thanked the three.

Augusta stayed. She said, "What can I do?"

"Right now nothing. Appreciate your hanging in there with me. This case has so many false roads leading nowhere. I think I'm at X and suddenly I'm at non-X. Promising becomes unpromising. Yet I think there's a dim light leading us forward."

She hugged him tightly before leaving. They kissed, she left.

CHAPTER 39

Hugh Concannon was also at a dead end. Agatha Pruitt was most likely slaughtered by one of the many bums in a suspect neighborhood, she was alone, probably, and above all seen as a vulnerable elderly lady, a perfect target. Stupid McAbee was trying to relate it back to Margaret Thode's murder. Good luck with that, he thought sourly. While it was one thing to financially pillage Agatha's brother of his monies on this useless pursuit it was still another to hinder his investigation by polluting his investigation. Of all people to use he brought Jack Scholz who was on the radar of every police department in Iowa and Illinois. What a rotten pair. Furthermore, McAbee had somehow won the affections of Augusta Satin. A fucking mockery of him as he felt bile surge up to his throat from his gut.

The last stab he took at the possible connection of Agatha Pruitt and the murder of Margaret Thode was his visit to Gretchen Heinz at the Kahl home. Between her starting to cry and the Nazi bitch of a nun, Ursula, he was escorted to the exit. Too much water over the dam. He was more than a month out and essentially nowhere in his inquiry.

In the meantime, four murders had taken place in Rock Island. Three blacks down as they continued to murder each other for some hidden offense, drugs or women, usually the propellant for those crimes and who really cared? Crap back to crap. The other murder, though, was of a student at Augustana College. She was car-jacked on the street that ran right through the campus, driven to the crime-ridden west end, raped, murdered, and her body dumped into the Mississippi River. His attention went to that incident. The media were hysterical. He'd work the Pruitt case some more but, for him, it was becoming a non-starter, although somewhere down the line he'd drag in McAbee and see if he had come up with anything. He figured that it would only be through the intervention of Augusta that the wily old bastard, McAbee, would share anything with him. But it was what it was.

Barry Fisk went to work diligently. He appreciated McAbee standing up for him in front of the Nazi, Scholz, and Bertrand's judgmental girlfriend, Augusta. He started on the three crones as he read some Facebook entries from some former students who were in the same class as they. Many years after graduation students would begin to share their recollections. And sure enough there was some running banter about the three. It wasn't kind. 'Has anyone seen the three witches-bitches?' 'By the end of our senior year their faces were beginning to turn green.' 'Maybe they jumped into the cauldron and they're gone.' 'I still dream about the curse they placed on me and Bob.' He started on Angela Diaz. Her senior picture showed a grim face, piercing eyes full of hatred, deep black makeup shading her eyebrows and under her lids. He understood why students stayed clear of her. He thought that if she was love making with either of the other two it would be porcupine love. He didn't pursue the fantasy. Angela Diaz graduated, moved to San Antonio, was arrested on three occasions for meth production and selling. Her last known address was in Waco, apparently making a living working for a Harley dealer. He was surprised by a picture on the dealer's site. All of the black makeup was gone, her hair was white and her fully tattooed arms were crossed over her chest. She and three other women were advertised as the Repair Chicks. So much for Angela.

Next, he pursued Maureen Blong. The search ended abruptly. Maureen was an overdose at age 22 in a Chicago hostel for single women.

He figured that this angle was going to quickly evaporate for McAbee not that there couldn't be involvement in the Thode murder. But McAbee's hypothesis that the Pruitt murder related back to 45 years ago was now on thin ice, especially his inquiry about the three witches.

He approached Samantha Ogden with the same skepticism as the other two wackos aware that Hilda, the high school counselor, had hopes for Ogden. Her picture, while full of the witch stare and look held little hope for her, but unlike the other two he could see clear beauty marred by baleful stares and blackened makeup. He pursued her life after high school only to be stumped. Samantha Ogden was off the grid. He tracked driver's licenses, none except for her 16th birthday, so also for an American passport at the same time. He combed through the student newspaper and saw that at 16 she went on a two week school trip to Russia. A goodwill exchange closely monitored by both the U.S. and the U.S.S.R. With the current climate involving the invasion of Ukraine by Russia such trips were surely off the table. There was also a summer trip to China, following year.

Was Samantha Ogden, a straight A student, off the grid by an unreported death, such as being a victim of a serial killer or was she off the grid by her own doings?

Banks, credit cards, mortgages, marriage licenses, Facebook, Samantha Ogden disappeared. Given her rebellious nature this wasn't a mystery, but could she have been done this by herself? Without assistance? The three girls were all doomed by their angry and defiant choices while in high school. McAbee would be surprised by Ogden's disappearance but perhaps he could close this piece of the investigation, a dry well. Before abandoning the search he googled her parents. Her father died of cancer in 2013. Her mother was in a nursing home in Moline, a further search led to her having onset dementia.

The next chore involved Margaret Thode's parents. McAbee told him that they were dead. It was close to the truth. Her father had suicided in 2002. Her mother was dead three months later, heart attack, 2003. McAbee had asked him to locate family members of the two of them. Barry thought this to be over the top, but he did as asked. Margaret's father had a brother in Hawaii. Dead two years ago. That was it for him. Another family extinguished. What was it? Science makes progress one death at a time, meaning that it was the young who saved science not the old Neanderthals.

Margaret's mother had three sisters. Only one was alive. Verna lived in Wheatland, Iowa, a small town of about 1,000 residents equidistant to Davenport and Cedar Rapids, off of Highway 30. She was a single woman living in a large house in the middle of the town, huge porch, singularly attractive as he used Google Street View.

His work done he went to his couch for a nap wondering about only one conundrum, Samantha Ogden, he would work her parents later.

CHAPTER 40

Augusta enjoyed the drive with Bertrand as they took Highway 61 out of Davenport to DeWitt, and then onto Highway 30 heading west as they edged the small farm towns of Grand Mound and Calamus before turning north, heading into Wheatland. Bertrand drove carefully but with determination. He was a good driver, easy to relax with. But he had a streak of impatience with drivers unlike himself, speeders, slow pokes, sloppy passers and street light runners. He would regularly send those annoying people to hell.

Verna Macy lived on Third Street in a house that was probably built in the early 20th century. As Barry had said it was surrounded on all sides by a large porch, probably eight feet wide. It wasn't even. There were slopes in it and as they neared the property it was clear that Verna was in over her head if she navigated the place by herself. The roof showed spot repairs, now the porch, close by, sorely needed paint as did the exterior of the house. She conjectured that a large family once occupied the place.

He hadn't called ahead. Bertrand was puzzling to Augusta when he did that. Another quirk in the man.

The grass was at least eight inches high and needed weeding badly. The cracks in the pavement leading toward the entrance were sporting a variety of weeds and encroached grass. Bertrand had updated the case on the drive. He was going on hunches. She was leery of that approach as eventually hunch-driven investigations tended to lead detectives astray. But Bertrand was enormously successful with it. Like he had a third eye.

She must have seen them as the screen door opened. "Can I help you?"

Verna's lingering look at her didn't surprise. Small town America eschewed Blacks. Fear of the new? Ignorant racism? Anxious curiosity? McAbee seemed unfazed.

"Verna Macy?" He said in good cheer.

"I am. What do you want? Who are the two of you?"

He introduced himself and Augusta and asked if they could come in and chat a bit. She looked them over carefully, "You selling something?"

"No. We're looking into the murder of your niece, Margaret. Some information has come our way."

Verna, yet to formally introduce herself went into full gaze. "My name is Verna, but you seem to know things, surely my name. Okay. Come in."

Her living room was darkened. The house was in chaotic orderliness. Augusta sensed a slight cat urine odor. They were told to sit on a couch that was placed under a picture window, blinds down. They did as told.

Verna, facing them, sat on an upright chair of blue and white fabric. It was frayed on the arms. She was built in geometric proportions. Her head was an almost perfect square and her body a rectangle. Curvature was absent to her, a toughness around her small lips and narrow eyes. Wary. "You realize, of course, that what you're saying makes little sense. No one is around anymore. After 45 years? But I'll listen to you."

Bertrand gave her the information necessary for her to be willing to bite into his inquiry. Augusta was not surprised at how much he excluded from his summary. She listened intently to the former professor who had mastered the art of lecturing and maintaining interest.

There was a slight pause before Verna spoke. "I don't know what you expect from me. Margaret's murder destroyed my sister and her husband. I'm the youngest but things in our family were never the same. You know that everyone in my family is dead except for one lousy nephew, my sister's kid. I wouldn't spit on the little bastard. I never married, worked at Deere for 30 years, pulled up stakes and bought this place. Obviously, it's beyond me. So, keep your opinions to yourself." She broke a smile, suddenly transforming herself into a pleasant woman.

Bertrand drew her out about Deere, what she did and why she chose Wheatland as her retirement haven. She opened up. He was masterful at this as she spoke of things in a relaxed way, glad for the company.

Apparently she realized that she had forgotten why they were here as she caught herself and said, "Okay, I've done enough talking. This is about Margaret. Again, I don't know how I could possibly help. Churning all this up is not my idea of fun."

"No. I don't want to take you through that. I'm sure the pain lingers. Doesn't need a new match," he said gently. "Margaret herself is a bit of a mystery to me and Augusta.

Someone I spoke with said that she reminded her of Amelia Earhart. Familiar?"

She thought for a bit and said, "Wow. That's well put. I watched some stuff on Earhart. I felt that Margaret was a one of a kind. Like her. I agree. Very apt. But I don't know where you're going with this?"

"Here's where you might help. Is there anything that you have from Margaret? Notes, letters, whatever."

"No. Well I have the leaflet that the funeral parlor put together. I have no idea where it is. Somewhere. Is that what you'd want?"

"No. Your sister, Margaret's mother, died in 2003. Right?"

"Yes. Florence, yes."

"When there's a death like that of Margaret, parents hang onto things. A way to stay attached to the life of the victim. That make sense?"

"Ah. Of course. I see your point. When Florence died I was given a trunk of hers. Mementos largely. I remember opening it, saw some of the stuff, for example, she was into linens and pressed flowers. I couldn't deal with it, closed it up. When I moved from Davenport to out here I did bring the trunk. It's in the attic. Lots of stuff up there. Under the linens. Did I look? Peeked. Stopped. Couldn't. Out of sight out of mind."

With his large smile he said, "Verna. This is where you're supposed to invite me to go up there and open the trunk."

She laughed. Amazingly they were in sync with each other. "Well yes. You led me along very shrewdly. All three of us will go up and take a look. But I warn you that I may scramble to the other side of the attic if it gets tough on me."

Augusta had yet to speak because she knew that Bertrand was on a winning streak with Verna. But she was damn curious about the trunk.

They climbed the narrow stairway up to the second floor. The runner that ran through the middle of the steps was badly worn, McAbee noticed. He reached for the railing to assist his ascent.

Verna turned around and said at the second floor landing, "This is where it gets tough. But we can do it." She pulled a chain off a hook and when it hung in the middle of the hatch that it guarded she gave a tug. The hatch didn't move. McAbee offered to tug at it until Augusta, forcefully he thought, said, "Let me have it." He backed away as Augusta with one quick yank pulled out the hatch and the attached stairs came down a few feet. She pulled the attached stair-ladder to the floor.

Verna said, "You're as strong as you look." She glanced at McAbee who observed a smile on her lips.

Verna grabbed onto the railing and with a sprightliness that surprised him went up the nine steps.

Augusta looking at Bertrand said, "You go first. I'll catch you if you fall." She raised her eyebrows and smiled at him.

When they walked on the attic floor the creaking was off-putting. A ghost story could have easily been contrived. There was one light in the center; a pull-cord brought the area to life as the light danced around the room on its loose hanging cord. At the other end of the attic was a small dirt-caked window that allowed a small shaft of light. As

McAbee got his bearings he observed how jammed up the place was. Verna had a touch of hoarding in her. In one area she pointed to two trunks, on top of each other. She said, "It's the bottom one. Sorry."

Without hesitation, Augusta went over and tested the weight of the top trunk. She said, "Bertrand, I need your help. Will you grab onto the strap on the side?" He did so and that trunk was placed to a side where there was room for it. They then lifted the Thode family trunk and brought it out to the center of the attic, under the 75 watt bulb. It didn't have a lock.

McAbee deferred to Verna. "Do you wish to open this? You're okay with us searching it?"

"Yes. Let me see how I do." With a creak the lid was opened, some of the trunk contents on full display. Verna said, "It's as I remember it. I don't want to deal with it. You can. There are some collapsible chairs over there," she pointed toward the small window, "I'll get them for you." With a rag that she found on her way to the chairs she brought them over, opened them, and dusted them. "Please sit and do what you have to. I'll be over across the way. Been meaning to bring some stuff down from that knitting box," she pointed across the floor.

McAbee sat at one side of the trunk, Augusta the other. He pulled out a large linen throw, probably meant for a couch. Some sheets and pillowcases followed along with a linen coat. All of them had a musty odor. Beneath these was an assortment of pressed flowers neatly laid out. That was the end of this section of the trunk, a tray of sorts, two parts in this trunk. Nothing of consequence on the top tray. He removed that section and saw an entirely different type of contents beneath it.

His knowledge of Margaret gave him an immediate meaning, sadness fell on him. As he looked over at Augusta, he felt that their expressions matched. Before he touched anything, he arose and went over to Verna who was poking through the contents of an old shopping bag. He said, very quietly, "There are two shelves in the trunk. You had it right about the first one. Linens and pressed flowers," he paused. She gave him a nod for him to continue. "I'm afraid the bottom tier is all about Margaret. Do you want to see it? We haven't removed anything yet."

Verna said, "Let me take a quick look," as she stepped over to the opened trunk. She saw what Bertrand and Augusta saw. There were three framed pictures, two of Margaret, one of them as an early teen, the other as a young woman. The other picture was of three individuals, presumably father and mother with smiles and Margaret as a young child, perhaps five or six. There was a teddy bear and a baby doll, a loose folder that seemed to have cut outs, pictures, two neatly folded dresses, five Nancy Drew books and some knickknacks. At the far end of the trunk under a scarf, earmuffs and mittens was a small book engraved with a title, 'My Diary.'

Verna said, "I need to sit." Her tears began. She told Bertrand through sobs to take the trunk but leave the linens and flowers on the now detached top tier of the trunk, Bertrand noticed that she never stopped crying.

Awkwardly, Bertrand and Augusta moved the lightened trunk downwards and out of the house placing it on the back seat of the Camry. Verna was on the porch, hunched over and still sobbing. She said, "I knew. I knew. I was afraid of that trunk. Do what you have to do with it and the contents. Whenever you're done with it call me or come back. I don't know if I can handle it. You're very kind McAbee. Please treat it with respect. You too Augusta," she said as an obvious afterthought.

The drive back to Davenport was done in complete silence.

CHAPTER 41

Augusta and Bertrand, each carrying an end of the bulky but lightened trunk, brought it into Bertrand's condo. Augusta opened the lid. They both stared at it, less menacing than in Verna's attic.

A teddy bear and the thought of any dead kids who had them as friends was toxic for Bertrand. He breathed deeply, holding his grief in his heart. Augusta, more in control of herself it seemed, removed the doll and teddy bear putting them out of view. She probably remembered, he couldn't, a bad reaction from some previous cases, she always one step ahead. She then removed two dresses. She said softly, "They're laundered and beautifully folded," putting them aside. He thought that in a way the process was like an exhumation. She opened the loose binder. On the pages were pasted remembrances, some pictures too, of her experiences. A kindergarten performance, a Girl Scout patch, a one-page paper where a teacher had pasted a gold star with a written, 'Most Excellent.' It went on like that for about 30 pages before the book went blank and unused for its back half.

Knickknacks were removed. A car from McDonalds with a clown sitting in the driver's seat. A bobble head of a player from the Chicago Cubs, name hard to read, maybe Ernie Banks. Each item had its own particular stab, reminders of lost innocence, a memorial to a particular time in her life, a happiness, a pleasant token to a moment that no longer meant anything to anyone except McAbee himself as he reflected on the items.

Augusta looked at him intently, "This is hard for you isn't it?"

"Yeah. The older I get the more it stings."

"Well, I did those. You ready to do the diary?" she asked somberly.

"Of course," he said hesitantly.

He picked up the diary and held it as though weighing it. It was an off-size, perhaps six by nine inches. 'My Diary' was centered on the light blue cardboard cover. It wasn't a tome, perhaps it had about 100-150 pages, unlined and unnumbered. He opened the front cover and read on the first page, 'If you come across this diary it is private and you should not read any further. If you do you will be cursed.' Hand-drawn was an image of snake-haired and wild-eyed Medusa. It was nicely drawn. "I'm going to read this but I feel lousy about it."

"Oh don't, Bertrand. It may prove to be material to the case. Margaret would want you to."

"I know, I know," he said crankily.

The personal revelations began on page two, her 16th birthday, November 14th. He flicked through the pages. It was written on a so-so basis. Months passed with no commentary. Sometimes dates were sequential, day by day, but this was rare. Back to page two. She had been given a new bicycle. Her joy was obvious as well as her gratitude to her parents, small hearts drawn on the page.

A beloved teacher, a despised teacher, some men, some women. She had neat penmanship, small, precise. Eleven pages in, she recounted some of her bicycle experiences. She rode it with the constancy that had been reported to him. Her joys at routes in the Quad Cities as well as a few close calls with cars and trucks. She seemed to have no fear, a problem for people of her age. Life was eternal.

November 14, again, now she was 17. She was troubled by some of her schoolmates, taunting but with self-talk spurring her to fight back. She was finding a spunkiness as the diary progressed. Boys were stared down as her middle finger was befriended by her. She loved seeing their reactions but privately, now, in her secret diary, she was concerned. She was increasingly aware of her surroundings while on her bike. She seemed to have lessened her running. Perhaps she wasn't eternal as the year progressed and the taunting and explicit threats toward her were increasing in frequency and in strength. No names until March. Scooter and his ilk. A one-armed freak! He scared her. He once drove by her and pulled so close that she almost fell over. She was now a lesbian bitch, a cunt, a freak. She worried for her parents, their health a concern, no particulars.

November 14, now she was 18. Her toughness doubled-down on. She was aggressive, her self-talk more daring and her retorts back to various freaks (a word she used often, regarding her tormentors) more explicit and graphic.

She liked science and math but eschewed English, history, and social studies. She went on a few dates but they were coded as disasters. She had a scholarship.

A new set of taunters. Girls! Jocks, she called them. Some basketball players, track girls. She suspected them of being bent, meaning gay. Comments made to her as crude as what the boys threw at her. She posited that she was good looking; she didn't need approval from a few that she designated as 'gawky bitches.' And then a new group of screwballs. Three witches. Three weird girls who blackened their eyes, wore a black Halloween type of lipstick, to her they were menacing. They came onto her as recruiters to their way of life. She was appalled by them. Upset that they saw in her a potential recruit. Was she that odd? She manifested doubt for the first time in the diary. As the three continued their pestering she lashed out at them. Their reaction was predictable. They tore into her verbally, hurling curses, insults, and threats.

Another incident with Roger Smalley. She got off her bike and ran after his car that sped away. None of this surprised him as his vision of Smalley as a teenager was harsh.

Toward the end of the diary one comment held his attention. One of the witches had cornered her in the girl's bathroom. She was groped by her. She'd had enough as she punched the unnamed witch in the face, a tooth was knocked out and the witch became hysterical. Margaret feared that she'd be kicked out of school. One guy, unnamed, came to her. He tried to console her. She alluded to him as one of the 'perfects.' McAbee wondered if this could be Forrest Graham, that maybe some kind of contact had occurred between them. No way to tell as he speculated about how many 'perfects' there could have been at Rock Island High School.

But nothing came of it except for glowering gazes from the three witches. To his annoyance no identification of which witch had groped her was ever made.

The last entry in the diary was her enthusiasm about the coming summer and her admission to the University of Chicago on a full scholarship. 'Finally getting out of this lousy environment at the high school.' Her last diary words.

He read off the salient pieces of the diary to Augusta; when he finished he asked her, "So, what do you think?"

"Pretty predictable. Gifted, tough, but also a teenager. Some vulnerabilities. Clearly, though, there are suspects and some of them have found their way into her diary. Scooter, one-armed Smalley, and the three witches, good confirmations. Smalley, in particular, acting out. Could easily have misjudged and hurt her. I admire her for knocking out a witch-tooth." She smiled.

"You better watch out with that language. You're sounding a bit like Jack Scholz," he said lightly.

She winced. "So now what?"

"Smalley is still a suspect. We'll have to put some pressure on him. Scooter, no. The three witches? Could be any of the three punched by Margaret. But it always comes back to a live person. One witch dead, the other in Vegas with no way to secure that device from her status out there. The other, Samantha Ogden probably dead."

"Forrest Graham?" she asked.

"Not a chink in his armor. Hard to see him as a suspect. But he's the one with the most access to that device."

"Working in concert with someone?"

"You mean Forrest Graham and Roger Smalley? No, I don't see it but all things are possible. I have Barry doing more work on Graham. It worries me when I hear someone is perfect," he said.

"Well, of course. Only you have that," she said with a laugh. "I'm going now. Will you drive me downtown Mistah?"

"Sure smarty. I will," he said.

CHAPTER 42

Fisk answered the call from McAbee. He knew that it was he but as always pretended otherwise. "Yeah?"

"Hello Barry. Have a minute?"

They both knew that he did but the game had to be played out. "Very tight here. What's up?"

"I don't like something about this case," McAbee said.

"What's to like? Seems as though it's a dead end. Enter the world of Concannon."

"Advice heard. Advice rejected. Do you know that I'm concerned with?"

"Yup. I've been at this for hours. You're referring to Samantha Ogden. Somehow, somewhere she just disappeared."

"Were there any requests by her parents to the police department in Rock Island? FBI?"

"Not that I could see. Not positive about that. Those records are not in the ones that were digitized. But what I can tell you is that no investigation file was ever opened on her. Poof, she disappears in the summer of 1978. I cannot for the life of me raise anything on her."

"This is so odd. Her parents?"

"Augustana profs."

"What's the deal with them?" McAbee asked.

"They got divorced in 1979 near the time of Ogden's disappearance. In 1973, Augustana College was awarded a grant to develop a program on Asian Studies. Augie hired both of them, a married couple. She was Chinese, a naturalized citizen. Her husband, an American, whom she met at Harvard. It awarded doctorates in Asian Studies. Requirement for entry into the program was fluency in Chinese, Japanese, or Korean. They were both fluent in Chinese. How he came by this fluency I don't know. They both graduated from Harvard in 1966, Ph.Ds. They both were employed by Random House before seeking the Augustana job. 1973."

"Samantha Ogden? Did she know Chinese?"

"Presumably. Nothing on the record. No programs of any kind at Rock Island High School. No way to tell. If I had to guess, I'd say yes. I imagine they wanted to practice with each other and would probably engage with their daughter. No way to tell."

"Recognition software?"

"Used it. No takes. Still trying to get more information on the saint, Forrest Graham. He is covered up by the CIA. I think that Samantha Ogden is probably in some unmarked grave, somewhere in some desert. She was last seen as a witch. Don't see any of them coming out of that costume party in one piece."

"Okay Barry. Stay on Forrest Graham. Samantha Ogden is probably just a trail run dry. But stay on her parents anyway, just in case."

CHAPTER 43

Pei-Ling Chén was a brilliant student. She was quickly noticed by the Mao government as someone special. A devoted Communist who seemingly was able to divine Mao's thinking before even thought it, her sour boss noted with respect and just a bit of fear.

The relationship between China and the USSR was strained back in the late 1950s. One had to step carefully in any instance where exchanges were tested. In the troublesome year of 1957 Zhou Enlai, the Premier of the People's Republic of China and close associate of Mao Zedong, ordered that a special bureau be established directly under his control. When the bureau was formed and the 31 specially ordained agents were situated in the then called city of Peking he personally interviewed 20 of these agents. He wanted new blood, a different way of thinking. Pei-Ling Chén was the 20th interview that he conducted. She was 23 years old, her academic career perfect; he secretly fell in doctrinal love with her. Her imagination, subtlety of mind, appearance, and interviewing skill-set overwhelmed him. Her boss, an ignorant and obstreperous fool tried to sabotage her when he was queried about her. That fool was quickly sent to a camp for thought reconstruction, essentially, he was disappeared.

Pei was chosen to lead the agency. She was told that this special bureau did not officially exist and was never to be publicly noticed. She would only report to him. When told of this she said, "Of course."

She was ordered to organize the agents and staff in a small non-descript building in an out of the way street toward the outer rim of the great city of Beijing, then still called Peking.

In further discussions, she was told that she would be welcomed in Moscow as an understudy to a special division of the KGB on Lubyanka Square. An old acquaintance Sergei, last name unreported, ran a special division in the KGB. At a meeting in the mid 50s over a private dinner between Sergei and Zhou he had mentioned that the KGB had successfully infiltrated many sectors of the American government with what were called 'deep plants' or sleepers, people nurtured over years and years to gain access into the affairs of the capitalistic pig of a nation, the USA. The Russians crowed at their success at obtaining the required information that enabled the USSR to develop atomic weapons, the Rosenbergs, Fuchs, in England, and a host of other patriots to the cause of international communism. The mission he went on was assiduous, lengthy, and even if only 20% of the plants proved successful it was a gold mine of information when the vein was hit. Someday, when Zhou was ready, he was willing to share his expertise with a designated agent. He gave one warning, 'This person must be of A+ skills.' There was no room for miscalculation or incompetency.

For Zhou the time had come. He was a strong believer in symmetries and when he was interviewing Pei-Ling Chén it all came together. This female genius was fluent in Russian, English, and Japanese besides her other gifts of acumen. Her photographic memory amazed him.

And so it was that in the autumn of 1958, Pei found herself in Moscow. Her first task, and it was always her task, was to win over this Russian by the first name only, Sergei. Within a week she had succeeded in doing so. His last name was Malken. He was a heavy drinker. Vodka was his drink of choice. Because of that and probably his age, he was a horrible lover. But it was all worth it as he gave to her what was probably the entire 'book' that the Soviets employed with such great success. She was also placed in an apartment in one of Stalin's poor imitations of the American Empire State Building. Semi-impotent Sergei had clout as the poor fool doted over her.

After four intense months of study, mixed with her feigned interest in the man, she left Moscow for China.

Ushered into the office of Zhao Enlai she submitted to him a thorough report of Russian efforts and their infiltrated enemies. It was much more elaborate than Zhao was given to understand. The KGB had sleepers in almost every country in the world. She indicated that a secret file that she had accessed in Sergei's office safe included the names of 36 Chinese citizens who were considered to be plants or sleepers for the KGB. Her photographic memory had retained the code that Malkin used on the safe. An aging and careless fool, she concluded. Zhao, a notoriously hard man to surprise was shocked as the Chinese had one formal agent in the USSR at the time. He reflected that

China was light years behind the hated CIA and now re-perceived USSR. More and more he threw his considerable power behind Pei-Ling Chén, a rising but hidden asset in the People's Republic. Those Russian plants in China? They were gone within the year.

The formal agency that was organized by the Chinese government for security, spying on Chinese citizens and foreign governments was formally called the Ministry of State Security, the MSS. It was composed of multiple divisions called Bureaus. Zhou knew that he had to place Pei's division into that network while keeping it independent and secretive, remembering how Pei had infiltrated Sergei's most closely held secrets. The MSS was a sloppy and staggering giant of an organization. With his profound skills he inserted Pei's group into a separate bureau that reported only to him. That took great finesse on his part but he was a master at the finagling of government agencies. The fear that he evoked was an additional propellant to his success.

Accordingly Pei-Ling Chén was given extraordinary authority, and given the times, a handsome budget. Catch-up was now a prime task for the People's Republic as Zhou Enlai knew in his heart that China must be prepared to eventually enter the world at large when Mao would soon realize that being a hermit nation was a foolish enterprise. Eventually, of course, the subtle efforts of Zhao with the Nixon administration and his malignant agent Kissinger would eventually change the hermit into a swaggering giant, a vision realized as Pei presently oversaw a multi-tentacled bureau of supreme importance. The light years of backwardness had now become microscopic as charts of success had taken on a vertical quality under Pei's direction.

CHAPTER 44

A restless woman of considerable talent had pestered the authorities for permission to study in the United States. Her name was Jia Wong. It was 1959; Zhou Enlai was impatient. Pei had impressed on him how far China was from having a first class security system.

Pei had Jia Wong brought to her office. She questioned her closely as to why Jia, a 20 year old woman, a newly minted degree from the University of Peking in foreign languages was so insistent in her requests to enter the country of a professed enemy. Her answers were satisfactory. She wanted to understand the American mind as well as educate them on the majesty of the People's Republic.

Would Jia be willing to be an informal agent for the Chinese government? Reporting only directly to Pei. There was a hesitation in her reply. Pei informed her that this was a necessary condition to any approval for such an enterprise. She informed Jia that her extended family, parents, grandparents, siblings, and other relatives would be held personally responsible if she failed to adhere to the contract. Jia was given two days to think it over and either completely and unquestionably accept the conditions outlined by Pei or she should ever abandon her hopes of going to the USA.

Two days later Jia Wong vowed her allegiance to Pei and was sworn in as a secret agent of the Peoples Republic of China. She was the fourth agent to be sent abroad, one already placed in the USA the others in Australia and Canada. Zhao had informed Pei that any show of interest in creating a bridge to the USA would be met with glee by the Americans. In fact, any possible manifestation of a split with the USSR was welcomed and encouraged. Yes, Jia Wong, would be watched closely by the FBI, an agency with a storied hatred of Communists but there could be no chance of disclosure as Jia was a deep plant, years and years of patience with perhaps nothing to show for the effort. It was a matter of sowing as many seeds as possible for the hopes of having one beautiful tree. That was the same game as described by Sergei Malken. It was the only way to think, patience and perseverance.

Jia was happily granted a student visa by the United States. An example of future cooperation between the two countries.

Jia was accepted into Harvard College and its program in Asian Studies. She was a find for the program. She was given a full ride scholarship, a monthly allowance, and a job assisting professors in mastering the difficult language of Mandarin.

Much to Jia's surprise she was left alone by China. In 1960 she noticed an American, a classmate, by the name of Joseph Ogden. He hovered over her as a protector. They would talk. His Chinese was very good and he appreciated being able to fine tune his skills. He was attractive to her, good looking, serious, but also with a good sense of humor. They began to date. Sex was off the table for her and he accepted that as he appreciated her reserve and the protection of her virginity as she falsely led him to believe.

Soon, after a few dates she was shocked to find a Chinese woman in her locked dorm room in Cambridge. To her, "Who are you?" she heard, "I am a cousin of yours. For your record my name is Rita. Your room is free of any listening devices. Do you understand?"

Befuddled, she said, "Yes. I think so," as she reflected back to her arrangements with Pei and her security agency.

"You have done well with Joseph. He is one of us. While he is an American he is a Communist with a deep love and commitment to our People's Republic. While this is true there will always be a slight reservation about him. Of you, though, none. Your parents send their love by the way," she said with a slight chill in her voice, a meant warning, of course. She was a heavy-set woman with a seriousness that matched her weight. "Besides Joseph you have been watched by others as well as myself. We are pleased and we wish you to continue here in the Boston area, tucked away and hopefully forgotten to the FBI. It is desired that you and Joseph marry."

Jia was taking each missive with as much grace as she could, realizing that the world she had consented to enter had a considerable number of constraining blades attached to it. She had appreciated the freedoms that America allowed but she had no recourse with which to challenge the authoritarian woman whose eyes were focused on her with scary intensity. She had to go along.

The fat one went on, "He will propose to you next week and you will marry him within the next month. Your status will not be disclosed. Your marriage and honeymoon will take place in a city by the name of Reno in the state of Nevada. You will continue your studies here until you both complete your doctorates. Children are encouraged. As you will see we require that offspring be brought up to be as Chinese as much as possible. Other than that I have just told you you are to fit in and follow the path that opens to you. Either myself or someone else will occasionally show up in your life to gather information and instruct you about our expectations. Always know your family unit in China is protected from some of the upheavals currently occurring in our great country."

"I understand," she said with as much gusto as she could summon up.

The fat one said, as she arose, "Our great country is preparing to enter this troubled world and bring Marxist thought throughout the world. It will take time and much sacrifice. You are the point of a huge knife," she left with a small bow.

Jia looked out her window and saw 'Rita', a supposed cousin, enter a car. The passenger seat. She was driven away. Jia wondered how many others would be visited by cousin fat woman.

CHAPTER 45

Jia and Joseph graduated from Harvard in 1960. Shortly after their marriage in Reno, observed by four unknown Chinese, Jia had conceived and nine months later Jia gave birth to a daughter. The name of Samantha was transmitted to Jia and Joseph by an unknown authority in China. Although China stayed in the background and ruled with a light hand it was clear to the couple that the upbringing of Samantha was not to be done without advice, that meant interference.

Samantha spoke Mandarin Chinese at home but was also fully capable with the English language. Her looks gave an unusual impression. Clearly she was Asian but her Nordic features softened her Chinese visage. People had to do a double take to capture her Asian race. She was abnormally pale, as she grew she was encouraged by her mother to avoid the sun. Her skin took on a pearl-like quality.

Joseph and Jia's relationship started to erode as they became editors at Random House for Chinese books that were beginning to trickle into America. New York was abhorrent to them during a period of time, the late 1960s and the early 1970s, when crime was omnipresent.

Samantha was educated at a pricey private academy in mid-town Manhattan. Financial assistance was provided by the People's Republic of China.

In 1973, Augustana College in Rock Island was awarded with a grant to establish an Asian Studies Program. Joseph and Jia touched base with an agent who now rather regularly and annoyingly monitored the education of Samantha. Joseph and Jia consistently put aside their personal problems for Samantha's sake but they thought that a fresh start in academia might help them to return to their lost love. Augustana leapt to hire them and in July of 1973 they moved to Rock Island, Illinois. Samantha, now 13 years old, was enrolled in a private school in Davenport. A new agent, there was constant change by the Chinese authorities, mandated that Samantha be enrolled in Rock Island High School. The aim was to guarantee that Samantha be fully Americanized, her too involved Chinese identity be softened, that she could learn to deal with the evil crassness of Americans.

Jia and Joseph's relationship did not improve in Rock Island. Their task of making Augustana's Asian Studies Program top notch was reasonably successful. They were both highly trained and professional scholars. But student interest never materialized to the point where the program could reach a top level. They both knew that their poor relationship was not helping the program.

In the meantime Samantha filled out, a beautiful and brilliant teenager who learned to absorb the racist comments of her classmates. She was active in some clubs and was reasonably popular in the cruel environment that permeated the high school.

Her relationship with her father was strained. He started to drink and when intoxicated he became vituperative and cutting towards her. In her sophomore year a very austere Chinese man came to her house for a visit. His demeanor and voice scared her. Never once did he smile as he seemed to command the house. Her mother and father went into subservience in his presence at first. As the meeting went on her father, Joseph, began to drink and with that he started to bear down on this man from China. The meeting became awkward and the man eventually left. For the first time in her life she observed the hatred between her mother and father, their verbal attacks toward each other after he left shocked Samantha. She thought her father to be a fool; she reached a closer relationship with her mother.

While Joseph was at a convention in Toronto, Canada, Jia opened up to Samantha about the connection to China and her place in this changing world. In her heart she was not surprised but she was of mixed opinion. Jia announced to her, 17 now, that she would be spending the summer, six weeks of it, in Beijing. Samantha was astute enough to see this as a branding exercise. She was troubled but part of her welcomed the opportunity to shed her quarrelsome parents.

She arrived in Beijing on June 3rd and was met at the airport by the very same austere man who had spent time at her house and who had come into conflict with her father, Joseph. He looked at her sternly and informed her that she would stay at the Hyatt Hotel for three nights and then she would be given a room in a dormitory at Beijing University.

On the second day at the Hyatt, now rested and oriented to the time change, there was a light knock at her door. When she opened the door she saw a 30ish woman, beautiful, self- assured, and in her way overwhelming. Something about her brought Samantha into awe. They spoke for three hours. The woman's name was Pei-Ling Chén. Pei, ever charming, began to question Samantha who realized that many of the questions asked came from a place where the answers were already known. She was praised for her school performance, her mastery of Mandarin, and her obedience to her parents. "It is of concern to us that your father seems to have lost his bearing?" Pei then stopped and peered closely at Samantha. By that time in the process she was mesmerized by Pei. She had never been in the presence of such a supreme person. With her, she concluded, she must always be totally honest. "They are headed for a disaster, I think. It's hard to be around my father. My mother is my inspiration," she said to Pei who merely smiled encouragingly.

As the meeting went on Samantha was steered into her take on China and the USA. Was she fully aware of what was expected of her? She wasn't, she answered honestly. "It is important that you be with me as the future unfolds. We have 71 current sleepers in America. Some of these are already seen to be useless. Such happens in this business. But, you? I have you on the top of my list. We can place you in a position where you can be one of the finest agents ever placed by us."

Samantha's heart skipped. What did this glorious woman mean? Me?

"For now Samantha I will leave you with this thought. I want you to wrestle with what I've said." With that last comment Pei left. Her gliding steps suggested an angel to the smitten Samantha.

CHAPTER 46

Samantha's six weeks stay in Beijing was an awakening for her. Instead of the announced plan the study of Chinese poetry in the 18th century nothing of that sort occurred. After she assented to becoming an agent she was placed with three other women in special training.

Two of the girls dropped out of this exercise after one week. The remaining girl in the session had a quality to her that Samantha distrusted. Yet this girl, Liu, made concerted efforts at establishing a friendship with Samantha. But for the entire six week stay Samantha kept her at a distance even as she was probed often about her feelings toward the program by this woman, Liu.

For the first week she was introduced to fashion and personal grooming. She was told by a short woman of exquisite skill and charm that her first weapon as an agent was her sexuality. The art of flirtation mixed with innocence was overwhelmingly successful with men. At the age of 17 there were few barriers to success. Men were easily finessed and overcome. By the end of this first week she was sent back to the Hyatt Hotel bar. She was to exert some of her skills on the foreign clientele. She knew that she was being monitored as she sat at an end table, very visible and very by herself. It was 6 p.m. on Saturday night. The first man to see her concealed his interest. He was balding, probably mid-40s and Western, nationality still unknown. His constant peeks in her direction supposedly went unnoticed by her as her tinted glasses were just right for concealment. Twice he was about to slide off his seat at the bar but he stopped. Finally, she caught his eye and gave him the tiniest of smiles behind her show of shyness.

Soon, he walked over and said, American clearly, "Are you alone? Need a drink? Do you mind if I sit?"

With a practiced smile and a flutter of her eyelids, and a blush that she learned how to manufacture during the week of training she said, "Yes, to all three. That would be nice. My name is Paula."

"You're American?"

"Well yes and no. I have lived in China for most of my life. But you?"

"Allow me to buy you a drink. Your preference? Oh, my name is Bob."

"Just a white wine Bob, thank you," she said demurely.

For an hour she drilled down on him. He was a businessman from Seattle. He was interested in the manufacture of automotive parts for Ford Motors. He explained his parts business, in particular, that he was interested in working with a start-up company in Shanghai. He was staying at the hotel. Great room. Would she like to see it? Of course not, she was instantly angered by his suggestion. "Do you think that I am a prostitute?" She arose and left him with a parting look of disgust and anger. Part of the training – you must be alluring but never perceived to be on the prowl as a whore. There was a distinction and she would have to work on her presentation.

An hour later, at a Marriott, she went to her task again. This time he was an Australian who was loud and pushy. He told her that he was in the business of exotic animals and their possible usage in Chinese medicine. Listening to him explain how many diseases could be cured through the usage of animal organs was seen to be an abandonment of reason by her. The more she listened to his bluster the angrier she became. Finally, after one hour or more of over-reach by him he asked her to go to a disco bar with him. She was disgusted and her innocence and virginal presentation slipped off of her demeanor. Anger rising, she said, "You're full of shit! Buffoon!"

He cursed at her parting figure. She heard words, 'bitch' 'Chinese whore' and others but they were obscured by table chatter and a dropped plate.

On Sunday, she was visited by Pei who was not as friendly as a week ago when she arrived. "Samantha. You have much to learn. Your conversations and interactions last night are seen to be failures. The American first. Yes, it is not good that he saw you as a prostitute. We think that you overacted your innocence. Let me show you." She took from her case a small projector and then she pointed to some facial gestures employed by Samantha. "Too soon, too conspicuous." They watched the interaction that had been edited down. Samantha took in the comments and criticism. She understood.

"But," Pei went on now a harshness in her voice, "You never show anger that you manifested in both interactions. Never are you to do that. We are noticing in you a streak of quick anger. You were repellent in either instance with the American and the Australian. I see it as a weakness. You must learn to harness it. Someday it will lead to your downfall. It is egregious and must be controlled. Do you see? Your anger must be subdued."

Samantha was taken aback. She was defending her honor, in one case the sexual invitation by the loutish American, and the other, the absurd intellectual crime being committed by the buffoonish Australian. She explained this to Pei who, as usual, listened with care, showing no emotion other than warmth.

Pei said in response. "You are not seasoned, of course. You are only 17 years old even as you were made up to look like you were 20 or 21. Let me say this and please think about it as you must eventually concur with this. Be cynical about heterosexual men. When they reach into their 70s they are more reliable, tamed as it were by nature. But anywhere from 30-70 be very, very, wary. They are almost universally drawn to a woman such as yourself and will employ extraordinary tactics to have sex with you. A magnetic field. See it for what it is. Do not reach into anger unless they are being violent or threatening. We will address that issue next week. Neither of those men from last night was threatening. They were what is predictable. You are beautiful, highly desirable. Play them out! Don't have sex with them unless absolutely necessary to a mission, otherwise keep your senses intact. The French have a phrase, '*sang froid*.' Emotions should never be on display such as you exhibited. Do not be discouraged, however, you were most adept at drawing those sex-driven fools to give away information that we can use as time goes by. But you threw away your advantage for future meetings with them. Never do that."

Samantha listened closely to Pei. Her wisdom was beyond anything that she had ever encountered.

When Pei left Samantha cried. She was in need of much training.

CHAPTER 47

Samantha's instructions in the martial arts went for two intense weeks with three experts. Their reports to Pei pretty much told of Samantha's softness as a woman, this was put down to her American laziness. That part of the reports did not surprise Pei. The general assumption in China being that Americans were fat and lazy. They couldn't criticize her weight but softness was another thing altogether. In some perverted way the instructors probably thought that they'd get high marks from Pei for patriotism by putting down the American.

Of the three instructors she was especially interested in what Kim said. She was a master at judo and also an astute judge of potential. After all, two weeks were totally inadequate for the training that Samantha would have to receive if Pei's plans materialized. Kim wrote that while Samantha had American softness, thank you Kim, I will notify the authorities of your patriotism, she had unique strengths. Her size was five feet, five inches, in the non-centimeter and archaic measurements used by American reactionaries. More tributes to patriotism Pei thought unkindly. Samantha instinctively knew how to use size to her advantage. The student was a subtle learner who would demonstrate skill at an opportune moment. But most noticeable were her reflexes. Kim judged them to be consistent with elite athletes. She was, in sum, a raw talent who could be brought up to high defensive and offensive skills in the martial arts. Her last comment, however, concerned Pei. "Samantha has hidden pockets of anger and hatred. When those are exhibited I see her as a danger to herself and others. It would not be wise to poke this tigress in the wrong way. If the tigress cannot control her fury she will eventually be trapped."

The other two instructors agreed with Kim but they failed to mention the anger and hatred that Kim had felt in her. But Kim's analysis of Samantha's psychological traits of anger and hatred had been observed by Pei herself, as with the foreigners.

Pei visited Samantha after her third week. She noticed that Samantha had improved self-assuredness, a greater maturity. This was good as she would need confidence in herself for the missions that she might have to undertake.

On the fourth week Samantha was given a trip around the country. Observations were made as to how she was able to relax and socialize, excellent was the judgment.

Samantha's fifth week was devoted to common techniques used by spies. Pei was told by Liu, Samantha's classmate in training, that Samantha was very remote and cold. Self-disclosures were not forthcoming, their conversations were one-sided and superficial. Liu wondered if she was onto her as a spy for Pei. Nothing was explicit but something was up. Pei would find out, of course. If it was true that Samantha had smelled a plant it was a tribute to her skills. Spycraft was, of course, a sophisticated and complicated arena. The techniques took place under a Russian-trained instructor with substantial skills. His take on Samantha was simple enough. Smart, smooth, unruffled and with an extraordinary command of details. He reported that on two occasions she became angry and cursed at him. He did not realize that she held such anger in her. If she was pushed by criticism she might eventually act out and cause harm to a perceived obstacle and ultimately to a mission, the only fault he found with her.

At the end of five weeks Pei knew that she had a high-strung thoroughbred in Samantha. She was aware of the incipient anger in Samantha. She knew that Samantha held her in high regard and was unlikely to ever manifest it in her presence.

The sixth week was going to be the most threatening. It was always fraught with emotional discharge. But it was the most essential of the weeks. All discussions were taped and transcripts were reviewed closely by Pei who used four highly trained interrogators for the week. Some of the transcriptions were red-lined by her.

Interrogator 2: "During the past five weeks you were befriended by your associate student Liu. Why were you so resistant to her? She might eventually be a colleague in espionage. Why treat her in such a manner?"

Samantha: "Why should I? She was nosy. I didn't trust her. She touched stuff in my room. Private."

Interrogator 2: "How would you know such a thing? Do you lie regularly?"

Samantha: "I lie sometimes. She was a lie always. I notice things. I set traps for her. She was too stupid to notice.

You should use smarter people. If you persist in making false inquiries then you're the liar aren't you?" Samantha concluded rudely.

Interrogator 2 note to self: 'She is an arrogant girl. Very tough and forthright. She clearly saw through our usage of Liu. I do not mean to insult Liu but she clearly gave herself away to Samantha.'

Interrogator 3: "You are seen to have superior intellectual skills. Must be the Chinese in you. But you have been observed as immature and given to anger and the lack of self-control. Perhaps you're not suited to espionage?"

Pei knew that interrogator 3 was a menacing man, heavyset and confrontational, eyes of fire.

Samantha: "If I won't make a good agent then I'll fly home and forget the past weeks. It's true that I cannot abide insulting, inane, and abusive people. In that regard I am a work in progress. But to know is the first step in victory over a part of oneself that needs training. But as I say, I'm prepared to leave here. However, I will only do so when Pei tells me that she agrees with someone like you."

Interrogator 3: "You see. You're angry right now. Out of control."

Samantha: "You and your false accusations can go straight to hell. Are you finished?" Samantha said heatedly.

Interrogator 1: "Please tell me of you home life? Your school? Your friends?"

Pei knew Interrogator 1 as the 'soft' one. Excellent at divining secrets. She spoke candidly of her father, Joseph, a man of great intellect but also one who was hypercritical and a drunk. He and her mother were at odds. The relationship was doomed. While she wished to get back to America she

261

did not wish to be with them. Her mother? Fine. Her father? No. Interrogator 1 was congratulatory of her candor about her mother, Jia, and her father Joseph.

Friends and contacts? She saw herself as a bit aloof, securing a few friends but if they were killed or moved she would not care very much. Other phenomena at the school? She mentioned a crazy type of girl, a cyclist, whom she admired from afar. She called her an alpha- girl. Samantha admired the way that she was true to herself. How she put down adversaries. Her name? Margaret Thode. She mentioned the two girls who gave themselves to witchcraft and were a cause of mayhem in the school. She spoke about how she wanted to transcend her environment and become important and successful. Interrogator 1 was, as usual, able to draw out, in elaborate detail, how Samantha saw her world and how she was prepared to go back for her last year at Rock Island High School.

Pei thought that she had a good sense of Samantha, only Samantha's flash anger worried her but she thought she could bleed it out of her when serious training was engaged in with her.

With all the reports in Pei decided to commit to her. She would be given every opportunity to excel and become one of the great spies of her time. She went back into her files from Sergei Malkin, trying to find a blueprint of success. It didn't take long to uncover how they planted Helen Murray deep into the English establishment. Much of Murray's success was still under top secret cover but she knew enough of it for Samantha's grooming process.

Two days before Samantha was to return to the USA, Pei met her in her office, ornate by Chinese standards, but impressive and studiously arranged. She could see that Samantha was overwhelmed, a girl who was made to be groomed.

After small talk and served tea Pei began, "I am convinced that you are part of our future. China needs you to succeed and I will be with you every step of the way. I have mapped out our road. You must adhere to it no matter how repellent you find it. Are you with me?"

"Yes, of course. But why were some of my interrogators this past week so obnoxious?"

Pei smiled. "That was their job. It all comes down to spycraft and its soulmate treachery. It was not personal except as a test. I would not be speaking with you now if you had failed."

"I see," Samantha said.

"At first what I will ask of you will not be easy and it may not make sense but you must follow my directions. I have directed State agencies to investigate certain conditions at your high school as well as students. At the end of your schooling we will have it that you are obliterated. Remembered but passed on as dead and lost. When you come back here next summer we will re-construct your existence. You will have a new name, a new birthplace, a new passport and you will eventually be placed in San Francisco. Your success there will be of your own diligence and skills and assisted by us. You will be a deep plant and it may take years for you to succeed. Do you follow?"

"Yes. Of course."

"We have studied closely the two girls who have become witches. They are unstable. Their futures are dim. We doubt that either of them will live to 25. They will be seen as fools, forgotten, lost teenagers who were doomed. I want you to be seen in the same way. Your disappearance back to here will be by freighter from California. The assumption about you is that you were killed because of your dangerous lifestyle. Being a witch will be a dramatic foil. Your mother will be told a few details. She is a devoted communist. She will understand. Your father will not be told of anything. He has become a lost cause to us because of his drug issues with alcohol. We must keep him in the dark."

"Me? A witch? Those two asses?"

"Yes. This is your first of many missions. Can you do it?"

"I will do whatever is necessary."

"From here on in you will find us by your side. But remember one thing Samantha, your temper! Keep it under control!"

CHAPTER 48

When Samantha flew back to the United States she was confused but also jubilant. She felt that she was in the hands of a greater authority that could interfere on her behalf if she ran into trouble. She was also excited about her mother's continued support. Her confusion was simple enough as her destiny as an agent for the People's Republic would always be a work in progress.

Her next to last day in Beijing was odd but fun. She was given a Vespa and taught how to drive it. When that was mastered she was instructed on a variety of techniques, parking, braking, turning, twisting, 360s and so on. She fell in love with the Vespa.

Picked up at O'Hare Airport in Chicago by her mother Jia, they drove back to Rock Island via the East-West toll road, two hours and 45 minutes westward. On the driveway to her house Jia paused before opening the garage door. She told Samantha that her father and she were separated. Joseph had taken a job at De Paul University in Chicago. He had already moved. There was a letter on the kitchen counter for her. Samantha took the news calmly if not joyfully. She felt that her father would be an encumbrance to her future.

Jia now opened the garage door. Samantha was overwhelmed with joy. In the space allotted to a second car there was a light green Vespa. Her mother's smile was lit with joy. When she jumped out of the car she ran to the Vespa. It was brand new. There was a card on the seat, her name written in Chinese script. She opened it and read a message off a small card, 'Samantha, ride, enjoy and stay safe.' It was signed by Pei.

She reported to her mother about the six weeks, her love and respect for Pei, and her buy-in to becoming a sleeper agent for China. Jia went over to her and they hugged, now companions in espionage.

Samantha's first mission was to make an effort to join the witches for whom she had no respect. Of the two she thought it best to approach Maureen Blong whom she perceived as an out and out drug addict. Angela Diaz was menacing besides being into heavy drugs. She parked her Vespa near Maureen's house. It was early August, Maureen sat on her porch, a beer in one hand. She was alone. Her neighborhood was shabby, her house was surrounded by grass uncut for weeks, a small dog was chained to a post. She yelled to Maureen, "Hey! Can I come up to talk?"

Maureen looked her up and down before saying, "It's a free country. What do *you* want?"

"I want to join you."

"A Jap? You gotta be kidding me."

"I'm half Chinese and half American white. I'm no Jap."

"Whatever," she said with practiced surliness.

"How do I do this? I'm tired of all the crap at Rocky, tired of my mother, tired of everything in this weird society. I want to be free like the two of you."

Maureen creased her eyes and went into deep thought. Samantha figured that the drugged up bitch didn't have any idea what to do. But she thought that one more witch would be a welcome addition to her.

"That'd be something," Blong said.

"What?" Samantha asked.

"A white, a spic, and a chink! I'll talk with Angela. There'd have to be an initiation. But we'll see."

Three days later, walking back home from pre-registration for her senior year she felt the presence of company, turning around she saw the two witches in full garb, odd smiles on their faces. Diaz said, "You wanna talk bitch?"

Samantha was repulsed by the two. From her martial arts training in China she knew that she could beat the hell out of both of them, but she stayed herself. "Yes. I do. I need to be taught your methods," she smiled within herself, she enjoyed the duplicity she was showing the two misfits.

In the next two days they performed their initiation rites. It included a sharp knife, the exchange of blood between them, the muttering of some unintelligible chants and the sacrifice of some scrawny cat that was placed on a stone in the old cemetery on Rockingham Road in the west end of Davenport. It was gutted by Diaz. To Samantha it was total bullshit. They instructed her in wearing a black garb that Maureen had fashioned into an outfit pretty masterfully. Her makeup was placed on her gently for such a witch of vicious looks, Angela Diaz.

On the first day of classes she zipped into the student parking lot on her Vespa. She had turned sharply near a group of boys who whistled and guffawed at her as she strode forth in her witch garb. She hurled curses at them. If one of them tried to attack her she was prepared to break an arm or a jaw. Secretly, although she felt embarrassed at this act, she also felt exhilarated as she was now fulfilling one of, she hoped, a long line of requests for the People's Republic.

The charade went on for two months before the administrative authorities at the school stepped in and started to issue warnings and penalties. Curses in the hallways, shrieks in classrooms were simply not allowed.

Vice Principal Fullbright had her into his office. "What's this about Samantha?" he asked kindly. He was a nice man but her acts of belligerence didn't allow for truth or candor. She played it tough with him. He kept shaking his head in disbelief that she, a super-talented student, could become so obnoxious, pairing herself with such a twosome. He required that she meet with a counselor named Hilda.

In Hilda's office she was surprised by how sharp the woman was. Her questions were knowledgeable and penetrating. It was good that Samantha had prepared her defenses against this prying woman.

In the meantime, she had once again run across Margaret Thode, an odd girl who stood up to her tormentors with the strength of a knight. She'd see her constantly biking her way around town in Illinois or Iowa as she went across the Centennial Bridge or the Arsenal Bridge into Iowa. She was tall, pretty, self-assured and she had heard about her scholastic abilities a year ago from an admiring teacher.

She experienced strange feelings toward Margaret. She was an alpha female. One day she observed her stop her bike and confront Angela Diaz who was taunting and cursing her. She heard her say to Diaz, who backed away from her,

"Hey sister. I don't want anymore shit from you." Samantha was embarrassed at that moment to be near Diaz. Margaret Thode was serious business and Samantha began to realize that secretly, very secretly, she was falling in love with her. This was a woman!

CHAPTER 49

Forrest Graham was upset. His older sister, Stephanie, had written to him, a private letter to his residence in Georgetown. Communications between the two of them were guided by CIA guidelines for an officer as high up as he. Her letter was short. A call would be appreciated upon receipt of her letter. No more was said. It was not a good sign. There was a trip wire in the communication. Something was amiss in the Quad Cities. A potential scandal for the family? His brother, Edgar, the alcoholic?

He asked his wife to secure a throwaway at the local Walmart. She knew the score. Scandals of any sort were to be squelched at the outstart. The agency had enemies all through Washington, D.C. Adversaries thrived on any scandal that could in any way damage the CIA. A high position such as he had was a primary target. Stephanie's letter was sensitive to all the nuances of his job.

Wife back with the throwaway he drove his wife's car in a zigzag way across the Potomac and eventually found himself in Virginia where he pulled into the driveway of a safe house known only to three men, *his men*, in the entire agency. He dialed Stephanie, she picked up immediately.

"Steph. Got your letter. What's up?"

"I've been approached by a guy named Bertrand McAbee, the PI referred to in the article I sent about Agatha Pruitt. Looking into the Thode case too, apparently."

"Go ahead" he said sharply.

"He wants to speak with you. He thinks you might know something."

"How'd he find you?"

"Age of Google. Come on Forrest."

"What did you tell him?" he asked edgily.

"I wanted to tell him to go to hell but something told me that was unwise. He wasn't pushy or anything but I didn't want to lock horns with him. It would be absurd for me to tell him you know nothing. You got that right?"

"Yeah. The reality is that I can't help. Agatha Pruitt I barely remember her."

"I get the feeling that she was not his primary concern. I may be wrong. He doesn't show his cards. But he seems to be more into the Margaret Thode case. You remember her right? I kinda thought you had the hots for her? Yes?"

He paused for a bit. He was trying to figure out how this could carom. "He doesn't think I'm a suspect surely."

"Don't think so. Very calm. Very indirect. But he has his teeth into something. Maybe just a confirmation of a fact? You were very upset about the murder, I remember well."

"Who wasn't?" He felt unnerved about this coming back up after all these years.

"Look Forrest. You always say that you have to be above any possible scandal. I'm just passing this on to you under the protocols you established. Bottom line. He wants to speak with you. Of course, he has no power and you can send him a note that you have nothing to add to these events. I have his address and phone number. "Write this down." She recited the information. "Don't be so uptight for God's sake about everything."

"You don't know what it's like out here. A snake under every object around me. I'll call him now and get this out of my life. Take care Steph. By the way how's Edgar?"

"Drinking his way to the casket. I fear for his life. Don't give him a thought. You have enough on your plate."

They disconnected.

McAbee saw the identification, private caller. He wavered about answering it, tired of so many spam calls. It was 8:30 p.m., an atypical time for spam calls. He answered, "Yes?"

"McAbee?"

"Yes."

"This is Forrest Graham. You approached my sister?"

"Yes, yes. Thanks for calling. I have a few questions."

"Right off the top I barely knew Agatha Pruitt. Sorry about her murder but I can't help you."

"Of course. I thought as much. My issue is not she. I'm convinced that her murder connects back to Margaret Thode. Agatha had re-opened the unsolved case about Margaret's murder. She was on to something, I think. So I'm re-working Margaret Thode. Your name has come up. Not as a suspect, of course, but rather as a brilliant observer of your classmates."

"Please with the flattery McAbee. Doesn't work with me. My name? How so?"

"Process of elimination. Every time my firm eliminated potentials you'd never go away. Will you allow me to ask a few questions."

"Shoot."

"How do you remember Margaret Thode?"

"Beautiful spirit. Smart. Loner. Standoffish. Confrontational with some of the clowns in our class. Loved her pluck. Maybe gay, but I don't know that. Just a guess. I liked her but at a distance. She didn't invite positive attention but she did draw a lot of negatives. Intellectually, she was in the upper percentiles. That's about it. Really don't want my name mixed into this. I assume that you know of my position?"

"I do. Your take on her is pretty much what I've heard from others. However, I have another question for you, okay?"

"Go ahead," Graham said with a touch of impatience.

"I accessed her diary. Very little in it. But there was an incident. There were three girls in your class. Witches was the act. Remember?"

"Yes. Horrid girls. Could not believe they were not expelled as 80% of their time was spent on deviancy of one sort or another. Those two, then three, were obscene."

"Close to the end of her senior year there was an incident between Margaret and one of the witches. In the women's bathroom. One of the witches groped Margaret who in turn punched the witch. That led to a crying witch and a lost tooth."

"I remember this. Margaret was in tears. Classes had ended and the building was close to empty. She sat on a bench. I saw the tears. I went over to her and asked if I could help. First time I ever spoke to her. She told me what had happened. She was afraid as she had a scholarship for college. She wasn't hysterical but she was very shaken. I tried to console her. For a minute I thought that we connected. Then she got up, said thanks, and just ran out one of the doors. I tried to follow her but she was on her bike and gone. Big cyclist!"

"There were three witches. Angela Diaz, Maureen Blong, and Samantha Ogden."

"Diaz and Blong were into that act for at least two years. Ogden, as I recall, only did the witch thing for her senior year. Don't know what got into her. Brilliant and then she became a walking catastrophe. She was worse than Diaz and Blong. Her parents were Augustana profs. They bought her a Vespa. Sometimes she carried a broom behind her. Scary. I think she was channeling the bad witch from the *Wizard of Oz*. Nothing good in her future."

"Do you know who groped Margaret by any chance?"

"Had to be Ogden, Chinese. Margaret was outspoken. Tough girl. One of the few I ever admired at Rocky. She was calling out a Chink bitch in her exasperation, that answer your question?"

"Yes."

"That's it for me McAbee."

CHAPTER 50

McAbee sat at Biaggi's Restaurant in Davenport. It was his first time there since the attack on him, weeks ago. He admitted to himself that he had a bit of trepidation in the parking lot even as it was still daylight. Alert and armed he was shown a booth at the back of the restaurant. He sat and waited for Augusta. As he looked around he noticed one of the guys who had saved him that night. The one who was hurt by his assailant. There weren't many people at 1:35 p.m. on a Wednesday afternoon. He was talking to another waiter. Bertrand waved at him. The waiter obviously didn't remember him from that night but he shrugged and came over to his table. He said, "This isn't my table sir. I'll get Katrina."

"No, no. That's not why I signaled to you. Do you remember that night a few weeks ago? You helped me when I was assaulted?"

"Oh. Of course. How can I forget? I'm still taking Advil for my shoulder. Are you okay? You took a few shots from the bastards."

"Yeah. I'm okay now. Took some time, though. I never really thanked you sufficiently. My friend was supposed to give you a reward. Did he?"

"Oh yeah, $200. He was really nice about things. Good man."

Bertrand was pleased with Sebastian for his generosity. "While you're here. Those two men who were out to get me. Did you notice anything about them?"

"Big bastards. I don't associate that largeness with Asians. For some reason I see them as small and quick. Movies probably. They were like cement bags."

This was a new piece of information. "Are you sure they were Asians? I recall the guy who warned me to stop an investigation that I was doing speaking without an accent." He caught himself in that inference. It was similar to the waiter's assumption about Asians.

"Absolutely sure. The masks didn't cover their eyes. It was dark but there was enough light. Nice seeing you. Tell your friend thanks for the money." He left.

Augusta came in a minute later "Sorry Bertrand. Last second call and the lights. Every one red. Forgive me Mistah?"

He was up by this time. They hugged. "Do I have a choice?" he whispered into her ear.

"Of course not. Just going through the motions with you," she laughed and they both sat.

They chatted about a few cases, her two daughters (both fine), and then they ordered a salad. Katrina, the waitress, was clearly surprised with the two of them. Reason? Bertrand thought to himself, who knew?

He told her about the revelation reported to him a few minutes ago.

"Asian? That's interesting. Very curious. I don't associate those activities to them. And why would they have any interest in your work? Odd. Not that many Asians in the Quad Cities. Never heard of them on a for hire basis to beat up someone. What's your take on it?"

"I'm very touchy about one piece relative to the Margaret Thode murder."

"What's that?"

"I'm hesitant to bring it up. Pretty far out. Remember I told you about the three witches?"

"Yeah?"

"One of them, Samantha Ogden, was half Chinese. Parents both profs at Augustana. Her mother was a naturalized citizen. Bright parents, ran their Asian Studies Program. Their daughter joined the other two witches in her senior year. Apparently she was off the wall. Worse than the original two who were themselves wild."

"Big reach Bertrand."

"I know. I keep hitting dead ends. So any sort of oddity draws me out."

"Ogden was the one who fell off the grid? Barry have any ideas?"

"No. He thinks that I should have a drink with Concannon and we should commiserate with each other. He is of the opinion that Ogden, weird as she was, probably got herself killed somewhere. Poof – gone. But I'm skeptical. Barry who always tells me that I'm lucky, metaphysical, poetical," he was smiling, "he then resorts to an explanation that is purely speculative, that is metaphysical in his world. A pure piece of guesswork because he has hit a wall about Ogden. The other day I had him run a check on the Vespa that Samantha Ogden used in her senior year. It took him a full day of grunts and head shaking but he ran it down in

Illinois vehicular records. You'd think that if she was hitting the road for some crazy run at self-destruction she'd keep the Vespa. It ended up in Chicago. Address in their Chinatown. Some guy name Wu. Then it just disappears from Illinois. Maybe it was sold in Indiana or Missouri but that Vespa is gone from any records."

"Sounds like you're reaching a bit. A straw?"

"I know. But Augusta I feel there's a hand here. An agency that is behind the scenes. I need a piece of luck."

CHAPTER 51

Jia called the school nurse at Augustana. "My daughter has lost an eye tooth. An accident. Does the school typically use a dentist? She needs treatment immediately."

"Not on hire but we have good connections with Dr. Martin Sedge. He treats our students pretty regularly. Football, basketball, fights in dorms. He's quite good. Practices just a few blocks from the campus. Let me give you his phone number." She did so and was thanked by Jia.

Sedge's receptionist, when told by Jia that she was an Augustana faculty member, scheduled in Samantha at 4:30 p.m. that day.

Samantha was in her room when Jia went to inform her of the appointment. She had a wet towel full of ice directed at her left jaw. She was still sobbing. Jia had not seen that in her daughter for ages. When asked, she refused to talk. Her witch's garb was thrown across the bed. She had put on a pair of jeans and an old sweatshirt. Jia was full of curiosity but she knew that when Samantha said no that was the end of any talk, that fierce side of her kicking in.

Dr. Sedge wore thick glasses, his eyes a deep brown. He had a gentle look to him as he spoke in a calm way through a set of white-washed teeth, a too large mustache, and a pair of ears that could fit a small elephant, Samantha thought meanly. Her tears had given way to red-hot fury that was devoted to Margaret Thode, the fucking Amazon who had gotten the best of her with a vicious punch that so shocked her that she became a whiny little girl.

"We'll have to take some x-rays Sam," he said.

Sam? Sam? She wanted to kick him in the balls the bastard. Sam! She breathed deeply and held her anger in check as three annoying x-rays were taken as she bit down on a hard piece of plastic that hurt the roof of her mouth and gum. She switched back to Margaret Thode and mulled over all of the happenings that caused her to grope the bitch that she recently lusted for, but that would be difficult to ever admit. She adored the way Thode asserted her independence and toughness with the asses who assailed her at every turn. Even that one-armed bastard, Smalley, was unsure of himself around her. Samantha noticed his body language, the tell, that Smalley exhibited as he tugged at his earlobe. He covered it up but Samantha saw through him and that gang of weirdos that he hung around with.

But she also saw on a few occasions Thode hanging around with that geeky Agatha Pruitt. They touched each other when they said goodbye in the parking lot. They looked at each other with knowing gazes. She concluded that they were lovers quickly enough. But why would Margaret Thode even look at Pruitt, a heavyset, plain-faced slob? Had to be brains. Pruitt was smart.

Then she observed that Thode had acquired a bracelet that she was fond of rattling around on her wrist. Probably from Agatha. Who knew? But she seethed in her jealousy fighting desires in herself toward Margaret Thode. She wanted to give her a love token, a necklace, a bracelet, anything. Beneath the witch's shrieks and curses, an act put on by her for the People's Republic, she desired to court Margaret whose every movement she observed with a kind of awe. She had rarely desired another female and parts of her were confused, ashamed, worried about the puritanical People's Republic and the suppression of lesbianism. But these concerns were quickly extinguished by the flames of lust that burned in her.

She had seen how Margaret had treated witch Diaz who had come at her in her usual vile way. But had Samantha not noticed a kindly look at her by Margaret? Another coal added to the fire.

"Okay Sam, we've got a real problem here. Car door? Punch? Are you hanging out with a bad guy?" Sedge asked with a smirk.

It was hard for her to speak. He had placed a wad of cotton in her mouth. She knew that she was still bleeding as the taste of her blood curdled her stomach. She had to keep herself under control with this fool of a dentist. "No. Accident."

"Whatever," he said skeptically. "I want to let this heal for a few days. You still have a bit of tooth in the gum. I'll have to pull it and then we'll talk about what to do. You're very beautiful. How do we restore that look?" He touched her arm but his hand stayed too long, it moved a few inches very gently down her forearm.

Pei came into her mind, now. Her talk about controlling her anger and how the inability to do so could cost her in the real world of espionage. Irretrievable mistakes that destroyed the lives of many agents. She gripped the sides of the chair and held herself in control of the white-hot rage that was in her heart toward the dentist and Margaret Thode.

Out of Sedge's office she was driven home by her mother, Jia, who was still in the dark as to the episode that led to this disgraceful day. She would have to concoct a story that would satisfy her mother's intelligence when she reported back to Pei in Beijing as Jia was required to do to satisfy them. As she thought through all of this her anger never subsided. What Margaret had done was not only an assault on her but it was an assault on China by the arrogant American.

However, her confusions maintained. She was still in love with the bicycle-riding bitch.

She told her mother that a witch act at Rocky had costs to it as she knew. She drew a lot of hatred and finally a kid threw a punch at her and caught her off guard. She was so stunned and confused that she just left the school. It was closing anyway for the day. She would not report the incident. That was final.

It took three weeks for Sedge to complete his work. The loss of the eyetooth was put right as well as he could. The slimy bastard continued to touch her in ways that she knew were beyond professionalism. But she held in her anger. She understood Pei's concern about the dangers of her flash anger. Ultimately she would have to convince her and other Chinese authorities that she had brought it under control. Perhaps, once in a while on a mission, she would have to unleash it and have it serve her interests.

She continued to behave in her role as an irritating witch at the school. She was of mixed emotions when her act required her to support Diaz and Blong through howling in classes and in the halls. When confronted by students or staff she would hurl curses in some pseudo-witch speak. There were times when she observed fear in the eyes of some of them when they heard her crazed language, amazed at the stupidity and superstitiousness of those who bit on the falsity of her act.

But then there was Margaret Thode who gave her a knowing look of disdain, perhaps hatred. She rued the spontaneous grope that cost any future with her as a lover. She had read enough about the thin line between love and hate as she pictured a continuum with pure love on one axis and pure hate on the other with all other nuances on that line. She wrestled with her ambivalence, sometimes overwhelmed by love and its accelerant lust on the one hand and then harshly replaced by hate and, in her case, its accelerant shame and embarrassment at being kicked to the side of the road by this malignant whore, Margaret.

She vowed to herself not to leave the country until she could resolve, in some way, the contradictions that tore at her.

Were they not alike? Independent, bright, pretty, gay, and over and above any girls at Rocky. The consummation of their love would be an explosive in their future. At times her infatuation could have her thinking that she would disavow her oath to Pei. She and Margaret could set up house and be free forever.

When an alternate narrative took hold a whole new series of thoughts rankled her. Margaret was a vile, arrogant, vicious and violent bitch who was in love with her cheap bicycle and a profoundly ugly woman. She could not meet the standards of Samantha. A hateful distraction, a racist cow, seriously in need of a lesson that would permanently take her down.

And so it went back and forth in a mind that came dangerously close to losing its center.

CHAPTER 52

The report from Jia discouraged Pei. Even in her worst moments, she, with many sleepers blown, agents captured and the demoralizing failures that haunted her, did not expect this news from the USA.

Samantha was one of a kind. Her mother, Jia, had been tellingly circumspect about the tooth incident. She reported that the witch performance had its dangers as some students were extremely upset with Samantha's shenanigans. But it was being handled, a good dentist, and Samantha had come to grips with it, the price to pay was how it was perceived by both of them, Jia and Samantha. Pei, ever suspicious, was unable to get more information other than it was a conflict in a bathroom with a very violent woman. In fact, it was reported that Samantha handled the whole matter with aplomb. Aplomb, Samantha, a punch to the jaw – it did not compute.

Pei would have to debrief Samantha when she was brought over to China. She felt that something was missing in the report due to a mother's protective embrace.

Samantha, now in April of her senior year, pictured the missing tooth as a signal to move on and away from Blong and Diaz who were doubling down on their outlandish behaviors. This caused her to begin to separate from them. She would announce to them a doctor's appointment or issues with her mother. Their time together became irregular and the buzz that she once got from her odd behaviors wore off. She would maintain the disguise until the end of the semester in late May, however.

But Margaret Thode? Samantha seethed in anger as well as a sexual craving for her that expressed itself in violent sadistic fantasies. There was a score to be settled. Nevertheless her time for departure was coming. The Vespa, she was told by her mother, would be taken by a man named John Wu. An imaginary cash payment would be made. She had a few weeks to get her affairs in order. This same John Wu would drive her to Long Beach, California, where she would be concealed on a freighter returning to China. Samantha Ogden would never exist again. Jia knew this; Samantha was overjoyed to be in a greater scheme under a woman of remarkable skill, Pei. The table was being set but one matter needed resolution.

When school ended she tossed away her witch's garb. That phase of her life was over. John Wu called and said that he was coming to Rock Island to pick up the Vespa and execute a formal but pseudo contract. She had another week with her two-wheeled love.

She committed herself to her Margaret Thode obsession. Perhaps her return to normal dress, some makeup touches, some tight fitting jeans, an alluring pair of glasses and a frank discussion with Margaret would resolve the issue between them. It was to be the one remaining agenda for her.

She began her hunt of Margaret. It was comparatively easy to follow her, a no-match contest between a stodgy bicycle and a quick Vespa. On several occasions, she was close to cornering Margaret for the necessary conversation. Her desires increased as the hunt continued. To her dismay, at one point, she saw Agatha Pruitt and Margaret meet up on the levee in Rock Island. They walked, held hands and acted as though their love was as deep as the Mississippi River that adjoined the Rock Island bike path and trail that they traversed. Anger ripped through Samantha. She felt the familiar surge of rage and the trembling of her entire body as she secretly observed this offense against reason and love.

She was in torment and was simply unable to control the thoughts that flew through her at what felt like the speed of light. She feared that her time in China would be cursed by her failure to secure a closure for her out of control lust and its counterpart an out of control hate.

Her time before departing for China was running out. She knew that she had to press the issue with Margaret. And then the golden moment had come up like a needed number in a lottery. Her memory of the entire meeting with Margaret would be forever etched in her mind.

Toward evening in late spring Margaret had biked her way into Sunset Marina, near a path that ultimately worked its way into the Rock Island bike path and trailway. The sun was setting, the coming night had a slight chill. Margaret had turned on a small headlight and a flashing red light on the back fender of her bicycle. She had a small pair of earphones. She was probably listening to music.

On a straight stretch of the road that circled the marina she sped up her trailing Vespa and cut off Margaret with a sharp slant that caused Thode to brake and peel off onto the grass beside the road. "Hey! What the hell are you doing?" Margaret yelled heatedly.

Samantha, with practiced speed, was off her Vespa. She ran toward Margaret and said, "Margaret! I need to speak with you very badly. Please."

Margaret looked at Samantha with surprised eyes. She hoped that it was a look of interest but wasn't sure. "Aren't you one of those fucked up witches? Are you the one from the bathroom? Jesus woman! What do you want?"

"Please hear me out. The witch act is done with. I had to do that. Another story. Please talk with me." She noticed a grass area beyond the shrubs, up a bit. "Can we talk privately up there," she pointed to the grassy area.

Thode was looking her over as she had hoped. Her tight fitting jeans, a loose sweatshirt that was studiously chosen as an enticement, and her carefully put together makeup was in full view. Hopefully, an arrow of love would blast into Thode's heart.

Hesitantly, Margaret said, "Hey listen. I'm sorry about the punch. Nobody ever groped me before. You startled me. Let's just leave it there."

"Please speak with me," Samantha begged.

Margaret looked at her watch. Then she said, "Okay, what's this about?"

Samantha said, "Can we go up there? It's private. Maybe we should move our stuff more off the road?"

"Sure," Thode said stiffly.

Having done so they proceeded up the small slope. They stood facing each other. "Can we sit?" Samantha said softly into a complying but reluctant Margaret who did as asked.

Samantha, reflecting about the events years later, felt that she made a strategic mistake. Instead of advancing the topic slowly she plowed into her feelings full speed ahead. "I have watched you for my entire time at Rocky. You and your bike." She smiled but Margaret was stone-faced. "I have admired you for most of my time. From a distance, of course. You would never know how over the time I have come to adore you and your ways. This past year with my crazy witch act, yes I know it was crazy, I have simply fallen in love with you. I think about you all the time. I love you. I would do anything for you. I'm supposed to go back to China in a few days. I would give that up if we could be together." There it was, all out there, she thought.

Margaret Thode never moved, never nodded, never showed any indication that she heard the love laments of Samantha. Finally, Margaret said, "Forget it. You're right, I'm gay. On every account there is simply nothing there. I have no desire for you. I have a girlfriend. I'm taken," she said resolutely as she shook a silly, loose-fitting bracelet back and forth on her right wrist and stood up.

"Can't be so. Not with that ugly Agatha Pruitt. Are you kidding me? Are you sane?"

"Hey! Fuck you witch. You're a crazy bitch. I'm checking out of here. Get some therapy." She looked down at Samantha with an arrogant and hateful stare. "Chink cunt!" She turned to leave with her normal strut.

It was all too much for Samantha whose anger sizzled into full hate. A rock beside her hand urged her to act. She arose rapidly and in full stride smashed it into the back of Margaret's head. She went down on her knees, moaned a bit, and then the rock was smashed into her head in a staccato fashion. Now out of control Samantha turned her over and beat her face with the rock, again and again. She tore off her shirt and bra and beat at her breasts. Then her pants were removed, her panties and again a savage beating upon her genitalia. She found a stick, spread Margaret's unresponsive legs apart and slammed the stick into her vagina repeatedly. As she did so, she cried uncontrollably.

Then she withdrew a small penknife from her back pocket, opened the right hand of Margaret and very quickly, lightly, and crudely scratched the Mandarin symbol for unrequited on her palm. It was barely noticeable but it was important to Samantha to do so.

She ran to the Vespa and surveyed the scene. No one was there. She picked up Margaret's bicycle and hurled it into some bushes, but with enough presence to pull down the sleeves of her sweatshirt to cover her hands. No fingerprints. She jumped on her Vespa and, with too quick a start, drove away with a skid from her tires.

CHAPTER 53

Samantha was picked up in Shanghai then flown to Beijing. Pei gave her two days of freedom, an opportunity to get her legs under her. Pei had a driver pick her up and drive her to her headquarters. She made her wait for a half hour, all by design. Samantha was now in the possession of the Chinese government. Young recruits needed this reminder.

Pei recognized the weight loss. She had been notified by the freighter's captain that Samantha seemed to be fasting during the trip across the Pacific Ocean. She hugged her and welcomed her into service in the special bureau that she ran, a part of the ever-growing MSS of the Chinese government. They sat and the customary tea ceremony that Pei had particularized took place. As she gazed at Samantha she observed a small tic on her left eyelid. That was new. The girl was nervous about something.

"So tell me Samantha. A year has passed. Much has happened?"

"Ah. Yes. I'm glad to be here in my true homeland."

An interesting deflection, a concealment? "Tell me about your trip across the ocean?"

"Oh, it was fine. Everyone treated me very kindly. Did a lot of reading, kept to myself mainly."

"Food on those freighters is sometimes good. Yes?"

"Yes. Very good. Plenty," she looked down at her hands, the couch they sat upon allowing little concealment.

Pei realized that the session was going to be lengthy. She went to her desk and issued an order to her secretary. "Except for my 7:30 dinner cancel everything else. Reschedule." She went back to her seat, unsure which side of herself she would manifest to Samantha who had never seen the confrontational and abusive Pei. Her next few answers would dictate the course of the conversation. "You seem to have lost some weight?" Pei asked neutrally.

"Oh just a few pounds," she said again with defensiveness or was it evasiveness.

"You seem different to me?"

"No, just a bit worried I guess about what's to come."

"I see. More tea?"

"Oh no thanks."

"Your senior year at the high school?"

"Very difficult. Joining with those witches made things tricky. But the Vespa helped. Thanks for that."

Pei nodded and smiled. Samantha had become, what is the phrase, as 'quiet as a church mouse.' "Let us go through things. The school? Your good mother? The lost tooth? By the way may I see?"

She opened her mouth and pointed to the left side of her jaw. "It's temporary," she said with a half-hearted smile.

"Tell me about that incident. Very unexpected. Had to be traumatic for you?"

"Oh, a roughhouse girl. Big, strong, didn't like my witch act. She saw an opportunity while we were in the bathroom alone. She just slugged me."

"Um. Did you react? Fight back?"

"Well... I... was too shocked. By the time I registered it she was gone."

"Interesting. You held that temper of yours." Pei smiled, but insincerely. This was not the same girl from last summer. "Are you tired? Still adjusting?" she asked in a conciliatory way.

"No, no. I'm ready to proceed," she looked down at her curling hands.

"Samantha? You know this Bureau is a very special agency of the government. I need your full candor, full disclosure. I feel that you are incomplete to me. Hiding? Of course, that will not do. The Mao government had special rituals for forcing confessions and having people admit to their faults. Total honesty to the State. Warts and all. I personally do not adhere to those Maoist policies. Citizens would sometimes say anything to avoid disgrace and humiliation. Many times truth was sacrificed to satisfy the tormentors. *But*, the principle is necessary to maintain. Do you see? Truth must be told."

Samantha looked down amidst the very slightest of a blush. "Yes," she said almost in a whisper.

"I have run much interference with some of the authorities who were opposed to the use of an American. You owe me a debt Samantha, it can only be paid with absolute loyalty and honesty. I do not accept evasion; furthermore, you are not good at it. I will never accept lies and deceit from you. Do you need another day at the hotel to collect yourself or are you ready to tell me all? Even your worthy mother Jia had descended into concealment in my judgment. Something is awry and I demand the truth from you," she said with a practiced firmness showing a side of herself that many of her subordinates bowed to in fear. Her look fastened onto Samantha, unyielding and intense.

Samantha said nothing. Her hands commingling as if in a dance.

Pei pressed, "I had great plans for you. Still do if you meet my conditions. Otherwise, I will send you back to the U.S., you will be on your own *if* the authorities approve such. Otherwise there are special camps," she said in a suggestive way, a threat. The authorities that she spoke of were none other than herself alone. What was happening now was necessary. She either had to break her down or somehow dispose of her. So much was at stake with this rising or falling star in front of her.

"I feel that you are disappointed in me. I am so sorry about that. I admire you. Please do not dismiss me. Some things have occurred. Not good, dangerous. I have done things that you will see as indefensible."

Her hesitancies in speech and meekness gave Pei the opportunity to propel into her. "Tell me about the tooth. The whole truth. Not a repeat of what your mother reported," she demanded.

Samantha was silent for some time. Her fingers flew back and forth into each other, head down. Finally, she looked at Pei and burst into tears. Then the confession came concerning the groping incident with Margaret Thode, a complete story that Pei did not interrupt in the telling.

Pei said, "I am pleased but frankly surprised by your restraint when she hit you. But I understand the immediacy of the situation. You are a homosexual?" she asked nonchalantly.

"In this case, Margaret Thode only, I am. But I have yearnings for males too."

"Margaret Thode? Why this woman? What is it about her?" Pei asked.

"There are only two women I admire. Adore. One now, you. You see I murdered her," she said with a boldness that threw Pei off course. Murder?

Pei stood and went to a cabinet. She removed a bottle of Jack Daniels from the shelf and brought it over to the table that sat in front of the couch. She went back and studiously removed two glasses. She called her secretary and asked for ice. It was brought within a minute and laid on the table besides the bottle and glasses. The secretary retreated swiftly, as if she had done this before and did not desire to linger.

Pei said mildly, through a smile, "We will drink to your future and to your complete honesty."

Samantha was timid with the alcohol but Pei's sipping example forced her hand. She drank and her features relaxed.

"So you have much to tell me. I have cancelled my entire day. I need to hear all." And so it went for the next four hours. She insisted that Samantha repeat both stories about Margaret Thode, especially her murder and the violence that surrounded it. She dug deep into Samantha's final dishonor to Thode's murder, the penknife strokes on the victim's palm, unrequited.

It wasn't a work of art she said, crude, but there. Her signature to the murder, Samantha said coldly, her words now showing a bit of a slur. Her initial embarrassment passed away and there was a blossoming truculence and pride in her. Pei construed that she was making up for her passivity in the bathroom while also striking out at a love that was unattainable, unrequited.

At the end of the recitation, Pei invited her to lay down on the couch for a nap. The alcohol had done its job. She fell asleep. Pei watched her for some time asking herself what this alpha woman could possibly do in her service. Samantha was a dangerous mix of talent, volatility, and psychopathology.

When Samantha awakened at 3:55 p.m., Pei made her repeat her stories. More questions occurred as she recounted her experiences. By 6:30 p.m. she sent Samantha back to the hotel. More interrogations tomorrow. She would bring in a few trusted experts on cross-examination. Samantha would be stripped clean of every idea she had. At the end Pei would decide. She either would serve the homeland or she would be eradicated from this earth. There was no middle ground. Before leaving the office she called security and ordered a complete search of all materials on the internet surrounding the death of Margaret Thode.

CHAPTER 54

McAbee hated that a dead end sign fronted the road to a solution. Richard Pruitt's voice had an echo of despair all over it, sensing that Bertrand was in a stalemate. Barry Fisk was matter of fact, as usual, "no place to go." Jack Scholz, on some secret mission for the CIA, had said before his departure, "My missions shouldn't take long. Looks like you have a bummer with that Pruitt case." And most importantly, Augusta offered her help in what they both knew was half-hearted. She did call Concannon. He had nothing except the offer of a drink later that day. She declined.

Then the call from Hilda in Galva, Illinois. She said, "Did you hear about Stan?"

No hello from her, pure business and he instinctively knew what she was going to say. "Hilda. I haven't." he said.

"Stan died last night. The cops in Cambridge usually go by and give his place an eye. Blinds down this morning. Door wasn't locked. One of them steps in and Groucho goes after him. Snarling, ready to kill. Or so they say. They shot the poor dog and then found Stan, McAbee!" She started to cry. McAbee's heart ached. He shook his head in despair.

They talked for a bit. He wondered why Hilda called him. Didn't she have real friends, not McAbee whose interest in the two, she and Stan Fullbright, was essentially transactional. And Groucho – loyal to the end? He said, at the end of the call, that he'd attend the wake. Bitterly, she said there would be none. Stan had told her that he had a contract with a Cambridge mortician, cremation and no memorial service. He had hoped that his neighbor would take Groucho but he wasn't convinced he would. He had a feeler out for someone else, unnamed. He might help he hoped. She concluded the call, "McAbee I'm going to tie one on, this is bullshit!" She disconnected.

He wondered if he was the unnamed? He shook his head. It was going to be a lousy day. He went back to the Thode case recalling an admonition from Aquinas who warned that a small mistake at the beginning of an inquiry could lead to huge errors at the end of an inquiry. He went back to the entire file around Margaret's gruesome murder. Many pages were of no significance, already tagged by him with different colored post-it notes. He spent the entire day in his house laboring over the materials. What if anything, did Agatha Pruitt discover? Perhaps nothing. Maybe her murder was, after all, a break-in and had nothing to do with her inquiries into her lover's murder, but he thought better of it. He never had a serious case without deadends.

He looked again at the folder with the pictures from the murder scene. They were black and white computer print copies of the real photos held by the Rock Island Police Department. Their quality was poor to middling but he studied each photo. The brutality was repulsive. He agreed with Detective Abe Snider, this had to be personal, not a random act. But there were exceptions to every norm that the cops held. Agatha Pruitt surely studied these vague photos. To see a lover so brutalized had to be horrific for her. Some of the pictures were very general, taking in the position of the body relative to her surroundings. Some were very precise, almost microscopic, wounds, disfigurement and so on. The photographer took care. He was diligent, thorough. He noted Margaret's right hand, her palm specifically, obscured by some kind of symbol or picture covered partially by blood or mud or perhaps both. Her hand was splayed, maybe even stretched, reminding him of some of the crucifixion scenes from Renaissance painters. He removed a magnifying glass from his desk drawer. Something was etched into the palm. Probably just some blood splatter or mud he thought. But as he looked more closely it appeared to have a quality of artistry or at least, order. No other photo showed the palm. When night fell he put aside all the materials.

At midnight just as he went to sleep a fleeting dream woke him up, it was the memory of the palm with the splatters closing over a symbol if sorts.

The next morning he drove over to Rock Island. He entered the police headquarters. He went to the same secretary at the same desk with the same attitude, non-caring defiance, Diane Furey at her best. He asked for Hugh Concannon.

"And you are?" she asked with a studied look of false innocence. After she was told she hit a switch and typed in the name of McAbee.

The new system was noted by McAbee.

Suddenly the door flew open from the area where Concannon's office was located. Concannon came into the waiting area with speed, his expression intense. "What do you want McAbee?" He said loudly.

"A meeting in your office," Bertrand said neutrally.

Concannon looked him up and down before saying, "Come on back then."

Nothing had changed in his office. The only missing ingredient was Augusta who McAbee had not invited. She was a third rail between the two of them, a jolt for hostilities between the two of them now facing each other.

They both sat. Concannon asked, "Well?"

He wasn't as belligerent as normal, his tone a little softer, more open. "You know that I've been working the Agatha Pruitt murder backwards through Margaret Thode."

"I do and as I told you it's pretty damn stupid."

"I understand. I need something from you. I think that I have a thread. But I have to have access to a file, actually Margaret's crime scene pictures, the originals."

"Off limits. Why don't you just retire. You're in over your head," he hit the desktop with his open hand, accenting his opinion.

McAbee lowered his head as he tried to figure out the man who sat across from him, the unnecessary belligerence that seemed to pulse in his veins. "I purposefully did not ask Augusta to come over here. I'm talking to you man to man. By your own admission, you've dead-ended on the Agatha Pruitt case. Not surprised. You've told me that my approach to the Agatha Pruitt case was wrong-headed. I've done a lot of work on the Margaret Thode case. I still think it's the key and now I need something from you. I work for Richard Pruitt. I don't need any credit if it comes to be that I'm right. I have this one favor. If I'm correct I think that both cases can be broken in one shot. You have nothing to lose, except maybe some pride, but a lot to gain. Breaking these cases would be a jewel in your crown of success as a detective."

"Tell me what you have. I'll check," he said, hand to his chin, receptive, perhaps.

"No. Not going to happen," Bertrand said firmly.

"Hah! Let's go at it this way. What exactly do you want with those original pictures?"

"What I want you already have. You've had it for years."

"You're fixated on Thode. I already looked at all of those materials. Nothing there."

"And maybe you're right. Let me check something."

"What do you want?" Concannon asked in a way that suggested that he was forcing McAbee to concede his interest in something that he could then discover.

"I want to study all of the original pictures that were taken at the Margaret Thode murder scene. Nothing more, nothing less. I can view them right here. Won't take anything."

"What something?" he asked again in a measuring way.

"If I find something there's still much work to do. But I promise that I'll let you in. It will be your solution, your solved case. I'm only interested in taking care of Dr. Pruitt, my client."

"Those pictures are off-limits. Very private and very difficult to view. The only thing that you have going for you McAbee is that Augusta speaks highly of you. I don't trust you enough to throw you. But she does."

Bertrand was tired. Concannon was an obstacle who might never concede. He didn't know any way around him.

Perhaps some later effort by Augusta might open it up but he doubted it as it would always revert back to McAbee himself. He started to push away from Concannon's desk. Perhaps Barry could pull up something in the dim printouts. Agatha, after all, did something to that effect, he conjectured.

"No, wait. I need to break this case. As long as you understand, it's my case. I'll get them out of records. But if you cross me McAbee I'll get you back. Understand?"

"We understand each other," McAbee said as gracefully as he could.

Twenty minutes later McAbee was in a different place, he knew that it was an interrogation room. There were three cameras all aimed at a square table that had four seats around it. Behind him was a picture window. He assumed that it was a two way. He was most likely being watched. There were two large folders. One was heavy. He opened it and he found the original 8 by 11 pictures of the murder scene. He slowly looked through them. Their austere and sharp quality, in contrast to the computer printouts, was stark and augmented the violence suffered by Margaret Thode. He searched for the one picture that showed the splayed hand. Indeed, there was some sort of character on her hand but it was submerged by blood and probably some mud, also a touch of green on her finger tips, maybe grass stains. He took out his iPhone and took three pictures, the last a close-up of the characterization on the hand, still hard to see clearly or interpret. All of the pictures were in the exact order as he found in the hacked file, but these originals had extraordinary clarity.

The other folder, not in the official file for reasons unknown, were photos of the body of Margaret, washed down for an autopsy. In their own way, these pictures were even more revolting than the ones at the murder scene. A steel table held the lifeless body of a woman who had suffered outrageous injuries. He looked closely for a clean and full picture of the right hand. It was only a partial, her hand half-turned, never in the fully splayed position. He saw approximately half of, was it a symbol? A tattoo? What he could see was clear, though. He again took three pictures on his iPhone.

If he was being observed or merely threatened by such he had no idea. In an effort at subterfuge, he took 21 more pictures, random shots. He very carefully placed the pictures back into the folders. Was it possible that he was not observed? He didn't know and as he left the building, having said thanks to Concannon, no indication of such was mentioned. He probably hadn't been was his surmise.

CHAPTER 55

At his office, Bertrand forwarded the pictures from his phone pertaining to the symbol on Margaret's hand to Barry Fisk. Immediately after sending them he called Barry to get the usual 'hmpfh.' "You get those pics I sent?"

"Just came across. What in God's name am I looking at?"

"Margaret Thode's hand. Look closely. There's a symbol there. See it? The palm."

"You know you're not the only person I work for. Maybe you could have asked me if I'm busy," he said acidly.

McAbee breathed deeply, careful not to say anything he'd regret. He held his silence hoping that Fisk would shake the grievance demons off his shoulders.

"Okay, let me look. I'm going to enlarge these two pictures. Well, they're not just random scratches. Let me see... Asian. I'm not familiar with the symbols in those languages. Where'd you get these from? They weren't in the file."

"You're right about the second one, on the autopsy table. Not in the file we had. The first one was. But it was of poor quality, a printer copy, what to me is clearly a symbol was overlooked because of the blood, mud and the poor quality of the transmitted files of the pictures taken at the scene. But these pictures in the original shots are clear, and even though they seem to be quick slashes they have reason behind them. Order. A mind at work. I think that Agatha Pruitt may have seen what was there in the hacked file, even off her printer. She could never access the original photos."

"Well, on the clear ones you just sent, yes. But if she picked that up from the blurry transmission, I bow to her. I would make her a partner. Am I free to isolate just the symbol and send them to a friend of mine who is Chinese and lives on the web? I'll call you back as soon as possible," Barry said with undisguised enthusiasm. "I can get the meaning on a translation site but there may be more to it."

The call came back about ten minutes later. "Yes Barry?"

"This is a big deal Bertrand. It's Chinese – the symbol for unrequited. He was as sure as sure can be. Where are you going with this?"

"I have to think about it but right off I have a connection between Margaret Thode and one of the witches, Samantha Ogden. Ogden may be dead as you suggested as the witches seemed to be heading to a doomed life. But the first thing is this. The symbol? Other murders? Has it ever shown up on other crime scenes? Can you get to work on that? The thing about Ogden is that she was a stellar student from an academic family. Maybe she caught herself from the inevitable fall that was awaiting her. There's more to her than there was for Blong and Diaz. For all we know she's still alive."

"Doubt it but who knows?" Barry said. "I'll start on it right away. Oh and Bertrand, congratulations on this."

Bertrand, surprised by a compliment from Fisk, sat and tried to put together possible scenarios. Unfortunately, he was on a road full of speculation and gaps if he tried to tie things back to Samantha Ogden.

Augusta stopped by and sat. She was happy. She said, "Great news. I finally got that crook at Midwest Energy. Been on her trail for four months," she looked at him. "Oh, oh. You're thinking. I've seen those signs before. What's up?"

He brought her up to the present including his meeting with Hugh Concannon. Her lips formed a whistle when she heard that he cooperated with Bertrand. "Perfect! You must have won him over with your charm," she said with a winced smile.

"I don't know what exactly caused this alliance. But my guess is that he feared your eventual presence if he didn't help me. But I did tell him he'd get the credit."

"Every once in a while Hugh can turn on a dime. By promising him credit, you became a dime. This is like coming out of a thick forest onto an open vista. There are possibilities all of a sudden about the case."

"I think that I have to test the hypothesis that Samantha Ogden is alive and possibly the killer of Margaret Thode."

"What can I do?"

"Samantha's mother is still alive. She's living in the Good Grace home in Moline. Barry said that she had some dementia."

"How did he come by that Bertrand?"

"Don't know. Don't care either," he said staring at Augusta. They both knew it had been a hack. Her question wasn't necessary in his view.

"Her name is Jia Ogden. I have a feeling that you could break through to her better than I could. You up to it?"

"Absolutely. I'm free this afternoon. I'll go over there. Let's just review what you want me to go after."

"It's all about Samantha, her daughter. Whatever you can pry from her. If you can, take advantage of her dementia. That's fine with me."

"Bertrand! You're getting closer and closer to Jack Scholz," she said with a bit of irritation.

"Murder is the issue here Augusta. Gloves off!"

Augusta drove across the I-74 bridge connecting Bettendorf to Moline. She proceeded on River Road that paralleled the Mississippi River. The waters were choppy, a thunder storm was predicted. She turned right and headed up the bluffs until she came to 11th Avenue. Good Grace was a relatively small complex, maybe 15 units each on two floors of an aging red brick building. She thought that perhaps it was a converted school. She entered into the lobby. There was a girl at a reception desk. She looked to be in her early teens. She was small, arms as thin as pencils. The badge on a thin white blouse said 'Sara.'

"Can I help you?"

"Yes, you could Sara. My name is Augusta Satin. I'm a licensed investigator in Illinois. I need some clarifications from one of your residents. Won't be long but I'd like to spend a few minutes with her *alone*."

"Oh. I know some of the residents. Name?"

"Yes. Dr. Jia Ogden. Used to teach at Augustana."

"I do know her. If you sign the register," she pointed to a large black ledger-type book on the right side of her desk. "I can see if she's up to it. And oh, not alone, I have to be present."

"Are you the boss around here?" Augusta asked pleasantly.

"Well, kinda. My mother owns the place. She's in Davenport for the day. So I'm in charge. It's assisted care only. The residents are in pretty good shape. No heavy cases here. Couldn't handle them. Our census is at 27. We have three units open."

"What do you do when they need more intensive care?"

"We get them transferred of course," she said with a touch of pique. "I'll get her for you. Just sit over there." She pointed to three chairs in front of which was a small coffee table with a newspaper and a few dog-eared magazines. The insides of the place matched the outside, aged. It had a sullen quality to it.

Jia, in a wheelchair, was rolled out in front of Augusta. She was very small, curled up into herself. Her short hair was fully white. Her Chinese features were augmented by her age, she had a determination around her small mouth and jaw. Her voice was reedy. "I'm sorry, happy to see old students. You look familiar." She was visually impaired, her eyes in studied squint. "Your name again?"

Augusta took this as a sign that she must resemble a past student. "My name is Augusta," she said carefully.

"Ah yes. I remember you well. How are you?"

Jia was confused; however, Augusta would not bite and try to enlighten her. "It's great to see you. So many years." She felt dirty, the PI business had a very bad side to it. "I was reminiscing about Rock Island High School. Your daughter Samantha? How's she?" The pause was agonizing. Augusta feared that she lost her.

Jia's body went into an even deeper curl. "My daughter!" she said in a despairing, yelling way, loud, for her at any rate.

Augusta said nothing, looking at Sara who seemed occupied with something on her computer.

"Gone with the wind!" Again a prolonged silence. "They took her and never gave her back!" Jia shouted.

After a wait from hell, Augusta said very gently, "They?"

"Pei Chén, Pei Chén, China!" It was then that she started to cry, her thin shoulders rocking back and forth.

Sara came over. "Are you okay Jia?" She, now appearing to be 17 rather than 12, "I want you to go. Whatever you wanted to know has upset her."

Augusta, forever suave, said, "I can see that. I'm so sorry."

Her last observation before leaving the building was the continuing wail of Jia and the consoling arms of Sara.

CHAPTER 56

As soon as Bertrand heard what had been said to Augusta by Jia Ogden he felt the heavy clouds that had concealed any progress began to shift, lifting. He called Barry Fisk, knowing that twice in one day was courting howls of protest. He was surprised.

"Bertrand, I might have something. Need some more time. Anything new?" he said excitedly.

"There is. But first I need to know more about this Chinese guy you're working with."

"Hong Kong resident. I call him Chou Chou. Fled when the mainland took over. He's now in London. Lots of Hong Kongers went there when the Communists subjugated Hong Kong. Why?"

"I have to know how secure he is. His position on the Chinese Republic?"

"Hates the bastards. Spends half his time trying to disrupt them."

"So," Bertrand persisted, "he can be trusted?"

"Have my word. What's up?"

Bertrand revealed to him Augusta's experience with Jia whose fury about her missing daughter and China also led to the revelation of a name. A longshot but perhaps the Hong Konger could try his luck. Augusta wrote it out as Pay Shen; however, she conceded that her spelling was probably wrong.

Barry was clearly pleased, an enthusiasm so rare for him. McAbee was, in turn, complimentary to Barry. They disconnected.

He called Jack Scholz who came on the line through an undercurrent of deep rumble. "Jack?"

"Yeah. Bertrand, I'm flying back from a mission. I'll be in Iowa tomorrow."

"Good. We'll call. We need a stroll."

"Got it." He disconnected.

On the spur of the moment he drove to Galva, Illinois, to visit with Hilda. There was still daylight in the town but it was disappearing rapidly. He hadn't called ahead.

She answered her door. McAbee immediately knew that he had sent a shock through her. Her bathrobe was loose-fitting, it fell open and exposed more than both of them wished. She reached up and touched her hair that was hopelessly tangled. Her eyes were laced with crimson crisscrosses and dried tears hung around her eyes like drying rain.

"Hilda," he said gently.

A cascade of tears fell from her eyes as she reached out and hugged McAbee. He just stood there, a receptor of grief for this woman who was full of spirit days ago. She took his hand and led him into her darkened house. They sat in her living room, a candle the only light, a bottle of Jim Beam and a glass was visible on the table beside her lounger.

"Told you I was going to tie one on. But I stopped drinking a few hours ago, napped, and threw up. Can't take old Jim Beam like I used to."

"I came to tell you personally how sad I am about Stan. He was a very gracious man. Classy."

"That and more," she said. "Can't believe what happened to Groucho," she said softly and another torrent of tears came from her. "You know McAbee. We were an item for about ten years back. I really loved him but he had his ways. So did I. We just couldn't foresee how it'd work. We just faded from each other. But, in a strange way, our love became deeper. I don't know how I'll fend without him. I appreciate your coming. I have some chocolate chip cookies in the freezer. Want some?"

Quickly, without his usual self-parsimony and stubbornness he said, "Two would be great."

He observed that Hilda not only moved unsteadily, probably due to the alcohol, but also her heavyset frame encumbered her. She brought the cookies and a napkin and handed them to McAbee who bit into the hard cookie. It was tasty to him. He'd remember the freezer when next he came into cookies in the course of his job.

They chatted about Stan Fullbright, Hilda too, as McAbee saw the grief lifting from her a bit.

Very gradually and indirectly, he brought his investigation into the conversation. Carefully editing he told her about Samantha and the puzzles left behind by her. He asked for any ideas she might have, any approaches recommended. He mentioned that Stan had thought Samantha started to show behaviors that were taking her away from Diaz and Blong.

"The last few weeks of a senior year are always hectic. I can't tell you I noticed any changes in her. But I do recall that she was alone a lot. Puzzled, her expression, like she was awaiting Jesus to come. Odd girl. Brilliant but a little off-center. Beautiful in an odd way. Stand-offish. Some of the faculty were a bit scared of her. Something lurking under there even before she actualized it by becoming a witch. Maybe a bit of a psycho."

"Did she speak Chinese? Would you know by any chance?"

"Oh for sure. Her parents were at Augie. Professors. Oriental Studies or something like that. I heard her over a pay phone outside the building. She was full speed into Chinese."

"Anyone know her. A friend?"

"Not that I remember. She did hang around with those other two witches. I don't know if that's friendship or porcupine love," she smiled for the first time from his entrance.

"Anything else?"

"Nah. Listen Bertrand I want to be by myself. Nothing personal. Thanks again for coming by. I have your card. I assume that Samantha is a target?"

"Kind of. Interesting girl for sure."

On his way back he ate the other cookie. All the arrows that had been shot out willy-nilly on this case were now becoming much more in line and focused.

CHAPTER 57

Bertrand did not appreciate calls at 5:50 a.m. He was still dealing, in a dream, with Hilda, Stan, and Groucho. "Yeah?" he said sleepily.

"It's me Barry. Sorry to wake you up. Do you want me to call later?" he said with studied innocence, knowing damn well that a call from him so early in the morning would set off an alarm in Bertrand.

McAbee sat up. "Give me a minute." He took a pad and pen from his side table, took several deep breaths and said, "Go ahead Barry."

"You think you're tired! I've been at this for 14 straight hours," accusatory as always, "and it's on your bill."

Just what I need thought Bertrand. "Barry. I get it. No argument, what's up?" If Barry kept pushing, McAbee would explode on him. He didn't.

"I have some extraordinary news. Two fronts. First, I have been on the databases of the FBI. Easier to hack into and more forthcoming than in the old days. I still had to finesse their systems. There have been three murders over the years where the symbol for unrequited was etched into the right palm of a murder victim, 1991, 2002, and 2013.

All women. San Diego, D.C., and New Orleans. Each with precision. Not like Margaret Thode, but perhaps that was the beginning, hurried, awkward. I think that Samantha Ogden is very likely alive. Can't be positive, of course."

Bertrand was processing the information as he went to his kitchen and started his espresso machine. Quickly, he wrote down the data given to him by Barry. He was feeling the adrenaline flowing into him. Yes, nothing was definitive but the lights were flashing green. "I suppose you don't have pictures of the unrequited symbol?"

"No. Just agent descriptions. It's considered to be a serial set of murders. Thus the FBI. But don't despair, I think that I can get into the files. Need more time on that."

"Anything else in the files?"

"Oh yeah! Sex crimes. The victims were mutilated in ways very similar to Thode. Very personal, very vindictive. *Unrestrained* was a term used at Quantico. The profilers, yes, they're still in business despite the woke nonsense, believe it to be a female murderer and no they have not linked the three murders back to Margaret and Rock Island."

"Great work Barry. Any way to tie a person to the specific places and years?"

"Sure. I was just hoping the stiffs at the FBI would use their super computers to do it. If they did connect they didn't indicate or they had no luck. My trust in them is very thin as you know. But I have some leads to pursue. This isn't the big news Bertrand."

"Oh?"

"You better believe it. So I've been in touch with Chou Chou. That's not his name by the way."

"Oh, really Barry. I would never have known," Bertrand said now armed with his espresso and lurching into mild sarcasm.

"Ha ha. You're really funny Bertrand. Don't distract me. So, Chou Chou takes the name given to you by Satin and he freaks out at the spelling. Augusta could use some instructions in fundamental Chinese for God's sake."

Bertrand wanted to instantly come to her defense but restrained himself from taking on Barry's backbiting ways.

"Anyway," Barry continued, "Chou Chou went ballistic at stupid Americans."

"I hope that you defended your colleague," Bertrand said with a touch of temper.

"Of course not, he's right. The first thing he did was to change the spelling from PAY to PEI, Chinese 101. Then SHEN to CHÉN, Chinese 201. Get it?"

"By the way, Barry, why didn't you change the spelling if it was so wrong?"

Barry hesitated, perhaps taken off guard. "Well, no. Had to use what I was given. Can't change the presented data," he said defensively.

"That the logic they taught you at Yale? Ph.D. to get to that level of sophistication," Bertrand now angry at the dismissal of Augusta's superb work and the smugness of Barry.

"Do you want to hear this or not? By the way we owe Chou Chou some consultant money."

"Please, continue."

"Here's the deal. Each name in itself is not uncommon. Pei and Chén. But the combination narrows things, obviously. So Chou Chou starts delving. He's looking at the famous Pei Chén as a most likely candidate as he patrols the other Pei Chéns. Yet he keeps coming back to the famous Pei. To make a long story short, given what I've transmitted to him, he lands on *the* Pei Chén."

"Go on, you say the famous. What's that about?"

"I hope that you're sitting. Pei Chén is the head of a Bureau in the MSS. The MSS is their CIA and FBI combined. Specifically she runs a unit totally dedicated to foreign espionage. Chou Chou worms his way into their systems as much as he could. There's a black wall that he can't climb totally but he got over it half way. This Pei Chén is a malevolent cow! He accesses some private communications about her from other officials. She's considered to be untouchable. An old bitch but she's hanging on. They're all petrified of her. She makes J. Edgar Hoover look like a kindly buffoon. They say that Xi himself is intimidated by her. Chou Chou infers serious paranoia about her. She has agents all over the world. Assassins, spies, you name it. Chou Chou says that China had hardly anything developed when Mao was fucking the Chinese populace. The country was introspective and isolationist. When they woke up to reality they put the pedal down on developing an espionage unit. Guess who was appointed? A young go-getter woman named Pei Chén who acquired power piece-by-piece over the years. The MSS that oversees all Chinese intelligence operations is itself fearful of Pei Chén even as she reports to their oversight committee. In other words, Bertrand McAbee, you are possibly touching against a fire exhaling dragon."

Bertrand made another espresso, now fully alert. Whoever Chou Chou was he admired him from afar. "But Barry. One problem. How can we tie these pieces together?

Even if Pei Chén is this one mentioned by Jia Ogden, how do we tie this back to Samantha? A real connection?"

"The real connection Bertrand is right there. The very words of Jia Ogden. Don't you see? Samantha gets into China. There are a million different ways to get that done. She's disappeared over there and comes back as a newborn. Passport, name, identity, everything. An incredible agent under the guidance of Pei Chén. Yes, no?"

Bertrand pondered the matter, aware of the gaps and logic leaps that Barry was making, very much unlike him and yet there certainly was a valid thread present in his thinking. "Okay Barry, let's say that your hypothesis proves correct. Let's even say that Samantha is in the USA as a spy, surely under another name and with sophisticated cover and the protection of the Chinese government. A needle in the haystack."

"Yes and no. There are the three murders. For all we know those three were off the books relative to her work for the Chinese. Personal!"

"From the very beginning I saw the murder of Agatha Pruitt running back to Margaret Thode, a love story underwritten by tragedy. A huge puzzle. And by the way Barry, your jumps are way beyond what you usually accuse me of doing. This is metaphysics on steroids and yet I'm pretty convinced that you're onto something. Maybe it's good that you're sleep deprived. What do you suggest is the next step?"

"Is Jia Ogden out of the picture for another visit?"

"Maybe not. What else?"

"Chou Chou is on the prowl. Don't underestimate him."

"I don't one bit." Bertrand said. "This is FBI domestically but CIA internationally. I'll talk with Jack, maybe he can move a mountain here."

Barry said, "Jack! Do you have to use him?"

"Barry, here's the deal. I'd use Satan if I had to."

CHAPTER 58

Ushi, her personal aide and bodyguard came into Pei's office too rapidly, urgency all over her face. Pei disconnected her phone immediately.

"Yes Ushi?"

"Our cyber team has detected still another probe into Quantico. Unrequited, hand, murder. Clearly relative to our asset. Someone else is coming at the same killings."

Pei sat back and looked at Ushi with a poker face but inside her mind she was furious. She believed that a hatch had closed on the matter of Meiling Tang, the former Samantha Ogden.

Pei was now 85 years old. She still held the power over a massive espionage agency in the MSS. China had at least 50 spies in every country in the world, the USA was tops of course, thousands, as America stupidly and sloppily gave themselves to the rape of their culture, its absurd thirst for money and its sheer ingenuousness. The USA could and would be taken, just a matter of time. She was proud of her contribution over those many years. Back to those early beginnings of her network development there came to her a gift, Samantha Ogden, an unpolished diamond.

Ogden was kept in China for two years after her arrival by freighter. Her greatest strength was her greatest weakness, a brilliant warrior and an intemperate brawler. The sculpting that was performed on her personality had been profound. Eventually, she had learned the art of assassination, an art that demanded intense patience and planning. Pei knew that professionally Samantha was prepared for the toughest assignments. But she also feared for her command of her personal relationships. She was given to what the French called the *coup de foudre*, the thunderbolt of love that became a dangerous obsession. Pei herself had been a target of such from Samantha. She calmed the waters when she saw it beginning to take shape. While she was quite tempted to take Samantha on as a lover she conquered that precarious yearning.

Two years and then Samantha's false marriage to Xi Fung, an established head of a travel agency in San Francisco. They married for the sake of her eventual citizenship. To the best of her knowledge, the marriage was never consummated. He, a committed Communist, did as asked and was never alerted to the fact that Meiling Tang (he would never know her true name or past) was a trained assassin at the service of the People's Republic of China.

Fake records were created for all of the time that she falsely spent in China. There was no fear of her discovery by someone who had known her, as it was well known that Americans were unable to discern one Chinese from another. But just in case, she was schooled on how to handle that remote possibility.

The travel agency provided her the cover to wreak mayhem in a number of cities throughout the world. She carried out 37 official assassinations as well as overseeing and/or engaging in numerous entrapments and other sordid practices necessary for the well-being of her adopted country.

But Pei knew that the private life of Meiling Tang was another matter altogether. When she fell in love, really lust on steroids, she was a danger to herself and to whomever the arrow of her love found a mark.

Samantha visited China eight times during her tenure as an agent in the USA. Her honesty with Pei was total. It was inconceivable to her that Meiling could lie to her even when she admitted that she had struck out and murdered three of her objects of desire. Two of them had rebuffed her harshly and paid a terrible price for it, as Meiling's ferocity was unleashed. The other was a lover who had strayed from their relationship. This last victim was detected and confronted. After her denial, she died the victim of a frantic and sustained savagery. All three murders, Meiling admitted, were patterned after that of Margaret Thode's murder.

Then some deranged investigator in a weird place called Rock Island somehow started to connect some dots. Pei's plants in the FBI alerted her to Agatha Pruitt's inquiries. Pei, not notifying Meiling, ordered the murder of this woman as well as surveillance on the woman's house with an advanced audio/visual system and a thorough search of her house. The two agents whom she sent were also assigned the task of beating some old man who ran a PI agency. He apparently took on the matter of Pruitt's murder. The sanctioned agents were half-successful, but they had been interfered with outside of some restaurant in Iowa. They were quickly assigned to Florida for another mission, out of the Midwest.

Maybe it was time to force repatriation on Meiling. Two separate inquiries within six weeks of each other were two too many. She recalled her original concerns about the then Samantha, her quick temper and out of control fury. Her warnings to her that someday these liabilities could undo her.

Ushi had been standing in front of her desk, probably for at least ten minutes, as Pei reflected on the dilemma of the marvelous Samantha, one of her first deep plants.

"Ushi, keep all of this in sight. Let me know of any further intrusions as soon as you hear." Ushi, forever sensitive to Pei's ways, left without another word.

Two fields of thought came at Pei. If, somehow, this whole nest of problems with Meiling came out and was discovered by her adversaries, too many to count, she would be done, her career over, perhaps to live in disgrace. Meiling would rather die than have that happen.

The second concern was more immediate. Meiling was overseeing an operation that had been worked on assiduously by her and a beautiful Chinese agent, Charlotte, who had managed to draw the attention of the United States Senator Hugh Powers from the state of Michigan. He was very close to assuming the chairmanship of the Foreign Relations Committee upon the retirement of an 84 year old curmudgeon who had been a bastard of an adversary to China. Simply, Hugh Powers had been laying his hands on some of the girl's sexually desirable parts. Meiling reported back that she was 80% positive that lust-driven Hugh could be compromised within the next few weeks.

And so Pei thought long and hard.

CHAPTER 59

Bertrand and Jack Scholz walked by an angry Mississippi River. A glorious April gave way to a sulky and moody May. Storms were prone to unpredictable patterns. Fair weather could be overwhelmed by clouds, wind, and rain within ten minutes. The river was an avatar of chaos as it flowed rapidly with white peaks warning of ever more coming disturbances.

"So Jack," Bertrand was concluding his thorough summary of the case, "that's where we are. There's definitely a China connection. When all the pieces of the puzzle are put in place the gaps end, things fit."

"So let's see. Samantha Ogden's about 63 years old by now. Your tie-ins with the MSS are very good. She'd be a great asset for the bastards. But much of this rests on some murders of women who had nothing of importance in their lives concerning national affairs. Crimes of love gone bad? Surely she's no longer Samantha Ogden. The Chinese would create a whole new identity for her. So, you're distinguishing a professional life from a personal life. Her personal life may be a wreck yet she might be able to keep a professional life separate. Possible? Yes. I've seen it in some people I've worked with. Disastrous drunks who could perform at A levels. Plenty of others too, philanderers, psychotics, and so on. The question is how do you smoke out such a creature. Yes?"

"That's it," McAbee said.

"Any identifiers?"

"Yearbook pics of Samantha. Also, I went to the daughter of Dr. Sedge in Rock Island. I asked her if she would have any records from her deceased father. She's living in a bit of poverty and looked to be at death's door. I offered her $500 if she could find X-rays from his practice. He was a dentist who also served the Augustana community. Long and short, she had every damn record that he ever kept including X-rays. It was as if she re-created his office in her basement. Eerie scene. Something was off about her. After I found Samantha's X-rays, neatly placed in a huge file cabinet, I sat with the dentist's daughter. She looked wretched. She was a meth user. Never made it to dental school. Broke her father's heart. The longer I live the sadder things become. The railroad tracks and stations that I have traversed on this case are full of sadness. So much broken," McAbee said.

Jack looked over at him in surprise. Fatalistically he said, "That's a constant for me. You just can't let it get into you. There are two paths that I see. Both federal, CIA, FBI." Jack touched Bertrand's shoulder. "I know, I know. One a bigger lizard than the other. It's hard for me to think that this Samantha is not on some radar in those outfits. Not about the Margaret Thode or Agatha Pruitt cases, rather her coming back here from China, I don't see her being clandestine here. She went through channels, immigration forms, green cards, maybe marriage and so on. Thousands and thousands fit that, I know, but it's a start. I can work the FBI a bit. They owe me lots from the last mission."

"I've got an idea for the CIA. A long shot. This is where I miss my brother. He could work something," he said wistfully.

"We done?"

"Yeah, thanks."

Bertrand, back in his office, was hesitant about calling Forrest Graham. He had locked his number. When he called it, he realized that the phone had been a burner, long gone from service. He called Graham's sister and asked her assistance. She was very quiet as he spoke. He thought that this was a hopeless angle as he finished his carefully edited synopsis of the case and a plea to talk with her brother.

"You know I helped you once. You also know that he's in a very sensitive position. But you persist. Personally, I think he's pretty uptight. So, at the risk of a bawling out, I'll pass your message on but don't get your hopes up. The Margaret Thode case, also Agatha Pruitt, something has to be done! I'm at my other brother's room, Edgar, in the hospital. I have to go."

He could only hope. A few minutes later his phone rang. 'Unknown Caller.' He hesitated but picked up. "Yes?"

"This is Forrest Graham. Some synchronicity, I'm flying into the Quad Cities tomorrow morning to visit my brother Edgar. I'll text you for a meeting. This better be good McAbee." He disconnected.

Barry Fisk abandoned his search for flights into the three cities where murders took place, where there was a symbol of unrequited found on the victim's palm. The task would require extraordinary computer power. The

FBI could pull it off but it probably hadn't, even though a serial killer had been identified. The killings took place at two Marriott hotels and one Hyatt. Old hotel records of the three were accessible. He doubted that he could find a common name for the specific dates concerned with each hotel. Nonetheless, he placed an inquiry for six days on either side of the murder.

Six days were too broad, TMI. He tightened to three days, while in doubt about the third day given that it could be a stay the day after the murder. Questionable, but anything was possible to divert suspicions.

Asian names were of great interest to him but they didn't preclude his search for all names. The Hyatt in Washington D.C. was his starting point. For the three days of inquiry, he was dealing with 1,032 names, 73 were Asian.

Next, he went to the Marriott. He secured the entire count of names relative to the parameters he set, three full days. The first Marriott in question had 971 names, 57 were Asian. Again, nothing was conclusive about the Asian names as the murderer could well be living with an English name through marriage.

With purpose, he hit the third hotel, a Marriott. He came up with 1205 names, 52 Asian. He brought up a sort/match application and ran the names for commonality. He found two matches, believing privately that there might be one match, if at all. His legs started to shake uncontrollably.

CHAPTER 60

Bertrand heard the specific phone sound he had given to Barry, crickets. He took the call, "Barry?"

"Sit down!" he said in an excited shout.

"I am."

"I have something. Big deal!"

Bertrand imagined Barry's legs shaking wildly. "Let's have it, Barry."

"I have two names of people staying at the three hotels during the times of the murders. Both women, one with an obvious Asian name. I checked her out. Travel agent. Has all the credentials. Came to the USA with a marriage proposal. Husband dead. She's in charge. Big agency in Frisco. Right age. Whole thing, name Meiling Tang."

"The other?"

"Belinda Cotton. Works for Amazon. District Manager. Age 51. Wrong fit, doesn't square up."

Bertrand saw immediately that a travel agency was a perfect cover. "No, Belinda Cotton is very unlikely given that 1991 was a murder year."

"I've got more on Meiling. She seems to be on the road, often. Extended periods sometimes. I've tried to hit on her profiles but she is very protective of her data. But I did get into her American Express account. She has been in Washington D.C. for the past three months. Throws a lot of cross signals. Like a whack a mole in a way. Considerable craftiness. She's very public with her business for a travel company but she herself is closed down and then when I get near her she evaporates. All the signs point to her."

"Where's she staying in Washington?"

"Oriental. Room 501."

"Have a picture in present time?"

"Yes, hotel camera. I've run it against her high school photos and I have an app that projects aging. Pretty good. Same person, 90% probability. That's considered to be an extremely high match by the app. I think that you have her. Now what?"

Bertrand hesitated in his answer. There were many calculations to be made by him. He needed time. One thing was sure, Jack Scholz would be part of the answer. He would not mention this to Barry; he didn't need the angry dismissals and retorts from him. "I have to think it through. Your work is outstanding as usual. Thanks Barry." He disconnected quickly.

A few minutes later, another ring. 'Unknown Caller.' He answered, "Hello."

"Forrest Graham. I'm in Davenport. Too late. My brother Edgar died before I got here. No time is good for me McAbee, at present. I put off coming here. Thought I had the time. I didn't. Lesson? Stay away from the pause button, don't hesitate, lollygag. When I get back to Washington perhaps we'll talk."

"We will," Bertrand said as Graham was disconnecting. He was unsure whether Graham had heard his comment. But he took one part of Graham's message to heart, don't delay. For all he knew this Meiling may be on the verge of leaving D.C.

He called Pat. He asked her to arrange a meeting with Augusta and Jack, not in his office but on the bike path by the Mississippi. The weather was perfect this day.

Two hours later, the three of them began their walk along the presently lightly travelled path. He recounted what he had on Meiling Tang up to and including room 501 at the Oriental, a three-month stay. When he stopped his recitation, a long silence fell on them as they walked.

Finally, Augusta said, "Extraordinary. I never thought you stood a chance on this Bertrand. But I should know better. But now what? You have some kind of promise to Concannon on top of all this."

"I do," he said. "I have a lot of IOUs on this case. I'll keep them as well as I can. Jack? Your thoughts?"

"Let's get the bitch and break her," he said sharply.

Augusta said, "I don't know about that approach. I think it's time to give the information to the FBI and the Rock Island P.D. They have the resources."

He figured that a disconnect between these two extraordinary talents would occur. He understood both of them. Wisdom led him to consider Augusta's approach. Legally, it was the way to go. The evidence was convincing to him, but the FBI? Their procedural approach and the time it would take to develop a case would probably take months. Furthermore, they'd probably finagle Concannon out of the matter with their concern about national security as surely espionage was in play. Concannon, belligerent indeed, still yielded the original crime scene and autopsy pictures that were essential to breaking this case. He was owed.

Then he thought of Forrest Graham. He didn't make it to his brother's bedside, seemingly brushing aside the proximity of death. What did he say? 'Stay away from the pause button,' in other words act when you can, don't procrastinate. He concluded that the FBI and even his thought of debt to Concannon was a form of procrastination. His client, Richard Pruitt, deserved justice, a more immediate kind.

They crossed under the entryways to the Centennial Bridge and continued westward. Another long silence fell. A bicycle zipped by them heading east. Some fishermen were sitting on a bench to their left, poles resting on the rails that protected pedestrians from the river and its dangerous and deadly currents.

He knew that he was slow to decide sometimes. It would be easy enough to hand everything over to the FBI. But he calculated that they'd cause trouble for Barry and his hacking. The agency had it in for Barry from long ago and when the FBI followed the chain of the investigation, they'd tread where they shouldn't.

He looked over at the river and saw a towboat pushing at least ten barges down river. A man was on the boat rail looking over at the three of them. He waved, cigarette in his hand. Bertrand waved back and then noticed that the man's face was deeply scarred, burns were his calculation. He shuddered.

He turned toward Jack and said, "How do we get her Jack? I want a full confession from her. I'm thinking that this angel of murder has at least five innocent women that she has to account for at the very least."

Augusta said, "Bertrand! Think twice about this. You're going over to the vigilante quality in you."

"I know," he looked at her in a way that said there was to be no compromise.

Jack said, "I'll have a plan by tonight. It will involve isolating her. If I can achieve that I'll break her."

"That's the plan I want to see. I keep dwelling on Margaret Thode and Agatha Pruitt. If I fix on them then my mind is made up."

Augusta shrugged, she said nothing further.

CHAPTER 61

Pei thought long and hard about how to proceed with Samantha who was very close to overseeing a major feat, the compromise of a U.S. senator. Not just any senator, but a power broker who would be towed into the shores of compromise and betrayal. Samantha was practiced and effective; she knew of no one who could replace her on this delicate assignment. The temptress Charlotte, being used by her, needed fulltime management.

But she was afraid, also. The most recent inquiries into the Margaret Thode and Agatha Pruitt cases told of danger. Had some agency or other put together a pattern on her? The inquiry after Agatha Pruitt's murder had been enough. But still another? And now another query about Samantha's pride, the unrequited signature at murder scenes. Her very open use of the travel agency was a benefit because it was so open and thus why would anyone suspect her? Subterfuge was usually the ignitor of suspicion, not transparency. But if a flaw in the very openness of her agency was discovered that very openness could become easily penetrable by enemies. If it wasn't for the coming trap of the senator she would have recalled Samantha immediately. An American-Chinese had already been through deep training to take over the travel agency. No, it was the Washington D.C. entrapment that paused Pei. The benefits outweighed the costs if Samantha could pull this off.

As a matter of course she placed two agents in the Oriental Hotel. Both of them were tough professionals who had been used by her on very sensitive matters, including the murder of Agatha Pruitt as directed by Pei herself.

Samantha saw both of the agents while crossing the lobby. She remembered one of them from 15 years back. A different case, a different time. The giveaway was a left foot that angled out about 30 degrees with the very slightest of drag. So, Pei was more concerned than she had said about those inquiries into FBI files. Pei had known about the three bitches she had murdered over the years yet she kept her on as an agent. Sure, they were quite happy when she took down a quarry seen as a state enemy, but they didn't want to hear about personal business. There was still a residual fury in her in those times of her youth when she was sexually rejected by Pei, not gently either. She knew that Pei admired her skills and was proud of the achievements that were made by them as a team but she also knew that deep down Pei always had a secret doubt about her explosive anger at slights, refusals, rejections, and obstacles. The Chinese had worked on her for almost two years. She feigned acceptance of their concern and she showed conquest of her fault. If she hadn't she would never have gotten out of China alive. But Pei? She was sure that she would always have that doubt about her even after these many years.

When that damn Agatha had reached into national data bases looking for the signature of her crimes of passion, Pei's secret suspicions had their fuse lit. What she found out, what she knew, Samantha didn't know. But whatever Pei had ascertained scared her, as she almost instantly forced the murder of Agatha Pruitt, while not informing her, and had put Samantha herself on notice that there was some entity working against her and ultimately Pei.

Then she received more information from her FBI source about a PI agency in Davenport, Iowa. ACJ! Some aging bastard named McAbee. But now any calm was interrupted by the two People's Republic goons who were in the hotel. If they in any way hindered the neutralization of the senator, she would never forgive Pei whose age and abilities she was now beginning to wonder about.

The senator had invited himself into Room 502 two nights ago to sit and chat with Charlotte who was an aide for a congressman from California. Her cover was that she supposedly was the stepdaughter of one of the hotel owners who arranged for her to stay in room 502. The Oriental was ordered to comply by the MSS and furthermore accept the legend surrounding Charlotte. Room 502 was wired through and through with audio and visual monitors. An unfortunate result of this was that the cute and inexperienced Charlotte couldn't piss without being observed. The virtuous senator sat near her on a small couch as he talked about how important he was and would she be interested in moving into his offices when time came for a change in staff? She put on a good act and grabbed his hand in appreciation. As she got up to refill his drink, he slid his hand down her back, across her ass and thighs. Neither said anything but Samantha knew where this was headed. Maybe just another week and then he'd be called into the Chinese embassy for a social affair only to be notified that he was on camera screwing himself into total compromise. At that point, Samantha's job as the manager for this entrapment would be done and she would head back to San Francisco awaiting her next assignment.

CHAPTER 62

Against his best judgment, Bertrand found himself in the Oriental. He seldom perceived himself as an operations agent. But Jack had insisted on the grounds that the venture would of necessity be messy with the capture and maybe kidnapping of Samantha Ogden now pretending to be Meiling Tang. The team had four connected rooms on the third floor; there were six individuals altogether including Bertrand himself.

The architectural layout of the entire hotel had been secured by Barry Fisk. Fake identities were created for all six who were supposedly employed by Microsoft. Jack had tapped into four of his former colleagues. McAbee was always impressed by their devotion to him. They proceeded toward the hotel as a team from Dulles Airport in an extended Expedition vehicle, even as three of them were local and had parked in the airport's long-term garage. When Bertrand was introduced to them, he felt that their eyes went askew. Surely, his age caused their disconnect.

Barry was on notice to stay alert back in Davenport. It was now 3:30 p.m. They knew that the target was in room 501, an end suite.

Each team member had an assignment for the mission whose objective was to remove Meiling from the hotel if possible. She was to be brought to a remote cabin in West Virginia where her interrogation would commence. The cabin belonged to one of his men who was named Gus. McAbee gathered he had been used on other jobs. When and about whom McAbee had no idea and didn't want one. Gus was apparently the driver and the overseer of the equipment necessary for the interrogation of Meiling in West Virginia.

An advanced remote camera had already been set up on the fifth floor by just a quick touch on the frame of doorway 540 that was two doors down and across from 501. Security cameras would not pick up the quick movement of Gus's hand. The rooms were oddly numbered.

Communications from Barry Fisk would be handled through Bertrand as Jack went into semi-fury at the mention of the 'midget's' name. In short order Barry called and mentioned that two Chinese, goon-like, were entrenched in the lobby and also frequently took the elevator to the fifth floor.

Besides Gus there was a woman of about 30. Her name was Jenny. To McAbee she looked like a linebacker for the Green Bay Packers. He wasn't sure how she'd be used. Paul, on the other hand, gave the impression of being a nerd of some sort, small of stature, thick glasses, he moved in an unsteady way. Every time he got up from his seat he stumbled and had to grab something to keep him upright. No heavy-lifting from him.

The remaining team member, Oats, also had linebacker qualities but his movements were quick and decisive. By comparison, Jenny was a lumberer. But there was a quality in each of them that McAbee saw as lethal, with a smartness about them that said failure was not going to happen. This wasn't their first rodeo, he thought, as he wondered where he had picked up that expression.

Barry reported that room 502 was also on Meiling's American Express card. Charlotte, a guest? Had been for almost three months, matching her own stay. Unfortunately, the hotel's security system was a closed circuit affair on each floor of the hotel, unlike their lobby, that for unknown reasons was a hackable system. There were a large number of Asians staying at the hotel. He was sure that he observed Meiling from the lobby cameras that included a camera devoted to the elevator and, of course, the floor demarcations on the plaque above the elevator doors. He froze the image and faxed it to Bertrand's iPhone. Meiling wore Western clothing, a very conservative black dress, knee length. Other than a pair of small gold earrings, she was unadorned. She looked to be in good shape, eyes particularly alert as she turned toward the lobby.

Barry called Bertrand at 10 p.m. Bertrand said, in his own room now, "Hey Barry."

"I have been on the lobby tapes most of the day. They keep them for about a week and then they're purged. This place surely is surveilled by the Feds. Little China. Anyway something amazing from two nights ago. Almost positive on this. You know of Senator Powers from Michigan, right?"

"Yeah."

"He's going into that hotel at 9:23 p.m.," he stopped.

McAbee knew it has his turn to play the straight man to Barry. "So what?"

"Well, so what? What if he's going to the elevator with a Chinese cutie about 30 years his junior? And what if they proceed to the fifth floor? And what if he leaves the lobby at 11:13 p.m. by himself."

"You're suggesting?" Bertrand asked with a slight smile on his face.

"Not suggesting a damn thing Bertrand. This is not an allegation like the stupid networks who tell us that the murderer of those kids in Uvalde, Texas, was alleged. Crap! I'm telling you something is amiss here."

"Barry, I thought you said that the Feds were probably all over this hotel."

"Sure. But they're Feds. Stupid bastards. What I'm saying is you better be careful there. You may be sitting in the middle of a pond of alligators."

"Understood. Anything else?"

"The two goons. They just seem to be cemented to the lobby chairs. Yesterday, Samantha went out, they followed. When she came back they suddenly show up, out of nowhere. She's being watched. So, she goes to the elevator, they sit in the lobby looking innocent, she gets into the elevator and very subtly gives them a quick look. She knows they're onto her. The camera catches her left eye wince when she spies them."

"Good to know."

"Give Jack my love," he disconnected.

CHAPTER 63

The next morning Jack and Bertrand went to a Starbucks, a block away from the hotel. They ordered a coffee and sat.

"Let's keep this coded. This is D.C., more cameras and listening devices than you can count. Lots of gray men and women being paid to listen into conversations. FBI and CIA are more cooperative than you'd think. Of course, if one of them crosses a line they sulk and retaliate for months. To hell with the country," Jack said in exasperation.

"Why do you say that if you think they're listening in?" Bertrand asked.

"So that you'll be cryptic and no one can figure out what the hell we're talking about," he looked at McAbee with a thin-lipped smile. "The hotel? Feds are all over that place."

"Clever Jack!"

"The West Virginia plan won't work. Logistics are bad. Too many variables. Get it?"

"Okay, backup?" Bertrand knew that Jack would have a backup plan.

"The occupied place," he took out a piece of paper and wrote on it 501. "Right there. We've got this down to 90%. Just a few wrinkles. When we succeed I'll call you."

Bertrand had told him, very quietly on the way over for coffee, about Senator Powers and Barry's concern that there might be an operation in play by the Chinese. Perhaps the Feds were onto it. Jack didn't respond, he merely jerked his hands upwards. No surprise there. Interestingly, Jack Scholz and Barry Fisk were probably in accord about certain departments of the U.S. government. Each in his own way had a cynical streak about things.

Bertrand walked around D.C. for two hours; he arrived back to his room just as the maid was about to leave. He gave her a ten dollar bill. Her eyes told of her appreciation along with her slight bow of her head.

He called Barry. He answered without the usual preamble of sourness. "Not much here Bertrand. Chinese goons are gone from the lobby trailing her. That woman who was with the senator? She came back about a half hour ago. Three big shopping bags, fancy, couldn't determine the stores but they seemed to come from plush places. No one following her. She goes to the fifth floor, and 502 probably. Lot of Asians staying at the hotel."

"Okay, I think we're circling around that. Stay in touch."

A few minutes later Augusta called. "I've been thinking of you out there Mistah. Any progress?"

"Things are coming together. Not sure how it will all play out."

"All is okay here. Pat sends her best. Be careful who you're hanging around with."

"Augusta, I'm always careful. You know that."

"Always?" she said flatly.

"Well, you're becoming quite the logician. I will. Promise."

"Need me out there?"

"No. It's a one man ACJ job."

"If I know Jack it's a regiment that he's using. Nonetheless please be careful."

McAbee had brought Homer's *Odyssey* with him. He opened the well-read book to the adventures with Polyphemus, the one-eyed cyclops. He thought that Odysseus was at his A level of treachery in the blocked cave with the recently blinded and raging son of Poseidon.

His iPhone rang. It was Jack.

"Almost ready to go. Be prepared," a quick disconnect.

Bertrand sat on his bed, anxious. Dealing with someone like Samantha Ogden was like playing chess against a master. She might be three or four steps ahead of Jack and his gang. On the other hand, he had known Jack for almost 25 years. He had never failed in a mission except for the killing of one of his men in Minneapolis a long time ago on one of McAbee's first cases. He felt that Jack had never let go of his grief over that loss. Bertrand assessed Jack's sorrow as a virtue. It probably was a main factor for his people to be so devoted to him.

"501." Jack said and disconnected to McAbee's "Yes."

Immediately, McAbee went to the elevator and went up to the fifth floor and walked to room 501. He knocked twice. It was opened, he entered, the door was shut immediately. His eyes fell on an unforgettable scene.

CHAPTER 64

Samantha stared out at them, her lips sealed with a sticky tape that she was unfamiliar with. Her arms were knotted against her sides and her legs were tied together. She was standing. There were five pigs in the room, one of them, a scrawny man who sat on her bed, not a worry. The big American bitch, six feet two or beyond stood next to her. Probably some kind of cow from Wisconsin. Next to her was a tough looking, equally tall, soldier-sort. She heard the tall cow call him Oats. Another man sat by the door, forties, out of shape. Did someone in the mayhem call him Gus? The four of them did not scare her. They probably wanted to rob her. But the fifth one scared her. He was a kindred soul she could tell by his eyes, cold and unblinking. *He* wasn't a robber. She heard two knocks at the door. An older man came in, allowed entry by the sentry Gus. Gus went to her desk and pulled out the wheeled desk chair for the old man. He sat and took in the scene eyes wandering around the room with movements that could match the flight of hummingbirds.

They were professionals. She no longer thought about robbery. The scary one came up to her and said, "I'll take the tape off if you give me your word that you won't yell or try anything."

She thought it time for maximum hubris, to back them down by being fearless. She nodded. The tape was removed. She licked her lips free of the gluey concoction and then she let out a half shriek before she was silenced, in agony, as he punched her brutally in her solar plexus. She dropped to the floor. She was gasping for air as he leaped on her and resealed her lips with the tape. He got up and then kicked her in the ribs, she was sure that he broke a few. Her pain was worse than anything that the MSS had done to her those many years back as they submitted her to training.

He turned and looked out at the others in the room. "Can you believe that she broke her word?"

She tried to bring herself back into a semblance of control, observing that her tormentor was looking very intensely at the old guy sitting in the desk chair who looked on with some kind of speculative gaze as if he was weighing something.

"Stand her up," the puncher said. The two big ones did as told, Oats and the big heifer, probably a transexual. Samantha didn't like the look of that one. "Let's try it again Meiling. Will you keep the peace as you promised? Just nod your head." She did as asked as she eyed the room for any possible defensive play. She found none, still unclear as to what was at stake, perhaps they were U.S. government agents onto the three-month entrapment setup. The Oriental was not as secure as the MSS had conjectured.

Her antagonist said to the scrawny one sitting on the bed, "Read to Samantha our first agenda item and the needed clarifications." Scrawny, of voice also, read from a card, "Senator Powers. Interesting quarry. You and your roommate next door. Not acceptable. Your equipment in this room is quite advanced. I've checked it out next door too. Same thing. Interesting material on your computer about Senator Powers' shows of affection. Question, how long have you worked for the MSS? Word of warning, none of us desire to see you in pain." Jack removed the tape from her mouth with a warning finger.

Samantha was trying to think past the pain that coursed through her body. She decided for another attempt. "I demand an attorney before I speak any further," she said in half gasps.

Her tormentor looked at her as if he was surprised, caught off guard. "Who would that be?"

"I need my phone. He's in there, his number and name," she said with a slight ray of hope. She didn't trust this tormentor, a dark man. Was he playing her? If he was FBI he might comply. CIA, never.

"You'll have your chance if we leave with what we've come for. Lot of attorneys in Washington. But not now, of course. There was a question asked of you. Answer it."

"MSS? I have never heard of that. I am an American. I demand my rights."

"You're not answering the question. I know that you're an American. By birth! But now you're someone else. Now you're Chinese and you work for the MSS. The question is how long? Last chance." He looked closely at her, a maniacal look in his eyes.

She shook her head, silence her chosen ally. He motioned backward toward the entry door where Gus sat. Gus brought over a small suitcase. When he opened it she knew what it was. He cuffed her ankles and fingers with hard metal clasps. The electrical current was turned on. She writhed in pain as the tormentor gave her a look from hell. He'd see just how tough she was. She tried to scream again. He clasped his hand over her mouth as the two guards held her upright. Her pain excruciating. "Next I'll double the current. Just keep it up, half China girl." So he knew of her parents, her Anglo father and Chinese mother. He knew her long ago name. The old guy got up from the chair and went toward the body breaker. Very quietly, but wanting her to hear, he said, "Give me a few minutes with her, Jack, before you go for broke." So, the tormentor's name was Jack.

"Do you need some pain medication?" the old guy asked gently.

The good cop/bad cop routine. The pain was the worst she had ever experienced physically. But psychologically, it was a trauma for her.

"Jack will find out how long you've worked for the MSS. Personally, it's not important to me. Not my mission, you see. Nor is the stunt that you're pulling next door with Senator Powers. My mission goes to the past, long ago, well before you left our native country for another. Just nod if you understand what I just said. You don't have to agree yet."

She looked at him closely. His eye color seemed to shift from a light blue to a gray and then back again. She gave him a short nod as she looked for Jack, whom she peripherally observed about three feet to her right.

"You were a student at Rock Island High School. A smart one. As a senior there you put on an act, a witch. Not appreciated by the authorities but who cares, right?"

347

She tried to stay calm. The bastard knew too much. Was he the PI from Iowa? She tried to corral her pain while staying focused on this character with his observant eyes, the fox-like Odysseus who stood three feet from ferocious Achilles, she now trying to focus on *The Iliad* of Homer as a distraction, but to little avail. She said, "That's not me. I don't know why you're saying this."

Jack whispered to the old man who nodded. The awkward man on the bed hobbled forth with a small envelope. Jack then held out his hand toward Samantha's face. The old man nodded. The two granite-like characters on each side of her held her tight as Jack forced open her mouth. The hobbler took out an X-ray from a tan envelope and looked closely into her left jaw. Seconds later, he nodded toward Jack who let her mouth relax. The awkward man looked at the old man and said, "Yes. Match," and then he stumbled back to the bed.

"You got your tooth knocked out by Margaret Thode," the old guy said softly, "the dentist's daughter kept all of his records, a basement of memory. He was a meticulous dentist. He kept your X-ray, Samantha. Unbelievable. Margaret Thode in her diary entry wrote of your encounter in the high school bathroom. A long time ago, I personally was groped in a crowd. It hurt and furthermore I was never able to identity the groper. *But* I was furious. Margaret was too. That's why you lost a tooth. Nod if you understand please."

She felt as though she was a mouse in an experiment, the coming result of an experiment's findings already known. She nodded as she cast a quick glance at Jack.

"So, Samantha. The conclusion is that there is a woman with great anger, proficient in Chinese, who in serious fits of rage kills her perceived adversaries, aka disappointments, and leaves a mark on her victims. The cops called it a signature. Right palm. Unrequited. Seems to be a connection among them, Margaret Thode to 1991, 2002, and 2013. But you didn't kill Agatha."

He stopped, observing her with great care. She tried to remain within herself controlling the pain and the revelations just made. Yet the man continued to look at her as though she was an ocean, something to be charted. Furthermore, she knew that she had been had. Serious homework had been done about her. And the crew in front of her? Would they kill her? She had little doubt that Jack would personally destroy her, her scalp hitched to his belt.

"I'm going to get a bottle of water from that fridge. Think about your answer in the time I need to get it." He looked to his right where Jack stood and said, "No more for right now Jack." Then he went to the small unit on the other side of the room, opened that door and withdrew a bottle of water. She dove into herself trying to find the correct response. She wondered if this was the end of her career, perhaps even her life. Pei who had rebuffed her sexual advances all those years back would now get her just desserts. And the little bitch Charlotte next door? How close she came to killing her, the same reason behind her other assaults. All this because some unseemly hag named Agatha Pruitt returned and opened an investigation on Thode's murder, this girlfriend working her own path to vengeance not by a carved Chinese symbol on a palm but by meticulous research. Well, she paid the price. Pei had her murdered and in doing so was she not only murdering Samantha, the bitch next door, but also ironically Pei herself, as the MSS would move on her, no longer a difficult adversary. He came back, water bottle in his hand. He said, toward Jack, "Please have your two friends take her very gently and sit her on the bed." They did, her ribs screamed at the motion, even as she was gently placed on the bed. The scrawny one moved to the other side of the bed as the old man retrieved his chair and rolled it over so as to be directly in front of her. She looked more closely at him, his face of high cheekbones, craggy features creased by age. He was weighing her as if she was a piece of unknown metal. If he knew so much why the bafflement on his visage? She was familiar with interrogations, all the approaches, all the games. But he was different. Was he confirming a judgment already made?

"My name is Bertrand McAbee. I run an agency in Davenport. ACJ. I was hired by the brother of Agatha Pruitt to run down the matter of her death. I don't think that it was your doing, directly anyway. You prefer Samantha or Meiling?"

"Meiling," she answered, almost as if he willed it from her.

"There's the phrase that comes to my mind when I look at you and the circumstances that we're in, *no way out*. You've had a good run given the business you're in and your training under none other than Pei Chén."

She winced just slightly, hoping he didn't notice. He knew everything. She was in a vise, the mission next door, her identity, the MSS, her life.

He went on, "Personal rejection of an erotic nature was the cause of this. Aristotle would say that you offended all of the virtues with this weakness. Temperance especially, but fortitude, justice and prudence also. I think he's right, of course."

She wanted to spit at him for his arrogance, his high-minded judgment, his weighing looks. But she couldn't. He was right.

"Give me a solution, a way out" he said softly.

"My mother?"

"She's in early dementia in Moline. But in a moment of clarity she expressed love for you but a supreme dislike for Pei."

"If I was playing chess I would have to concede the game. To your question, there is only one way out. Would you trust me to do it by myself?"

"No," he said quickly.

"That's fair," she said. "Good spycraft," she said with a wan smile.

"I'm not a spy."

"There are definitions that could prove that to be untrue. Next door. She is napping. Always does at this time. A night creature. Not a deserving girl in many ways. She has lived beyond her days. She is callous, wrong-headed. I have an answer to no way out if you would allow."

"Yes?"

"I need my knife back. That Jack of yours has it. I will go to her room, it's opened between us, and I will take her to her bathroom as a ruse. I will lock the door of the bathroom from its inside. The matter will end. My word of honor."

Bertrand looked at Jack who shrugged, as if it was Bertrand's call, his case, his decision.

CHAPTER 65

Bertrand went to Jack. He pulled him aside and spoke softly to him. A minute later Meiling's hands and legs were set free by Oats and Jenny together. The knife had not been handed back to her. Bertrand went back to her and sat beside her. "Not sure that giving you a knife is a good idea. You see that don't you?"

"Of course. You have my word," she said half gasping from pain.

"You violated it with Jack."

There was a long pause. She said, "You're not Jack. You went about this properly. He went about things like a Russian. You'll see that my word is to be taken sincerely. Would you please go to my mother, kiss her on the head and tell her that I love her. If you believe I am lying to you, you are more like Jack that I thought." She looked at him sternly.

"Tell me your plan exactly," he said as non-accusatory as he could.

"My plan? Simple. I will go next door and take Charlotte into her bathroom. She will be dead thereof. Then my turn. All will be as quiet as possible. Knowing your Jack, he will desire to confirm. So I expect you to remain in this room.

That's a Jack thing." She looked over at Scholz with a certain kind of respect. She had never met an adversary who was on the same frequency as she. "Can you get rid of this crowd? Just you and Jack. I will need only a few minutes. Revenge is a strange master. Once you're in bed with it it's always there. A soul eater."

Bertrand went back to Jack. He gave him the scenario. He saw Jack looking closely at Samantha, not in trust. He said, after Bertrand explained the course of events, "You're sure?"

"Almost 100%. I have a ritual to perform, her mother in Moline."

"Well, if you say so. I'm armed. She won't get the best of me if it comes to that." Jack turned and dismissed his team from room 501. He removed the switchblade knife taken from Meiling when they barged into the room with the bought keycard. He handed it to McAbee who took it and went to Meiling.

She took the knife from Bertrand, bowed toward Jack and Bertrand and proceeded to the pass through her connecting door into Room 502.

AFTERWORD

- McAbee went to Moline and visited Jia Ogden. She took him for a professor from Augustana. He held her hand, kissed her head very gently and told her that Samantha sent her love. Her look back to him was one of understanding.

- Hugh Concannon was visited by the FBI. He was told that both files, that of Margaret Thode and Agatha Pruitt, should be closed as solved. A sting operation was in play against the Chinese. There would be no public announcements. Angrily he thought of McAbee, somehow he was involved.

- McAbee visited Gretchen Heinz at the Kahl Home. He poured a few ounces from a new bottle of Bushmills for her and gave her an edited version of the solution to the two murders. She cried a bit and when this was noticed by Sister Ursula, McAbee was told to leave.

- The FBI associated the symbol etched onto the right palm of the woman referred to as Charlotte in room 502 of the Oriental. A connection to other murders. A massive sting operation on the Chinese would now commence. ACJ and its operation were ordered to stand down or else.

- Dr. Richard Pruitt was pleased that ACJ had solved the mystery of the murder of his sister even as he was notified that the two Chinese agents had left for Beijing the morning after the two bodies were found in room 502 of the Oriental Hotel. He paid a bill of $173,000 dollars to ACJ. Barry complained that his share was late in coming.

- Roger Smalley was sued by his receptionist, Ginny, who had detailed recordings of his sexual aggressions towards her. He is being forced by Major League Baseball and the National Football League to sell his partial ownerships in the two clubs.

- McAbee and Satin returned Margaret Thode's trunk to her aunt Verna in Wheatland, Iowa. It was a sad affair.

- Both Bertrand and Augusta feel that something is askew in their relationship. It will need work.

- On a minor inquiry for the City of Davenport, McAbee visited the Dog Rescue Building. Before he knew it, he adopted a dog named Tipsy. She was in worse shape than he.